D1825967

Mapleshire

Secrets of Rose Manor

Kimberleigh Dixon

Sea Maiden Publishing LLC

Front Cover by Kimberleigh Dixon
Back Cover by Lisa Martineau
Publishing Imprint by Christy Boughan

First Edition: 2024

Edited by Courtney Hanan. Instagram @c.hanan.editing
The text for this book was set in Garamond
Manufactured in the United States of America
First Edition ISBN Hardcover: 978-1-963873-99-3
First Edition ISBN Paperback: 979-8-218-37715-1

Sea Maiden Publishing LLC

To Holly

You were with me every step of the way

Thank you for all of your help and support!

Mount Gravensburg

Stennton

The Forest of Faiden Dell

Mapleshire

Hempsure

Entry

The long stone corridor echoed with terrified screams from the young maiden.

Rope fibers bit into her wrists every time she fought against them.

Warm, sticky blood slithered down her arms like a snake hunting for prey.

She tried to blink against the pressure, but the blindfold around her eyes was excessively tight.

The smell of blood and sweat pierced her nostrils, making her feel woozy.

Suddenly he halted. She tried focusing on what was happening, but the dizziness crept into every corner of her mind.

The sound of keys rustling and the creaking groan of a metal door met her pleas for freedom.

His grip around her arm tightened as he thrust her through the door.

She stumbled over her dress and fell against a wooden surface.

"Get in" were the only words she heard from her captor.

When she tried to remember anything about him, pain radiated through her head.

Chapter 1

Jeanette pulled open the door to the town's only fabric shoppe. She needed to get more linen to refill her stock and, being the only tailor, she went through more fabric than anyone else.

"Good afternoon, Jeanette," Kurt greeted her as she walked in. "What fabric can I help you with today?" The heavy weight of his cutting shears shined out the side pocket of his favorite tan vest, pulling it down against his thin frame.

"I need to stock up. I'm running low," Jeanette said as she looked at the bolts lining the walls. The fabric shoppe was small but full of options— linens, silks, velvets, and some lace.

Reaching out, she ran her hand over the smooth silk, loving how it caressed her skin. If only she could afford it. It was a wonder Kurt even had any in stock to begin with. Such novelties were usually only found in large, bustling kingdoms. Every time she'd ask him where he got it, he'd always say the same response— that he's had them as long as he could remember.

"Oh, Jeanette!" Beth stood up from behind a pile of cotton. "Perfect! I was hoping I would see you. Could you make a couple new dresses for me?" she asked with a wide smile. Her green eyes sparkled above her round cheeks.

"Of course. You are my best customer, after all." She'd made at least a dozen dresses for Beth. It came with the territory though.

"Fabulous! I'll come by later for the fitting." She shoved four bolts of fabric into Jeanette's arms. Stumbling back, she watched Beth prance out of the fabric shoppe.

Jeanette turned to Kurt. "Do you have anything new?" She'd suggested ordering some warmer fabrics the last time she was in so she could prepare for the Fall Winds. However, the selection looked the same.

"Not today." Kurt took the bolts Jeanette had gathered and laid them on the cutting counter. "The delivery you requested was supposed to be here yesterday, but they never showed up. I think the storm knocked down a tree on the road. Why don't you come back tomorrow? We should have the shipment by then."

"Alright. I'll just take this for Beth then."

Kurt smiled and measured the fabric. He didn't ask how much was needed, only who the client was. It helped that the town was small, he knew each and every person, along with their measurements. Plus, he'd always cut a little bit extra for Jeanette to keep in her stash. She paid for her wares and waved goodbye to Kurt as she left to finish her other errands.

The wind picked up and a chill ran through Jeanette as she walked through the village of Mapleshire. The bit of cold never bothered her though, she loved the weather. The way nature would react to the elements. The leaves rustling in the wind would soon change colors in the fall. Jeanette looked forward to watching the magic of the earth change with the seasons.

That was the only exciting thing that ever happened in Mapleshire. The sun peeked through the thick layer of clouds, giving sunshine to the previously shaded path. In the distance, fog covered the tip of Mount Gravensburg.

There had been stories of dragons populating the mountain, but that was ages ago. Tales go that they all died with the olden rulers of the lands. Some days, she wished she could leave Mapleshire and go on a real adventure or travel the world. But as much as she wanted adventure, the thought of danger kept her chained to her little town. The town's mundanity enveloped her as she strolled among the shoppes.

The next stop on her list of errands was the library. The only adventures she ever had were through books— though she figured she was the only one that felt like this. Everyone else fell into their humdrum routine and was happy to do the same thing day after day, year after year.

The library, which, truth be told, was a tiny house that Mrs. Glover rented a handful of years ago, was a building that sang to Jeanette as though they were old friends. She was happy that someone arrived in town who had a love for books just as she did.

Opening the door, the smell of old books embraced her. She took a deep breath and returned the one she had borrowed.

"Care to check anything else out today, love?" Mrs. Glover asked and filed the book into the returns section.

"Not today. I actually still have the other book you recommended. I'm planning to start that next," Jeanette explained.

"That's nice, dear." Mrs. Glover was sweet, but she never really cared to chat. The books in her library were her friends.

Jeanette double-checked that her list was complete as she left the little library.

Storm clouds brewed overhead, so she quickly headed home knowing that Beth would probably be waiting at her door.

Sure enough, Beth was sitting on the steps leading to her porch. "I came for the fitting."

"Of course." Jeanette smiled and opened the door for her.

Beth sat in the sewing room and stroked the purple fabric that she'd ordered. "Isn't this lovely? I'm excited to wear a dress with this material."

Jeanette nodded. "Let's get started."

Beth stood on the tailor's platform while Jeanette took her measurements. Then she took them again. She marked all the updated measurements; obviously now was not the time to mention any weight gain. However, Beth grabbed the paper with wide eyes.

"I can retake them." Jeanette pulled out her measuring tape again.

Beth laughed. "It's okay. That's actually one reason why I need new dresses. I hope you have enough fabric." She rubbed her belly.

Happy goosebumps ran over Jeanette's arms; fire filled her heart. "I'm so excited for you! I know you'll be an amazing mom! You raised me after my parents died, and I think I turned out pretty great!" She beamed at Beth and turned to her workbench.

"Thank you for that. I have to admit, I do have this nervous feeling in my stomach. I can't believe this is finally happening. I think I'm still in shock. I'm not sure I can do this."

"You'll do great! And I'll always be here to help you." Jeanette smiled.

Rain pelted the window and forced its way inside. It made both women jump at the intrusion.

"That latch needs to be fixed. Every storm blows the window open," Jeanette explained. But she honestly didn't mind it, the rain water wasn't hard to clean up.

"This must be one of the last summer rainstorms," Beth replied.

Jeanette's hands clasped each side of the window as she took a deep breath. The earthy scent of wet foliage filled her lungs. The gentle breeze and the soft rhythmic drum of drizzling rain called to her. She wished she could stay at the window for hours soaking in the last whisper of summer, but there was work to be done. She closed the window and turned back to Beth who shoved one of the accent pillows under her dress and was staring at herself in the mirror.

Jeanette laughed. "Of course you can do this! You guys have waited so long. When my parents died, I thought that I was going to have to go to the orphanage, or worse. You made it possible for me to stay here." She glanced at the portrait of her parents.

"I'm sorry they're not here."

"Do you remember anything else about them?" Jeanette's eyes moistened with unshed tears. She knew what Beth's response would be before she answered. This question was one she had asked regularly in the years since they'd been gone. Yet she still asked, hopeful a new memory would appear.

Beth was quiet for a moment. Her mind seemingly searching for something that she hadn't shared with Jeanette before. "Only bits and pieces. Your father was my tailor, so I have more memories of him. But still, all about clothes. I can't really remember your mother." With furrowed brows, she shook her head.

Neither could she. It was strange not remembering her mom. Like Beth, Jeanette's memories of her father were only about clothes and teaching her how to sew, but her mother, just blurry images.

Beth pulled Jeanette in for a deep hug. The tears could not remain in her eyes and fell silently down her cheeks "Thank you for talking with me. Sometimes I feel like I'm so alone here."

"Maybe it would be good to travel."

"Haven't we been over that? It's not safe for a woman to travel alone." Jeanette shook her head.

"Just think about it." Beth kissed the top of her head. "It might be really good for you."

Jeanette nodded. "I'll get to work on these dresses and I'll make sure to give some extra room." She winked. "Give my best to Clint." She walked Beth out and closed the door behind her.

A new baby. The town won't know what to do with themselves.

When she got back to her sewing room, she stood on the platform and looked into the mirror. Just as her mother had.

Her mother.

A fuzzy image of her mother mirroring her actions came to mind. This was the only memory she could recall and often thought it may have been a dream. She never could make out her mother's face, but she could see her blurry reflection. Her mother would stare at the glass for what seemed like forever to a small child.

No, not stare— search.

But search for what? Jeanette often pondered this question. What was she trying to find in the reflection that stared back at her?

She felt like a child as she copied her mother. If only she knew what she was searching for before she died. A deep ache blossomed in the center of her chest and she wrapped her arms around herself to hug the pain away.

After several moments, Jeanette left her reflection. She got to work on sketching different designs for the dresses. Crumpled balls of paper filled her trash bin. Figuring out a dress pattern that could grow with Beth was frustrating, and kept her up long into the night.

She hadn't had to make maternity dresses for anyone in five years, and even then, it wasn't one single dress that could grow with the young mother— she had requested a few dresses at different stages of her pregnancy. Though she'd also had hand-me-downs from her own mother, so she didn't need as many as Beth did.

It was hard for the people of Mapleshire to conceive, which worried Jeanette. With so few new arrivals, she wondered how this town would thrive and continue on. It made her wonder if other towns had issues as well, or if it was secluded to Mapleshire.

In truth, a part of her was glad though. If there weren't children in town, then no one would have to go through the heartache of losing parents like she had. She was only thirteen when her parents died, and although she should have been old enough to remember what happened, she didn't. No one in town really knew either. They never caught the man who murdered them in plain day and nobody was there to witness it.

She shook her head at the troubling thoughts, trying to focus on the task at hand.

Finally! She designed a series of pleats on the waistband that would expand with Beth's growing belly.

The next day, a new shipment of fabric came into the store while Jeanette was examining the current wares.

"Hello Kurt." A burly, bearded man hefted the delivery on the counter. "Should I come back next month?"

"Oh, I'd say so. I also need you to deliver this to Hempsure." Kurt handed the delivery man a package.

"Will do." He tipped his hat and left the building.

Jeanette made her way over to look at the new arrivals. "What's in Hempsure?"

"Eavesdropping again, are we?" Kurt raised one eyebrow at Jeanette.

"I'm sorry. I guess I can't help myself." She gave a sly smile. The last time she got caught eavesdropping, Kurt had asked Rosetta out. It did not go well.

Kurt bellowed a laugh. "My nephew lives in Hempsure. He's about your age, I think. It's been a while since I've seen him."

He had a nephew around her age? She should've guessed there were others her age in different towns, but not one so close.

"I didn't know you had family in the next town over."

Kurt nodded. "Oh, yeah. I have a ton of family around. Funny thing is, they're all in our neighboring towns. And yet," he paused, "I don't see them enough."

He must miss them. What must it be like to be able to visit when the pain of missing them sets in? The soft edges of grief twisted her heart, a pain she'd known for the past twelve years. Oh, how she longed to be able to visit her parents. Time may soften grief, but it never takes it away.

"Well, I think I'll come back later. Once you've had time to catalog these new bolts." Jeanette grazed her hand over the new fabric.

"Alright, have a nice rest of your day."

As Jeanette left the fabric shoppe, she knew she needed to find Beth. She needed to talk to someone, and Beth was as close to a mother as she had. She looked around the market, knowing that this was the usual time Beth would be running her daily errands.

Jeanette found her sitting outside the town's bakery, a steaming cup of hot cocoa in her hands.

Words spilled out of Jeanette's mouth as she told her all about Kurt's nephew in the neighboring town who might be around her age.

There weren't many people Jeanette's age in Mapleshire. In fact, the closest age gap in town was Meredith, who was still seven years her senior.

Beth just sat there listening, sipping her cocoa.

"Don't you have anything to say?" Jeanette fiddled with her skirt.

"You know what I'm going to say."

Not this again. Jeanette raised her head toward the heavens and closed her eyes.

"I think it might be good for you to travel. We have four neighboring towns. It wouldn't be that dangerous to go to one of those." She had a point.

It was less than a day's travel to Hempsure, which was supposedly a bustling town. At least, that's what she always heard when vendors would complain about deliveries being late. Beth and Clint had gone to Hempsure on their honeymoon, but they were together. Stennton was mostly a farm town though, not much to do there. The Gravensburg Pass was apparently hard to get to. But that didn't stop rumors of monsters lurking in the depths of the mountain pass and the caves surrounding it. That seemed pretty dangerous to Jeanette. Then there was The Forest of Faiden Dell, which she had never heard anything about. There was no trade with them, no deliveries, nothing.

"Maybe," she said, but it didn't stop the thoughts of danger for a woman to travel alone.

They sat in silence while they finished their cocoa. "I'll see you later." Jeanette gave Beth a hug and left. As she did so, she bumped into a man in a long black cloak carrying a loaf of bread. "Oh, I'm sorry. Excuse me."

"Travelling is a good idea, you should go," the stranger said with a groan.

Before she had time to question it, he quickly rushed away. It was weird that a stranger would tell her that, but her conversation was in public; he was probably just one of the delivery men for Kurt. Which reminded her of her errands.

Jeanette returned to buy some fabric and was then finished with her shopping. She turned toward the dirt path that ran between the shoppes, the villagers' homes, and led out past the lake. Her house sat in the clearing near the water, a straight route from the market. It was the way back home.

Although there was another way.

A longer path led through the overgrown forest that surrounded the valley. Even though she lived in this town, she was not about to take the boring, straight route that everyone else preferred. She smiled. Turning her back on the little path, she walked toward the forest.

The trail had a thick canopy of overhanging trees with spots of sunlight breaking through, causing sparkles of dappled light to glitter the bark.

Around her was the sound of whispers; the trees were talking to each other. She wished she could understand what they said, but that would take a different kind of magic, one that died out long ago. Thick brush covered a once-worn walkway; evidence of life that once traveled smoothly, now abandoned to nature.

Inhaling deeply, Jeanette was enraptured by the smell of forest. It had the constant fragrance of wet rocks and moss. Her presence startled something in the undergrowth. A charming squirrel scurried in front of her, weaving its way through the tangled leaves in its search for dinner.

There was another reason why she loved taking this overgrown forest path— it led to Rose Manor. No one seemed to care about the old, abandoned mansion. She, however, didn't mind stepping over weeds or having to duck under branches. Something about it called to her— it felt familiar, even though she had never stepped foot on the grounds.

A tall iron fence surrounded the property, doing its job to keep unwanted visitors out— to keep *her* out.

She came to the spot she loved to stop at; the spot with an engraved rose on a gate in the fence. Her fingers traced around it. The mid-bloom rose was on a stone plaque with carved vines surrounding it. The large lock on the gate was cold in her hands. She shook it, wishing she could go in to explore the grounds and get a better look. She knew that would never happen. It would be too dangerous to go exploring an abandoned building. She didn't want to risk falling through the floorboards, or becoming trapped in the cellar.

Besides, there was no way in. She had accepted it was better to admire from afar.

The grounds contained remains of stone statues and a once beautiful fountain; now dry and overrun with weeds and ivy. In her mind, she pictured the fountain full and flowing with pink or purple water, a sweet mist rising into the air like the mist that settled over the lake in the summer dusk. That was her favorite bit of magic.

Her gaze moved to the Victorian stone mansion with its tall spires pointing toward the heavens. Overgrown ivy laid claim to its salmon colored stones. Giant windows adorned the front with dusty drapes covering any view to the inside. The tall, wooden doors were emblazoned with carved lion head doorknockers.

What kind of adventures have happened in that house? Maybe a great prince would move in and save the town from a dragon, or a troll, or some other sort of disaster. Or maybe she would be a damsel in distress and the prince would save her and they would fall in love and live happily ever after like the stories in her books. However, the abandoned Rose Manor was not what it used to be. What kind of prince would want to live there? Even if it was the most beautiful place that she had ever seen.

Leaves crinkled behind her. The hair on the back of her neck stood on end. She spun around trying to find who or what it was. The trees cast long fingers of shadows across the path. She tried peering through the dark bushes and undergrowth.

It had become dusk while she was lost in her thoughts. The mysterious sound brought her awareness back to the present. She stepped toward the sound to try to get a better look. A deep rough growl met her curiosity, causing her to jump back. It didn't sound purely animal, but she couldn't tell what else it was either. A tall, dark shadow moved between the trees.

She shook her head and tried to calm her nerves. Her eyes were playing tricks on her. They had to be. Her heart threw itself against her ribs. No one was supposed to be in the forest after dusk. Rumors of terrible beasts generally kept the townspeople away.

Jeanette thought it was just old myths people used to tell to keep their children in line. *Stay out of the forests or you'll be lost to the fairies. Don't go out at night or cave monsters will devour you.* She wasn't sure if she really believed those stories, but she sure enough wasn't going to linger and find out if they were true.

She tore down the small path and through the dark trees to find her way home. Branches whipped her face, stinging her skin with small scratches. The sounds of the forest at night were different from that of the day. Instead of quiet whispering, the woods screeched and groaned around her.

Darkness settled and she stumbled and tripped on rocks and roots. Sparks of moonlight broke through the canopy, creating faces in the trees with its ominous glow. She felt her heart tighten with each twig that snapped beneath her feet.

Finally, she broke through the trees, the glaring moon hanging above her. After taking a moment for her eyes to adjust, she ran home to her safe cottage.

She had never been out after dark before. It was forbidden. There were dangers in the world that lurked in the darkness. Stories that kept people tied to their home and their hometown. She always thought they were just tall tales, but this fear in her chest told her to get inside where it was safe.

She tugged on the key in her pocket as she reached her door, pulling at the handle to open. Neither would budge. The sound of howling in the distance caused her heart to race.

"Open. Please open," she said aloud, desperation in her voice. As she tried the handle again, it opened and she rushed inside, slamming the door behind her.

She leaned against its frame as she caught her breath. Tears fell down her cheeks and her body shivered. She was thankful she'd left the door unlocked that morning.

She had never felt this type of fear. Once she managed to relax, she thought about her experience again. It was exciting. It wasn't exactly pleasant, but she kind of liked it. It was different. Her mind wouldn't let go of the adrenaline rush.

Her fingertips were still tingling as she got ready for bed hours later. Having a dip into adventure made her yearn for that feeling again. She wasn't sure what she could do that would make her heart pound like that. None of her adventure books had ever given her that rush before. It was the first time she really felt alive.

Chapter 2

A few days passed, and the town buzzed with excitement. Perhaps Beth had announced her news. But no— Beth was waiting until the Fall Winds. Surely she would have told Jeanette if she'd announced earlier.

This was something different.

It seemed as if everyone in town was out to shop, or at least gossip, today. Townspeople gathered in small clutches around the market, peering over one another's shoulders and speaking in hushed tones. This excitement was caused by something else, and Jeanette seemed to be the only person in town who had not heard the news.

"Rose Manor has been sold, Miss Warren," Mr. Quint, a short plump man, told her as she bought some apples.

Rose Manor.

Her Rose Manor.

Jeanette's heart jumped, then promptly sank. The very thing she'd daydreamed about was now happening, but her dreams were unlikely to be reality. It was no longer *her* Rose Manor, it was someone else's home.

A stranger.

She was glad it wouldn't be sitting vacant anymore, but she wished she hadn't been the last one to know. Maybe the new owners would repair it to its former glory.

Jeanette veered closer to the whispering groups as she headed to the fabric shoppe, hoping to hear more about this mysterious buyer. Depending on who it was, she may still have a chance at exploring inside the gates of her dream home.

"I hope a single man bought it." Two young women were speculating near the bakery. Their giggles made it clear of their hopes. "Ooh, maybe it's a runaway prince!" One of them swooned.

Jeanette's chest tightened at the possibility. If she had been better friends with those girls, maybe she would've joined in their conversation. But they were eight years younger than her, and they had already started thinking of her as an old maid.

"Maybe a family with a beautiful daughter lives there now," a few men said their wonders outloud. A flame of irritation heated Jeanette's chest. They had never paid any attention to her, but then again, she wasn't interested in them either.

The rumors were not as hopeful as a handsome prince, but a new friend was always welcomed.

The truth was, new people never moved to Mapleshire. The possibility of the unknown caused Jeanette's stomach to lurch, similarly to the way it had in the woods the other night.

"Do you know who bought Rose Manor?" she asked as she bought a few yards of blue linen for a new dress.

"No. No one knows, my dear. All we know is that it's taken up. Apparently they've been moving their items at night, so no one has seen them." Kurt rolled up her fabric and slid it into her satchel.

The mystery and intrigue were only surpassed by rumors about whoever the new neighbors might be.

"I overheard one girl say it might be a runaway prince," Jeanette said as she sifted through extra fabric scraps.

"I doubt that," Kurt said as he looked over his sales book. "More likely an older couple tired of all the gossip that travels through towns, who just want to live out their years in peace and quiet."

Jeanette chuckled. "Sounds like something you'd like to do."

Kurt smiled. "If only I had someone to live out the rest of my years with."

"You know, Rosetta is still single." They both laughed, but Jeanette caught Kurt glancing out his shop window and across the market to the flower booth where Rosetta sold beautiful pieces of her garden.

After she finished shopping and listening to the gossip, she headed home. She decided to take the longer path in order to walk by the mansion on the way; she needed to see it for herself.

She started on the familiar, overgrown path into the forest, dodging low branches and stepping over spiky weeds.

When the town was almost out of sight, hidden by the dense woods, the path she followed became easier to navigate. In fact, this part of the abandoned path was clear, revealing cobblestones once hidden by brush.

Surprise ran through her as she followed the path to her favorite spot in the fence. She ran her fingers along the rose and stared at the house, trying to see if she could spot anything, or anyone. Contrary to the path outside, the mansion looked the same as always.

She wondered if she'd ever be able to see inside, or at least make friends with the new residents. But if they were moving their things in at night, that told her maybe they weren't as friendly as she'd hoped they'd be. She gazed upon the house and couldn't help but feel a rush of a dark aura that urged her to run away. She wanted to follow her gut reaction, but a chill crept through her veins, freezing her in place. She looked around to see if anyone was nearby, but the closest people were in that house.

Shaking off the feeling, she looked at the building again. This time, as she scanned the windows, she saw a figure, though she couldn't make out any details. The heavy looking drapes quickly shut, the swiftness of the movement surprising her.

The rest of her walk back to her little cottage was calm but she couldn't help thinking about that foreboding feeling and the rumors around town. She continued on the renewed path until it met with its old overgrown self.

Her head swam with the new intake of knowledge, which wasn't much. There were too many rumors to figure out which was the truth. The feeling of darkness continued its hold on her mind. She had never thought she'd feel like that when looking upon her favorite place.

Maybe it was a sign that she would never see the inside.

Once she got back to her home, she decided to work on a new dress for herself. She needed something to occupy her mind. Every time she thought about Rose Manor, it made her sad to think about the ominous feeling that froze her insides out of fear.

Hours passed while she worked, but she finally finished. It took her longer than she thought, but that didn't surprise her since her mind was so distracted.

The dress was a tightly fitted bodice and a flowing skirt. She buttoned up the back and twirled in the mirror. Something was missing. She stared at herself until she thought of it. She walked to her ribbon drawer, found the dusty rose ribbon that her father had given her before he died, and cut it to her desired length. She fastened it along the waistline and let the ends hang down the back. That's more like it. It was her favorite ribbon; she had saved it for a special dress.

Jeanette loved the skill her father had passed down to her as well as becoming the town tailor. Although she felt she was destined for more. Something meaningful where she could make a difference.

Just then, a sense of determination filled her. She closed her eyes and pictured what destiny held for her. Maybe then she could find the future she could be excited about. Her mother's face came into view. If only it wasn't blurry. Just as she was focusing on her features, trying to make them clear, a crack of thunder boomed around her. She jumped and looked out the window at the clear night sky

"How are you doing, Clint?" Jeanette arrived early at the Marvins' home for dinner. Ever since they bought their own home they'd been inviting her for dinner once a week. An extra special evening was ahead for them as the Fall Winds were expected to arrive that night. A yearly tradition the town looked forward to, especially on warm summer days. Jeanette walked inside and put another handful of garment bags on the sofa.

"Good." He greeted her with a hug. He never was one for words, but he did make an excellent stand-in father. "Beth isn't back yet."

"Oh? Where did she go?" Jeanette looked around at the usually tidy home. Her eyebrows peaked. Dishes in the sink. Laundry on the dining table. The trash bin overflowing.

"She had a doctor's appointment. I just got home from work. I'm beat." He said with a yawn, he was still in his blue shirt from the school.

"That's okay. You go change and I'll start on this." Jeanette picked up a large towel and started folding it.

Clint smiled. "Thank you. You're such a sweet girl." He kissed the side of her head, grabbed a shirt and pants out of the pile, and went to the bedroom.

A couple hours passed. Jeanette smiled at the nicely folded piles on the table and the clean dishes drying on the counter. She returned from emptying the trash bin just as Clint walked out from his nap. His snoring had resonated from the closed bedroom door. He stretched and plopped down on the couch. Jeanette joined him.

Beth walked in shortly after wearing her new purple dress. Her baby bump was now visible under the layers of fabric. It had grown since the last time Jeanette had seen her. "I'm so sorry I'm late. You'll never guess what happened." She laid her bag down and turned toward them. Her eyes widened at the sight of her home. Dishes put away, laundry folded, trash empty. Tears flooded her eyes. "What— you didn't have to do that!" She placed her hand to her heart.

"It was no problem. Those were always my chores anyway." Jeanette laughed.

"So tell us what happened," Clint said.

Beth sat next to him on the sofa. "Frank sliced his hand, it was so gross— my morning sickness hit me. Hard. I tried to hold it back." She let out a shudder. "It was right about to be my appointment time and he came running in, blood gushing everywhere. I think Dr. Caldwell forgot that I was there." She shook her head. "But he got stitched up and went back to the butcher's shop."

"Oh my goodness! I hope he's okay," Jeanette said as she felt a stabbing pain form in her hand. Instinctively she rubbed the spot, knowing the pain was nothing. She often felt others' physical pain, all it took was for her to hear about it or see it. A strange quirk she'd had since she was young, although she's never been able to figure out why.

"Oh yeah? Worried about our Frank, are we?" Clint wiggled his eyebrows.

Jeanette grimaced. "Not in that way. He's too old for me." Most of the men in town were Clint's age. While he was only ten years her senior, she only thought of them as father-figures.

"He seemed fine when he left." Beth waved her hand as if waving away the topic. "Ooh! What's that?"

About time she saw the garment bags. Jeanette chuckled. "I couldn't resist." Unzipping the bag, she pulled out a burgundy dress.

"Oh, Jeanette, it's beautiful." She reached out and stroked the embroidered neckline.

"It has pleats as well." Jeanette pointed out the waistline.

Beth grinned as she rubbed her hand over her belly. "I love your handiwork."

"Well, now you have five more dresses. Come on, I'll help you get dinner ready."

As usual, dinner was delicious. She was lucky that Beth was such an amazing cook. They'd spent hours in the kitchen together throughout the years— time Jeanette cherished.

"It's almost time for the Fall Winds." Beth looked out the window at the setting sun. The Fall Winds were one of their favorite events. They came once a year marking the official end of summer and the true beginning of autumn.

"I'm so excited. Are we going to attempt our tradition this year?"

Beth laughed. "I think I can manage it."

Together they climbed onto the roof, cocooning themselves in blankets, like two caterpillars waiting to experience the change that was coming. Clint had his own blanket.

From their vantage point they could see the other townspeople around them, gathering by fires and bundled in blankets of their own. Everyone had their own way of celebrating.

It was time. The breeze came gently and kissed their cheeks with a coolness that only autumn could bring. It went from group to group and then through the trees. Everyone was silent and listened to the song it sang. Each year it seemed to sing a different tune.

The blanket nearly got blown off of them when the stronger winds came. Strong winds were rare. They represented a big change.

"I bet that's for you." Jeanette rubbed Beth's tummy.

"Or you—" She winked. "You'll have to make sure you're back before the next Fall Winds. Can't have you missing this little one's first."

"I never said that I was going to travel." Jeanette was still unsure of the idea.

Beth squeezed her hand. "I know change can be scary. But you have gone through so much already. I don't see the harm of trying something new."

Jeanette nodded.

"I can't wait for you to experience your first Fall Winds," she whispered to her baby. It would definitely be exciting to have a new baby in town. The youngest child was five.

"Oh look, the leaves!" Jeanette pointed toward the forest trees. The leaves changed colors right before their eyes. That was one of her favorite parts. The winds changed the foliage as they watched, like an artist with a paintbrush refining their work. The colors changed from bright summery green to a perfect mix of red, orange and yellow.

Autumn had officially arrived.

Fall was in full swing. As the temperatures dropped, so did the leaves. Creating a beautiful ombre of oranges, yellows, and reds on the ground. Jeanette was at her cottage, and with the weather changing so quickly, she was sewing larger jackets for the handful of children in town before it got too cold. She didn't actually *need* to sew jackets for the younger kids, they could have the hand-me-downs from the older ones, but that felt unfair. And she didn't mind sewing new ones each year for the children, it was a nice gift she could give to them.

Falling leaves flitted across the sky and danced in the gentle breeze. A golden frond landed on her blue dress. She picked it up, turned it in her hands, and leaned back, letting herself rest on the railing. She loved this time of year. With her eyes closed, she listened to the wind-song through the trees and the chirping of the birds. It was a peaceful time while she sewed.

"Well, that's done." She finished the last of the jackets, folded them in her arms, and carried them inside. She'd need to make sure she delivered them today.

Jeanette gathered her things and headed toward the market. The leaves crunched under her feet. She meandered out of her way to step on an extra crunchy leaf to let her escape the reality of the hardship of being grown and alone. To simply feel the freedom of childhood again.

Laughter echoed in her ears. Heat stung her cheeks; how silly she was for going out of her way to step on leaves. She looked around for the cause of the mocking, the broken leaf still under foot, but the laughter wasn't aimed at her. Thank goodness.

On the sands of the lake at the base of Mount Gravensburg, two men were fishing, laughing with each other.

One fisherman was reeling in a fighter. He leaned back to keep himself from falling in the lake, while his friend waited by the side with a net. The fish disturbed the calm water, splashed and flailed about. He pulled the line in, and the fish flopped in the net as the fisherman wiped the sweat from his hairline. His friend patted him on the shoulder. It must be nice to be able to do things like that.

Her father tried to teach her a little before he died. Her heart yearned for the time she'd missed with her parents. The knowledge they could've passed down to her if only they were still here.

Shaking the thoughts from her head, she stared at the lake. The water, once again calm, let the golden mist float back onto the surface. It was beautiful. She breathed in the fog, the taste of salt and cinnamon filled her mouth.

The natural magic made the mist change with the seasons. On spring days, it would be blue and taste of wet stones. Sunny, summer days, it would be pink and taste of sweet strawberries. She was so relieved it had not died off. So many of the different types of magic were just legends now. Somehow the natural magic lingered.

Jeanette arrived in town and found everyone in a frenzy. Usually, only the sound of small talk hummed as people bought their groceries. This time, there was an audible buzz throughout the market.

Beth had announced her news! The town was elated about the future little bundle of joy.

She looked around the market and saw smiling faces everywhere. People were buying their groceries and talking about the special addition coming. She had never seen so many happy people.

She made her way to the center of town and found people hugging and congratulating Beth.

"Beth! My goodness, everyone is so happy! Congratulations," Jeanette said and gave her mother-figure a hug.

"I know, I couldn't believe the response I got. I mean, I feel like everyone views this as their own miracle."

"Is that okay?" Jeanette asked.

"Oh, yes. Of course. I just didn't realize that this miracle of mine would mean so much to the rest of the town too." Beth gestured at all the townspeople celebrating.

Jeanette saw everyone thrilled. She tried to think back to five years ago when the last pregnancy announcement had happened. The town acted the same way then too. She glanced from group to group who were hugging each other as if this news would completely change their way of life. Mr. Quint was juggling apples, and Braxton was giving away free loaves of bread as part of the celebration.

Her gaze turned toward Rosetta, who was handing out flowers. She watched as Kurt slowly approached her. Although Jeanette couldn't hear what they were saying, she saw Rosetta nod and hug Kurt. Hopefully that was the good news Jeanette had been hoping for for the two of them.

She felt a happy chill run through her as she watched the celebration around her— then she caught a glimpse of a dark, hooded figure. The happy chill turned sour as she felt that dreaded feeling again. The sun came out from behind clouds and temporarily blinded her for a moment. She blinked against the light and tried to find the figure again, but there was no one there.

She turned back to Beth, gave her another hug, and left to finish her errands.

As she walked toward the fabric shoppe, she couldn't help but feel as if she was being followed. But every time she looked behind her, there was no one there. At one point she thought she saw a black cloak flow between villagers, but when she looked closer— well, she figured it was her mind playing tricks on her.

Pulling open the door to Kurt's store, she felt more at ease being somewhere that she enjoyed so much.

"Jeanette! What happy news!" Kurt smiled.

"I know! It's so exciting!" Jeanette said. "It was a good thing you cut me a few extra yards of fabric for her."

He laughed. "Oh, yeah. I guess so."

"So... uh, I wasn't eavesdropping again, but uh... you and Rosetta?"

"You stinker, how do you always seem to know about that?" He laughed again. "Well, I thought about what you said and decided that it was time I did something about my feelings for her. Turns out that since her rejection before, she's had a change of heart."

"Aww, well, I'm glad. I'm happy for the two of you," Jeanette said. It was true too, but at the same time a pang rang through her own heart, yearning for someone she could spend her time with. She left the shop without buying anything and headed toward the school.

With each step, she felt that ominous feeling once more. Something she couldn't shake. She couldn't tell if it was actually something to worry about, or if it was somehow her jealousy that others were having good news and she remained the same. The same in her job that helped the town but felt as if it wasn't what she was made for. There was always something hinting behind her heart that led her to believe that she was meant for more.

Arriving at the school, she found her father-figure. "I have a delivery," she said to Clint. "New coats for the children."

"Oh, perfect timing, Jeanette," Clint rallied the children and Jeanette handed out the new coats. They all thanked her and examined their new jackets.

"Congratulations on announcing! The town is so excited," she said and gave him a hug.

"Thank you. The children haven't stopped talking about it all day either."

Once Jeanette arrived back home and put her things away, she sighed vocally, her lips twilling with movement and sound.

A shiver crawled down her spine. Her body stiffened and she felt again as though someone was watching her. She looked around at her empty home.

Strange.

No one was there, but her heart burned in her chest. She cringed, her shoulders rising at the action. "I need to get out of here for a while." Something definitely felt wrong.

Once her picnic basket was filled with her blanket, book, and some leftover chicken, she wondered where to go for her picnic. She wanted to be further away from town. She smiled, knowing the perfect place— Mount Gravensburg. Surely she wouldn't feel like this surrounded by nature.

It was not a long hike to the small clearing that had a perfect view of the town. She had been there many times. Spreading her blanket out, she got comfortable. She reached into the basket, got her book, and set it beside her. Her stomach growled as she grabbed the chicken and started eating. She gazed out on the town. The trees broke at her spot giving her a clear shot of the valley, she saw everything from her perch.

The town looked so small. She *felt* small as she pondered on how truly tiny this place was compared to the rest of the world. She wondered if this was what her life would always be like. Maybe Beth was right— maybe she should travel.

After her lunch, she lay on her blanket and watched the puffy, gray clouds roll in. She stared at the shapes they made. One was a bunny, another a dragon.

Jeanette relaxed deeper into the blanket. The birds chirped; the leaves whispered as the wind whistled through the thick, fall trees. She always imagined that the wind was trying to tell her something.

As it blew across her face, she wished that she could've spent this picnic with her parents. Nevertheless, she closed her eyes and enjoyed the sounds of nature.

The rumble of thunder echoed through her bones. Gray haze surrounded her. The previously peaceful, sunny day turned into a stormy night. She squinted and blinked as she tried to focus but couldn't see through the woods. "Why do I keep doing this? I need to be home *before* dark," she scolded herself.

Carrying her basket, she stumbled over rocks and roots as she felt her way through the woods. None of the trees looked familiar. She should've reached the bottom of the mountain by now.

It started to rain. *Great, this'll make things easier.* She let a groan vibrate through her chest. Normally, she would've loved feeling the tiny cold raindrops tickle her skin, but it was dark, and she was lost. In her woods— she was lost.

Her heartbeat throbbed in her ears. She barely navigated over the rough terrain. Her ribs shivered in the cold. Instead of enjoying the racing of her heart, she wished it would slow. She regretted yearning for adventure. It was different when she could run home. When she could just dip her toes into excitement. This did not feel like dipping her toes, this was jumping off the cliff.

A howl ripped through the trees. She jumped and turned toward the direction of the sound. A pair of red, glowing eyes stared at her, and then they were gone. Something was out there. She took a couple steps backward, not wanting to turn her back to possible danger.

Slippery mud moved beneath her feet and she slid down the mountainside. Her hands flailed as she tried to grab onto anything that could stabilize her. She wasn't sure if she was falling toward a cliff or if eventually her momentum would cease.

The ground stopped abruptly but her heart continued to fall. No, it was her whole body that continued to fall. Her back hit the hard ground and her lungs tightened. She couldn't breathe. The rain lashed at her face, attacking her with pins and needles on her skin.

Finally, she had enough strength to stand. She'd landed in some sort of pit. She reached for the top so she could climb out, but it was too high. Fingers from a low hanging branch stretched toward the opening of the pit. If only she could grab that branch, she could pull herself out. What was she going to do now?

Lightning leapt across the sky and spurred on stronger rain. Mud came like a waterfall over the edge of the pit, spilling down on her. It swallowed her shoes. She needed to get out of this hole. Wiggling her toes, she managed to free her feet, but her shoes were lost.

The sound of branches snapping echoed on the wind. Her blood ran cold. Something was up there. She became quiet, still, not wanting her helplessness to attract a predator.

She listened for a sound. It was quiet for a moment. Then she heard the crackling of a torch. Light flickered at the opening of the hole. Shadows spread like oil. A tall man in a black cloak appeared at the top of the hole.

"Help! Sir, I need help getting out! Please!" Her voice cracked as she begged the stranger. That's all she could do. She needed help, and there was no one else.

He looked down and tilted his head at her. "Humph." He pulled her from the hole with one smooth movement. As he did, his hood came off exposing his face.

Jeanette let out a gasping scream.

His grotesque face, pale as snow, shone between bursts of lightning over deeply sunken eyes, with pupils that glowed red and black. His angular cheekbones cast dark shadows on thin cheeks. Patches of stringy hair fell over his three-pointed ears. The grip on her arm was so tight, she felt his long nails dig into her flesh. And worst of all, he smelled of rotten meat. The stench stung her eyes and made the hair on the back of her neck stand on end.

"Well, you were easier than I thought you'd be." He grabbed a large rock. Her breathing caught. "We can't have you telling all the townspeople what you've seen, now, can we?" His deep, rough voice sent spiders crawling down her spine. He lifted the rock with a fierce sneer.

"No!" She trembled, her body shaking. Lightning flashed across the sky again. She pushed and kicked against him to no avail.

Then, with one sudden movement, blackness crept through her senses.

A dull throb pulsed from one point on her head and radiated throughout her body. Her mind raced as she tried to remember what had happened. The rain swirled in a muddled memory. She had fallen in a hole and then— the man! Her stomach hurt from bony pressure. Was he carrying her? He must be. How long had it been since she got captured? She could have been unconscious for days. She tried listening to her surroundings, but it was quiet aside from his heavy footsteps on stone echoing around her.

Her eyes wouldn't open, though she kept trying to blink. Wiggling her eyebrows, she felt fabric across her eyes. The blindfold was excessively tight; she felt dizzy. The smell of blood and sweat pierced her nostrils— she felt as if she was about to be sick. Was that her blood she smelled or someone else's? Warm, sticky liquid slithered down her arms, like a snake hunting for prey.

Her breathing quickened. She tried to move around, but there was something restraining her arms behind her back. Whatever it was made her wrists burn.

She tried to speak but her mouth was dry. She fought through the pain and screamed. The corridor echoed her scream back. Her heart pounded once more with that new, now familiar feeling. The one that longed for adventure. She now regretted that longing even more.

"Oh good, you're awake," he growled and set her down. Her bare feet met cold stones and Jeanette knew this was her chance. She turned away from his heavy footsteps and tried to run. Blindfolded. She knew it was a dumb choice, but she had to get away. She took two steps before getting pulled back. Not only had he tied her hands behind her back, he also tied the rope around her waist to bind her. He yanked on the rope and tugged her forward.

Her terrified shrieks reverberated through the halls.

"Please let me go!" She sounded like a mouse, her voice barely squeaked out. She ran into her captor and fell onto the hard stone floor.

The sound of keys rustling and the creaking groan of a metal door met her pleas for freedom. His grip on her arm tightened as he thrust her through the door. She stumbled over her dress and fell against a wooden surface.

"Get in." The door rattled her teeth as it slammed shut. His deep rough voice jostled in her mind, sticking to the edges, marking her memory as its territory.

She hit the surface so hard that it made the air escape her lungs. Her mouth was so dry, it hurt just trying to breathe.

She had to get the blindfold off. The rope tightened against her hands as she struggled to free them.

She caressed the wooden object she had fallen against, which turned out to be a small table. With her hands still bound behind her, she knelt next to it. Her face searched the air until she collided with the corner of the table. Lightning danced across her eyelids.

The corner of the table would be able to get the blindfold off. It had to. She just needed to get in the right position as she nudged her head in different angles. But as she started working, the blindfold barely budged. This had to work. Nearly frantic, she returned to the table and finally hooked the blindfold onto the corner, tugging her head back quickly.

Freedom.

Chapter 3

Banging and clanging of some kind echoed through the stone corridor. He wondered what was going on in there. She must be scared. He stood in front of the dungeon door holding a bowl of soup. He didn't want to think of what punishment his master would inflict if he knew he was down here. Unease filled his stomach as he opened the door and entered.

"Who are you?" Jeanette's hands were on her hips, sweat marked her brow, and she was breathing heavily. His own brows furrowed as he looked around at the tiny prison.

Frayed, bloody rope lay on the floor under a sharp rock that protruded from the wall. He looked toward the small window, the table broken to pieces underneath it. She must have tried to stand on it to reach the bars. The yellow and brown stained cot was pulled from its normal spot in the corner. Jagged scuff marks in the stone flaunted her determination to move it.

He smirked. *That's my girl.* He liked to see that she still had her spirit after all these years. She'd tried to fight back, and now, she'd tried to escape.

"Who are you?" She demanded once more.

"I'm the one who brought you some soup," he replied. He wasn't sure if he could tell her his name. The pain of disobedience was not worth the risk right now. He held out the soup for her to take. She recoiled, but the growling in her stomach betrayed her. "I promise it's good." He started to walk toward her.

"Stop." She held her hand out and took a step back.

"It's not poisoned," he said and ate a small spoonful. Her eyes widened and she grabbed the bowl, shoveling the soup into her mouth.

She looked beautifully terrible. Dried mud and leaves coated her hair, clothes, and skin.

Her skin.

It was moonlit pale beneath the dirt. Even being covered in mud, she was a beautiful young woman. She hunched over the bowl. Her curly, brown hair, caked with gunk, swung against her shoulders as she ate. Her slender arms cradled the bowl against her. For warmth, probably. Her dress was still wet from the rain. The breeze came through the window, stippling her arms with goosebumps.

"Here." He took off his overcoat. She glanced at him, seemingly having forgotten he was there. "This will help keep you warm."

"Um..."

"Please. It's the least I can do."

"Thank you..." She reached out her hand, but hesitated. She stared at him; a vulnerability breaking through before her expression hardened again. Of course she's unsure.

He pulled his gaze. "Are you okay?" Ugh. Why did he say that? Obviously she's not okay. She's just been kidnapped, she's soaked to the bone, and she doesn't remember— anything.

"I... I am feeling a little better now that I've had that soup. Thank you." She handed the empty bowl back to him. His mouth went dry at the touch of their hands.

He took the bowl, gave a curt bow, and left the room. That was risky, bringing her food. Hopefully his master wouldn't find out about it, but the risk was worth it, he needed to see her.

She's a prisoner, he reminded himself.

Well— they both were.

Jeanette stood in the middle of the tiny room, holding a stranger's coat. She wondered who he was— he never did give her his name. Looking around, she was unsure of what she should do next.

The table didn't work, it barely held her weight before it buckled under her and she crashed to the cold stones below. The window looked large enough, if only she could reach it. Her breathing was already labored, and her aching muscles protested every movement, but she couldn't give up. She needed to escape.

The warmth from the soup spread through her veins, but it did little for her exposed skin. Jeanette looked down at the gesture; a leather coat with wool lining. Just the sight of it made her body convulse with shivers. She turned the coat around in her arms and put it on, sighing mightily at the embrace of warmth.

It smelled of fire, wood, and something else. It was familiar in some way, although she had a hard time placing the strange scent in her mind. His aroma, mixed with the smell of rain and wet dirt, permeated her senses. It calmed her in a way, and the smell of dirt gave her hope for freedom. Making her feel as though she was outside, as if she could run back home. She needed to get out of there. Somehow, there had to be a way to escape.

Death was an escape.

Would her captor kill her? She sighed at the disturbing thoughts that haunted her and shook her head. No. If he wanted to kill her, she'd be dead.

Returning to the task at hand, now full and warm, she continued to pull the cot toward the window. It was sturdier than the table, maybe she would be able to reach.

Finally, it was close enough for her to balance on the thin padding. Her hand gripped the bars of the small window. They wouldn't budge. But maybe if she hoisted herself up, she could squeeze through them.

Jeanette tried again and again to no avail. The bars were just too high. If she had any hope of escape, she'd have to tilt the metal frame of the bed and lean it against the wall. Her arms were already shaking, she wasn't sure she had enough strength for that, but it seemed to be the only option.

Jeanette heard footsteps in the corridor growing louder and closer. Her heartbeat doubled and a clammy sweat clung to her skin. She had barely reached the top of the frame and froze. Could it be the soup boy again? Or the hooded... beast? She wasn't quite sure what to call the man who had captured her last night. Everything about him screamed "monster."

As the door opened, the frame slid out from under her. She landed on her back and her head hit the floor, adding more insult to injury.

"Oh," the soup boy said and ran over to her. He held his hand out for her to take, although she wasn't sure if she could fully trust him. He was working with her captor. Even if he did bring her food and give her his coat, she wasn't sure. "I came to tell you that he's coming, I need my coat back. We can't let him know that I was down here."

Jeanette studied his face— unreadable. She accepted his help, and once she was standing, she slid out of his jacket. "Thank you, it was very warm." Before she could say anything else, he nodded and left the small dungeon.

She paced as she waited for whatever was awaiting her. She didn't have the strength to righten the frame and try again. Besides, her head was throbbing in two places now. But she wasn't going to give up. She needed to try to get away, despite her previous attempts ending in failure. She was willing to try anything.

Her train of thought vanished when the heavy iron door swung inward. It was too late for her plan to hide behind the door and slip out without him noticing, everything happened so fast. How strange it was that she didn't hear any footsteps.

The hooded man came into her tiny room. He was tall and had broad shoulders. His bony hands wrapped around a twisted wooden walking staff. He didn't have that last night.

No way was she going to wait for him to come any closer. She took a readying breath and bolted out of the room, bumping into him as she exited. She ran as fast as she could in the direction she thought would lead to the outside world.

His growl shook her bones. "Enough!"

She felt arms around her, but when she looked down, there was nothing there. She tried to move, to take a step, but her feet were glued to the floor. A hefty weight held her down. His heavy footsteps came closer to her.

A shadow darkened her vision— he was upon her. His stench burned her throat. She could tell he was close. He hovered over her shoulder.

"You think you can run from me?" The sharpness of his whisper drained the blood from her face.

"Who are you?"

He let out a cold, blood-curdling laugh which sent ice through her veins. "Do you really think I'd tell you?"

She squared her shoulders. "What do you want with me?"

"Humph." He turned and took a few steps in front of her, ignoring her question. "Follow me."

"And why should I do that? You kidnapped me!"

"Silence." His voice was no louder than a whisper. Her feet betrayed her wishes and followed him. He jingled as they walked, she tried to see what was making the sound, but all she saw were a handful of pouches dangling from his waist.

They stopped at a wooden door. She knew the unlikely probability, but the hope of freedom itched the corners of her mind.

He did something in the shadows, and the door opened. Light flooded the dim corridor. It took her a moment for her eyes to adjust to the new surroundings. Her feet continued following him through to a great hall.

The roaring fireplace cast tall, monstrous shadows on the painted walls. The massive rugs could swallow her whole. If she was his prisoner, he'd want her to stay in the dungeon, so if they're going somewhere else, he must want her for something specific— a repulsed shudder escaped.

Her eyes scanned the room. There had to be a way out. A hallway gaped from each of the three walls. The fourth wall had two double wooden doors leading somewhere unknown. Maybe that was the exit. If only she could get away from him— if her feet would just listen to her— she could try those doors.

With all her might, she resisted taking any more steps. Her captor stopped, his shoulders tensed, and he let out a low growl as he muttered something incomprehensible. Her feet betrayed her once more, dragging her down the middle hallway.

The wall was lined with pictures. Some were of meadows while others were of wild horses. The one at the end was different from the others. It was a simple sitting room; two oversized chairs faced a cold fireplace, a small empty table between the chairs. There was something enchanting and calming about it.

If only she could go sit in that room. To curl up in one of the large chairs, read one of her books, and pretend that none of this was happening. She stared at it as long as she could until he pulled her away.

Her captor led her up a winding marble staircase. Her gaze caught on a small window, and she stretched to her tippy-toes to try to get a better look, but her feet kept moving under her and she stumbled. The only thing she saw was the moon shining behind wispy clouds. It made her wonder how many days she had been unconscious for. When he took her, it was a massive fall storm, which was rare. This sky looked as though there hadn't been a storm in days, maybe even weeks.

He was controlling her somehow. He had to be using magic of some kind. But how was that even possible? Magic people could use died off long ago— didn't it?

They got to a landing. Another long hallway lined with an astonishing number of doors. She wondered what mysteries lay behind them. She wasn't sure she wanted to know. They came to a sudden stop at the end of the hallway. He unlocked the gold doorknob and pushed it open.

Despite her fear, she gasped in awe. A crystal chandelier hung above a gracious canopy bed with tall white pillars. Walls painted gold accented the dark cherry wooden furniture. It was as if she were a guest at a palace instead of a beat-up and bruised captive.

Her mind turned to questions— why would he take her to such a gracious room instead of leaving her in that tiny prison? If he kidnapped her, wouldn't he want her to suffer?

He placed a cold grip on her arm and shoved her in the room. She stumbled and caught herself on the bed. She turned to look at him, to see if he was entering the bedroom too.

He wasn't.

Her heart settled knowing that he wasn't leading her to a bedroom for something sinister, but that didn't mean she was just going to stand there.

She tested her feet.

Yes!

They moved under her free will and she ran to the opposite corner of the room. If he wanted to enter the room, he'd have to come in and away from the door. That could be the perfect time for an escape. She would run as fast as she could to those double doors she saw, and hopefully, they led to freedom.

"This will be your new chamber, courtesy of the servant boy." He slammed the door shut.

A breath of relief escaped. Thank goodness for that. But what did he mean by "courtesy of the servant boy"? Why would he have any control of where she stayed, let alone why would he care? She couldn't dwell on it, she needed to find an escape.

Now was her chance. There had to be a way out. She ran to the door.

Locked.

She should've known it would be locked. Confusion crowded her mind. She hadn't heard any keys jingling. She rattled it, pulling on the handle trying desperately to get it to open. Nothing happened. She put her forehead against the door, panic starting to rise. There was no way out.

No.

There had to be another way. Another door stood to the right. She ripped it open; the blue glow of moonlight shone through the small window, revealing a simple bathroom. That opening wasn't large enough to climb through, but the other one might be. She turned around and raced to the window on the opposite side of the room.

She climbed on top of the desk and felt all around the frame. There was no latch. She pushed, banged, even laid on the desk and kicked the glass. It wouldn't budge. Frustration rose in her chest. She hopped off, grabbed the wooden desk chair, and threw it against the window. It bounced off and clattered to the ground, knocking a small box to the floor as it fell.

There had to be something in this room that would help her. She turned toward the wardrobe, half expecting to find it empty. But maybe there would be something in there that she could use. To her surprise, the wardrobe was full of gowns for all occasions. Although beautiful, they wouldn't be of much help.

Anger screamed out of her.

She stared at the window for a long moment, breathing heavily. The moon glowed dark and ominous in the black sky. Something glinted in her peripheral vision. She turned to see the moon reflecting in a mirror built straight into the wall opposite the bed.

She moved in front of it and took herself in. Her blue dress had dried mud on it, and the bottom hem was torn. The slit made its way all the way up her thigh. Her bodice was ripped across her stomach with the tattered fabric hanging loosely by her side. No wonder she was so cold. Dirt streaked across her body. Dried mud and leaves snarled her hair. She took another step toward the mirror. The bump on her forehead already darkened with a bruise.

Her eyes stared at the mirror. What could she find in there? She knew this was not what her mother would be searching for. She wiped a tear from her face, berating herself for crying at a time like this.

Looking away, she heaved a deep breath and heard a whisper echoing her sigh back to her. She took a step toward the sound and found a golden grate on the corner wall of the room. It was hidden behind a large plush chair, and looked as though it could fit a small person. Luckily for her, she *was* a small person.

Kneeling down, she placed her hands on the edges of the metal and pulled. The grate shuddered and groaned. One more pull and it would be free. She rubbed her hands together and braced her feet against the wall. The entirety of it came free in her hands. Smiling at her accomplishment, she tossed it aside with a clank and peered into the unknown.

A cool breeze wafted from the darkness.

She took a steadying breath and started crawling.

Chapter 4

J eanette inched her way through the small space. Her shoulders had barely squeezed through the opening, but once inside, there was enough space for her to keep moving forward. This had to be a way out, she'd found no other options. Suddenly the ground in front of her crumbled, the world turned sideways, and the hard packed dirt rose to meet her. The air was ripped from her lungs.

Gasping for breath, she looked up from the flat of her back toward the light that glowed at the top of the hole she was now stuck in.

Just her luck.

Another hole.

Once she caught her breath, she stood and rubbed the small of her back.

The ledge she had fallen from was too high, no chance of getting back in the room that way. But now she was stuck in a dark hole. The earth surrounded her; there was no way out unless she wanted to start digging.

Closing her eyes, she leaned against the cold dirt surrounding her. She could call for help, but that wouldn't do much in the way of escaping. No, she had to figure out something else. Even being in this hole, surrounded by the earth, felt better than being trapped with that monster.

She felt the sides of the packed dirt around her. There had to be something she could do. There was a breeze blowing across her ankles and bare feet, she knelt down to examine where the air was coming from. The darkness of the tunnel made it hard for her to see, but as she felt the gentle wind coming from the depths, she found another crawl space.

It had to be an escape.

Jeanette hadn't realized how tight this new tunnel would be when she first started down the narrow path. The cold earth hugged her hips and shoulders as she pushed forward. Every inch she moved, more dirt sprinkled on top of her. The fear of the tunnel collapsing in on her made her body shake. Her fingers tingled with numbness, but she was determined to find freedom. The smell of soil filled her lungs, reminding her of the path she loved to walk daily and motivating her to keep going.

She tried to crawl forward but couldn't move.

Something had a hold of her dress. A claw dug in and inhibited her from progressing any farther. She wasn't alone.

Jeanette's arms turned to jelly and she kicked backward at whatever it was, hoping to free herself from its grip. She didn't feel anything. She tried to glance behind her the best she could, but darkness enveloped her vision— she couldn't see anyone. She tried moving more forcefully this time and heard the fabric of her skirt rip. Whatever had a hold of her was no longer keeping her trapped.

She quickened her pace. Her shoulders ached from rubbing against the sides of the tunnel and her knees throbbed from crawling. The echo of a squeak and a hiss from somewhere in the passage scurried across her ears.

Followed by a loud clunk in front of her. Or maybe that was from behind. Either way, it was too late to turn back.

Besides, she couldn't turn around even if she wanted to. It was hard enough crawling forward in the unyielding space. Her mind threatened to close in on itself as she focused on each small movement forward, knowing it had to end somewhere, hoping that it would lead her to freedom.

As she continued, she noticed at times the smell of wet earth or dragon's breath. She'd heard stories of dragons. How their breath smelled like burning heat, with hints of charred wood. She closed her eyes, breathing in the scent. She let her imagination take her to a mountainside with dragons that she had visited before only through the books she'd read. Back then, they kept her mind occupied, distracting her from the loneliness she hid in her heart. Now, she tried to focus on the memory of those books to keep her from the reality of being held captive by a villain worse than she'd ever read about. Never in her life had she thought she'd rather be surrounded by dragons, but never in her life had she ever been in a situation like this.

She came to a fork in her path. The stench of rotten meat pierced her senses, replacing her hope for freedom with dread.

"I wonder where that leads?" She heard her words bounce off the walls. She halted in fear, hoping no one heard that. *I really need to stop talking to myself.*

Go left or continue straight? She didn't want to get lost in a tunnel that led to who knows where. After a few moments, she decided to follow the straight path.

She felt something hard under her hand. Her fingers caressed it.

A tree root.

Is that what caught her before? She let out a sigh of relief that it was just a root and not something sinister lurking in the darkness. She continued on, being careful not to get caught again.

The pain in her knees made it seem like she'd been crawling for hours. She had no idea how long she'd actually been moving through this tunnel. The exertion made her lightheaded. Or maybe that was the freezing air. It had gotten more and more frigid the farther she went. She wiggled her fingers and toes to get some feeling back into them.

Her captor's voice echoed through the dark tunnel.

Fear turned her blood to ice. Although she couldn't tell what he was saying, she didn't want to go toward him.

Hesitation made it impossible to move. She couldn't turn around— the tunnel was too tight. She had to keep going. She closed her eyes and took a deep breath. She could do this, she had to. There was no other option. Inching closer to his voice, nausea burned her throat.

A light glowed a few feet in front of her. A small grate dead-ended her route, blocking the tunnel to a room. Phew! At least he wouldn't see her. She crawled closer to the opening and laid down with her legs stretched out behind her. It gave her knees a reprieve. She propped her head on her arms and peered through the slats.

The great hall's plush rugs came into view.

Then two pairs of feet.

Her breathing caught as she listened to the monster in the room in front of her. Who was that wretch talking to? She listened to the voices. That soup boy.

"You can't possibly do that!" the boy shouted at her captor. "She's just a girl! What do you really want with her, Larkus?" So that's her captor's name. She noticed how quickly he spat the question out.

"Shut up, boy!" Larkus roared. "Why would you possibly care?" The boy was silent. Larkus gave a deep sigh and continued. "You know why we need her. She has to undo it."

Her heart burned at the thought that they were talking about her and she'd missed a vital step. This was a monster's plan and he wanted her to undo... something.

The unknown had Jeanette panicking. She heard her heartbeat in her ears. *Calm down; stressing won't help anything.* She scolded herself.

"But Larkus, please be reasonable. There must be another way—"

Jeanette heard a loud clash and a hard thud. It made her jump as the boy landed a few feet in front of the grate, laying on his left side with Larkus towering over him. If the grate wasn't there, they'd be face to face.

Larkus's walking stick rolled toward her. It had an intricately carved swirl at the top and a pendant on a chain wrapped around the shaft. The pendant had a distinct design upon it.

One that Jeanette was familiar with.

One she remembered.

Jeanette ran into the house. "Mommy! Mommy! I brought you some flowers." She held the tulip bouquet up to her mother. Dirt sprinkled off the roots.

"Oh, thank you sweetheart!" Her mother turned to see the gift. She couldn't contain her laughter. "Did you get into the Conrads' garden again?" She picked up her daughter. "I guess it's time for a bath." She took her into the bathroom and stripped her down. "Oh, you have mommy's necklace. I've been looking for that."

"Yeah. It's so pretty." Jeanette stroked the image of the four seasons on the pendant.

"Yes. It is. That's mommy's special necklace and someday it'll be yours. But it's not a toy." Removing the amulet from her daughter's neck, she covered it with a golden silk handkerchief as she placed it back in its velvet-lined box.

Jeanette's head spun, the memory swirling away like water down a drain. She was surprised at how vividly she remembered that moment, as if it had just happened yesterday. This memory came clearly to her, unlike her memories of her mother in the mirror. It was the first time she'd been able to clearly see her mother in her mind. She was beautiful. But the pendant— That necklace was her mother's. It's supposed to be hers. Anger burned in her chest upon seeing it wrapped around Larkus's staff. She had to get it back.

It *will* be hers again.

"You ask too many questions, boy," Larkus snarled. "Remember who I am." He stepped over him— toward Jeanette. Heat scalded her cheeks. She pressed herself into the darkness as he leaned down and grabbed his walking stick. She watched as he exited down the left hallway. Finally releasing her breath, she exhaled the worry that she'd been caught.

The boy lay there for a moment. He grimaced and started to get up. His eyes panned over to where Jeanette hid. He squinted, then his eyes widened.

He turned his gaze toward the direction that Larkus went, then looked back at her and put one finger to his lips. She watched as he slowly got up and came toward the tunnel.

"What are you doing in there?" He gripped the slats of the grate and lifted it free. That was easy.

"I," she paused. "I was looking for a way out." He held out his hand for her to take, but she crawled out on her own. "How did you get the grate off so easily?"

"There's no way out. Not down there."

"Well, that's nice to know." Foolishness burned her cheeks.

"We need to get you back to your room. You need to get cleaned up."
He held his arm out for her.

Jeanette stared at him. Still unsure. She looked toward the left hallway.

"You can't leave."

"No. I can't." She knew she couldn't leave this place without her
mother's necklace. So, she placed her hand in the crook of his elbow and
let him lead her back to the bedroom.

She stared at the sitting room picture while they passed. This time, the
crackling fire in the hearth looked so welcoming. An inward smile burned
in her chest. If only she could sit in one of those chairs and enjoy the heat
of the fire.

They walked in silence for a while. She felt him next to her, the
warmth he gave off was doing strange things to her; her heart beat fast,
sweat soaked her palms, her breathing became shallow as she breathed in
his unique scent. She glanced at him to see if he noticed the blush on her
cheeks.

She saw details of his face she hadn't noticed before— a sharp jaw,
tanned skin, and bright blue eyes. She couldn't help but stare at him. A
red welt along his left temple emerged where Larkus had struck him. The
side of her face burned in response. She wondered what happened to him
to be stuck serving a monster like Larkus.

"Thank you for getting me out of the dungeon." Jeanette broke the
silence. She wished her voice didn't quiver. She hoped he hadn't noticed.

"Um... you're welcome." He looked down at her.

His blue eyes were welcoming and just a little mysterious. He seemed
friendly enough. She always was a good judge of character. Though, a part
of her told her that she should stay hesitant of him; trusting her gut too

soon could be dangerous. But there was something about him that felt familiar.

"Here we are." He opened the door and led her inside.

"How did you do that? It was locked." She took a few steps away from him. Was it possible for him to have magic too? As much as her heart was telling her to trust him, he and Larkus could be working together.

"It's not locked for servants." A pain of the past sparked in his eyes. He tensed his shoulders and back. "Is there anything else?"

She looked around her room. She'd made a right mess in her escape attempts. "Um..." She sighed and shook her head.

He came close to her, his expression was hard to read. "I know this is hard. I'm sorry about all of this. I'm sure all you want is to go home."

She nodded, fighting tears in her eyes. She did want to go home, but not without that necklace. She stiffened. "I just don't understand what's going on. Please tell me!"

"I..." he shook his head and turned to leave.

"No, wait. Please," she begged as she grabbed his wrist to stop him.

He turned back and stared at her. She saw a longing in his eyes and dropped his hand. His eyes burned into hers as he stood there, silently studying her.

"I need to know a few things before you go." Jeanette twisted her skirt in her fingers. "What does he want me for? I heard him say that I have to undo it. Undo what?"

"I can't divulge that information. I'm sorry." He was looking at her. No, past her. "So that's how you got in the vent." He pointed toward the grate. "You didn't need to rip it off the wall, it just slides up and off." He grinned.

She wasn't sure if he changed the subject on purpose, but a softness came over him, and he turned to leave again. Her gut was right, he was kind.

"Well, can you at least tell me your name?" Jeanette asked earnestly. She was grateful to him for having brought her soup, and despite whatever connection he had with Larkus, he *was* able to get her out of the dungeons.

He turned his body back toward her and a smoldering look came over him. A look that made a flush spread across her face. He took a few steps in her direction before he answered. They were only inches apart. Part of her wanted to take a step back, while another part wanted to take a step forward.

"Hugh. My name is Hugh," he said in almost a whisper. He took a deep breath and hurried away. The door shut behind him.

Chapter 5

Hugh needed answers. He wasn't sure he'd get any, but he needed them nonetheless. His evening chores consisted of cleaning, tending to the garden, and making sure there was enough firewood, among other mundane servant tasks. However, they mostly revolved around Larkus— making sure he had enough parchment, refilling his water, and serving him dinner. That could be an opportunity to get the answers he so desperately needed.

He held the tray and knocked on Larkus's door, taking one last breath of fresh air.

"Enter."

The stench of rotten meat slapped him in the face as he entered the room. "I've brought your dinner, as you requested."

"Just put it over there." Larkus waved toward the table near his fireplace.

The room was dreary. The burning embers in the fireplace fought against the looming darkness. Hugh glanced at Larkus as he scribbled something on a scroll. The letters meshed together into unrecognizable words.

"Don't you have chores to get to?" Larkus lit another candle on his desk. Even if the fire was roaring, it would do little for this room. The murk emanating from Larkus choked out the majority of light.

"I need to know something," Hugh started and then stood waiting for Larkus to either let him proceed, or expel him from the room.

Larkus turned toward Hugh. "I thought we finished our discussion." He tapped his own temple.

Hugh squared his shoulders even though the welt on his forehead still burned. "I took the liberty of taking her food." It wasn't exactly a lie, he *did* take her soup. "She thanked me for the room, but why would she think that I had anything to do with it?"

With others, Larkus kept them in the dungeons. There must be something more he wants with her if he decided to move her to her own quarters.

"I told her it was because of you. I need to be able to watch her closely, and I can't do that if she is in the dungeon."

"Are you still planning on letting her go after she fixes it?" he asked all in one breath. Hugh knew it was the only way to get any real answers.

Larkus let out a low growl and grabbed his staff. "I should have just cast a loyalty spell on you instead of that damn servitude spell. Then, at least I wouldn't be bothered with these incessant questions. One way or another, she'll be free."

The next thing Hugh knew, he stood in the hallway, his back against Larkus's door.

At least he got one answer.

The next morning Jeanette stood in front of the window, the sun shining through champagne curtains cast colorful shadows across the room. She couldn't say the night before was the best sleep she'd ever had; distressing images popped into her mind with each foreign creak and groan of the unfamiliar room. If the door wasn't locked for Hugh, that meant it wasn't locked for Larkus either.

Last night she managed to drag the desk to blockade the door. Although if they were magic, she wasn't sure if that would stop them.

She started pacing again. That seemed to be something she did more and more while being trapped in this room. Clumps of dried mud flecked off her skin, every movement she made sprinkled more dirt. She brushed the crumbs off her arms.

After her adventure in the tunnels, and then her attempt at keeping unwanted visitors out, her body protested at any further movements. This morning, those aches turned to stiffness and bruises.

She reached behind her to undo her dress but pain seared across her wrists. There had to be a way to undress without causing pain. She already felt like a prisoner in this place, she didn't need to feel like one in her clothes too.

She tried to pull the fabric off over her head. She hefted and yanked. Her feet slid out from under her, and she stumbled backward and landed in front of the mirror.

She almost didn't recognize herself. The dirt and mud stained her skin dark, as if she was a different person. Her hair was matted and tangled. Her clothing was ripped and barely covered her. The mirror was helpful to see where she might be able to use the fabric's weaknesses to escape from the cloth though.

Come on, she could do this.

Holding her breath, she grabbed a slit in her skirt and ripped.

The dress chose its own direction to tear. It followed the curve of her hips, and met at the large hole across her abdomen. There— at least it was halfway gone. She turned to see if there was another weakness in the threads that she could start tearing at. She found a frayed patch below her breast. As she tore it, the rip in the fabric traveled across her chest, finally releasing her from the rest of the garment.

Sadness pulled her heart down as she held her favorite dress, now ruined. She was grateful to be freed though.

Her naked body reflected back at her. Mud covered nearly every inch. She felt a longingness to be clean; living next to a lake made regular bathing easy. She had never gotten this dirty before.

The sound of something clattering to the ground came from outside her door, causing a wave of vulnerability to crash over her. She searched desperately for something to cover herself with, initially thinking the dresses in the wardrobe would be enough. But if someone was right outside, she wouldn't have enough time to put one on. Besides, all that would do is turn a nice, clean dress filthy. No, she needed something quicker. She grabbed the blanket from the bed.

She held still trying to listen for footsteps tapping against the stone. Her stomach turned and nausea burned her throat.

The desk would have to be good enough. There wasn't a way for her to lock the door on her side.

After listening for a moment, she heard no other signs of life outside the room. Taking a calming breath, she returned the blanket and went into the bathroom.

She messed with the knobs on the bathtub, checking the water until it reached a warmness level she approved of. As the water filled the tub, she looked for a towel.

There had to be one in here somewhere. The bathroom was small, no towel rack, empty shelves under the sink. No towel.

She would have to air dry or use the dirt covered blanket. Either way, she still needed to take a bath, and would likely need to refill the water more than once. She sighed. If only her focus could be on healing her sore muscles and not on the dirty water that would soon surround her.

She carefully stepped into the tub. Goosebumps prickled her skin as she sank against the cool marble. Warm water surrounded her, warming the tub, as well as her body.

Mud melted off of her, but didn't seem to turn the water murky. It was as clear as when she first stepped in.

A pleasant fragrance tickled her nose, her senses relaxing with the fruity earth scent. Her mind wandered to where it might be coming from. Her relaxation quickly drifted away as the thought of someone breaking into her room entered her mind.

She glanced toward the bathroom door. She hadn't heard anyone enter— the desk certainly would have caused some ruckus. As she moved her gaze away from the door, she spotted a small basket on the shelves under the sink.

That wasn't there before.

Her curiosity took control as she reached over and grabbed it. The unexpected scent intensified as she opened the lid.

Inside she found a large towel layered under a washcloth and two bottles.

Jeanette did a double take, closing the lid once more to examine the small basket, barely larger than one of her hands. Surely not big enough to hold all of what she'd just seen.

She opened it again and, sure enough, it was all there, sitting in a nice little pile. She didn't understand how the size of the inside didn't match that of the outside. She knew she was in the house with a monster who could use magic, maybe this was part of his magic too. But then why would his magic provide something so pleasant? She couldn't think of anything pleasant coming from that creature.

She pulled out the two bottles, one had a silhouette image of a head with long flowing hair, the other a silhouette of a feminine body. Together these bottles were the source of the scent.

Jeanette allowed herself to relax once again, the smell enchanting her senses as she cleaned herself with the sparkling liquid inside. The stiffness of her muscles loosened as she scrubbed; the tangles in her hair melted away. Even the pain in her wrists and back softened.

She dried herself off and stopped in front of the mirror to see herself refreshed. Even though she was still stuck in this prison, at least she wasn't covered in mud anymore. But now she could see the purple bruises on her backside where she landed, and the scratches on her extremities.

Finally feeling clean, she opened the doors to the wardrobe to pick one of those dresses.

Some of the gowns were made of solid, simple colored linen, like hers. However, others were more elegant with beading all over the bodices and flowing skirts. They were all beautiful. The thought that she wasn't the first captive to stay in this room crossed her mind. A cold wave washed down her spine, but she closed her eyes and let out a breath. She had no other option, and she didn't want to remain naked.

Underneath the hanging dresses was a large drawer. Inside, she discovered nightgowns in a variety of colors and fabrics. Cotton, fleece, flannel and— silk! Jeanette's heart leapt. If there were silk nightgowns, there had to be silk day gowns as well.

Jeanette examined the hanging gowns once more, this time spotting a dark purple dress that had been hiding to the side. Her hand massaged the smooth silk as she removed it from its hanger. It made her feel as though she was back in Kurt's shop, caressing the material he had acquired.

The towel fell to the floor as she slid the dress over her head. The fabric flowed as she twirled in front of the mirror. It was a lovely gown— whoever made it was clearly talented.

Being clean and well dressed gave her renewed courage. She felt ready to address the day, and to find the answers she needed.

Mainly, why did Larkus have her mother's necklace, and how was she going to get it back? It was tied to his walking stick. She wondered if he always carried it. That would make the recovery much harder. Although, when he grabbed her from the muddy hole that night, he didn't have it. That meant he must keep it somewhere. She just needed to figure out where. Her bedroom was at the end of this corridor, and with all those other doors, perhaps one of them led to his bedroom.

She took a deep breath. Her sweet smell reminded her of Larkus's overwhelming stench. He couldn't be in the same hallway, she'd be able to smell him.

She looked out the window again. The view of nature helped to calm her nerves. Although, what she saw wasn't entirely calming. There was a black mist surrounding the grounds, enveloping nearly all the trees in sight. Nothing familiar enough to place where she was though.

He had to have taken her far away from Mapleshire.

From her home.

From Beth.

Had anyone noticed that she was gone yet? Surely Beth and Clint had. Though she wasn't sure they'd be able to find her if they sent out a search party. *She* wasn't even sure where she was.

Her stomach growled. She tried to breathe through the pangs in her body, but knew that she wouldn't be able to focus on anything until she satisfied that urge. If she could explore this place, maybe she'd be able to find the kitchen. She might even be able to work out where Larkus kept her mother's necklace.

Her mother's necklace.

A blinding pain split Jeanette right between the eyes. An image of her mother wearing the necklace popped into her head. Only this time, she was laying in the grass next to her father. Dead. A dark shadow hovered over her.

Jeanette let out a shriek of pain. She shook her head to get rid of the image. It wasn't the first time she'd been haunted by her parents' death. She had recurring nightmares about it; each one being slightly different. This was the first time her mother was wearing the necklace.

It called to her, she could almost hear it. It pulled at every string of her heart.

She needed more information about Larkus before she could figure out a plan. Maybe if she ran into Hugh. There was something about him, something familiar. She could see kindness in his eyes. He might try to help her. But... he could be working with Larkus.

Gurgling hunger distracted her from the dilemma.

She pushed the desk just enough to try to open the door. Her stomach dropped at the rigid wood blockading her in the room. It was locked. Bubbles rose in her stomach. She fell to her knees, her body shaking from frustration and lack of food.

"I really need food," she whispered.

She could try to crawl through the tunnel and exit through the great hall. Then she'd be able to find the kitchen. She sat with her back against the door, her body unwilling to move. The vent would take too much effort to crawl through again.

If only this door would open! She banged her head against the wood. Just then, she heard a faint click. Did she do that or was someone coming in? She jumped up and stared at the door, waiting for someone to enter.

When no one came, she reached out her hand and grabbed the cold metal of the handle.

A sense of relief rushed through her entire body as she felt it move under her command. She knew she would have to be careful as she slowly opened the door and peered into the empty corridor.

There was no one there— at least not that she could see. She waited a moment to listen. Nothing. A faint glimmer caught the corner of her eye; a lone fork lay in the hallway.

Hesitation halted her at every turn.

She found herself in the same hallway as before. The one with pictures lining the wall. Her gaze was once again captured by the picture of the sitting room. She wasn't sure what it was about this painting that kept drawing her attention.

Warm fire embers were alight inside the fireplace. A pile of books sat on the small table, inviting her to pick one up and spend a rainy afternoon curled up in one of the large chairs. She felt a feeling of calm wash over her body as she examined the painting.

She reached her hand out to touch it, not knowing why, aside from feeling drawn to it. Zap! She pulled her hand away, rubbing the spot on her finger that had just been shocked. *What am I doing?* She thought as she shook her head and realized she had not been paying attention to her surroundings. She didn't want to know what would happen if Larkus found her.

H ugh finished stocking fresh firewood in Larkus's room— a daily chore. His fire burned through wood quicker than anywhere else in the mansion. The dimness of the stoked fire left a pit in his stomach.

Hugh first noticed the effect Larkus had around fire when he was just a small boy. They had been staying at a cabin when one day, Larkus left. Hugh found he was stuck at the cabin— alone.

Three days later, Larkus returned. As soon as he stepped into the cabin, something changed.

The room darkened.

When Hugh checked on the fire, it was still lit. The blaze was just as high as before. However, the flames looked pale, like a face that had gone white with fear.

He didn't understand why the fire reacted to Larkus this way. It had burned normally when he was home a few days before and it returned to normal by the next day.

That's when he began to watch Larkus closer, taking mental note of the effect he had on things— and when.

It wasn't long before he figured it out. The evil the fire feared was a mark that dark magic had been used. Ever since then, he was always cautious when the flames lost their color.

Hugh shook his head when he got back to the library. He took a deep breath. The smell of the old books filled his lungs. It freshened his senses from the foul odor in Larkus's room.

He descended the steps and saw Jeanette pull open the double doors that led from the great hall. His satchel dropped to the floor with a thud. She's wearing... that dress. How beautiful she looked in it. It suited her.

"What are you doing?" He gathered his satchel and straightened his brown overcoat. "You're not trying to escape are you? If Larkus found out, it would be the end of both of us." His voice wavered.

Hugh wondered how she got out of her room. She must be stronger than even Larkus had thought. Maybe she really could undo it.

"I'm just looking for the kitchen. I'm quite hungry. I haven't had much to eat." Her stomach growled, proving her point further. Her cheeks turned a lovely shade of rose.

Hugh felt relieved. He knew he shouldn't; she was Larkus's prisoner. As soon as he got what he wanted from her, he'd let her go. That's what he said anyway. Hugh didn't fully trust him— how could he? But he had no other choice.

"Allow me to show you the way." The tension softened from his shoulders. He held his hand gesturing back toward the double doors. "I'm sorry, I tried to bring you a breakfast tray, but when I got to your door... I was called away and accidentally dropped the tray."

"Oh, that's what the clattering sound was." Jeanette glanced around, her eyebrows peaked.

"Don't worry, Larkus is out of the house today. That's actually why I was distracted from bringing you food. He demanded I finish the morning chores right away, and then he left."

Jeanette nodded and seemed to relax a bit.

They went back through the double doors and down the far left hallway.

Hugh watched Jeanette as they traveled down the hall, wondering what was going on inside her head. She studied the walls. They were split into sections by pillars, each a different color. Hugh watched Jeanette's attention go from the deep red, to the gold, then over to the dark green wall.

She stopped in front of the light blue section.

"It looks as though it's shimmering." Her voice was trance-like. Jeanette reached out to touch the wall. Hugh wasn't sure what would happen if she touched it, so he grabbed her hand and pulled her away.

"It's this way." His heart jumped as he held her hand. Her skin was smooth and soft. She must hate feeling his rough hands. He needed to remember that he was still a stranger to her. Shock coursed through his veins as her thumb stroked the side of his hand.

He glanced at her.

She did not make eye contact. However, her cheeks looked flushed.

They got to the end of the hall and entered a tall wooden door.

"Here we are." Hugh let go of her hand as they approached and held the door open for her. He didn't want to let go. His hand ached at the loss of her touch, longing for her soft skin.

She looked like she was struggling with herself. What did she want? Probably to go home. Maybe that flush was disgust at having to hold his hand. He did just grab a hold of her— but he needed to pull her away from that wall. What must she think of him?

Just as he was about to speak, to say anything that would help break the tension, her stomach growled.

The struggle faded from her eyes.

Chapter 6

Jeanette gasped as they entered the kitchen. This place was like nowhere else, this she knew, but still, the surroundings were unexpected.

The kitchen was opulent. Wooden cabinets with glass windows lined one wall. Inside she saw sparkling white plates, cups, and bowls that made perfectly matched place settings. Her mismatched dinnerware back home popped into her mind.

On the far back wall were two stoves and two ovens, each large enough to fully fit the fixings of a Spring Bloom. She hoped she wouldn't still be trapped here during the holiday marking the official beginning of spring. Her favorite part of the Spring Bloom was always watching the flowers pop out of the snow and bloom instantly. She loved watching the ice and snow melt into water droplets that float away, kissing her skin as they leave. Beth would be due right around that holiday.

Hunger panged through her stomach and brought her back to her horrid reality.

Her eyes glanced to the right of the stoves where there were two steel doors. More doors that led to new discoveries. She moved to the center of the room where a long granite countertop stood. Goosebumps rose on her skin as she ran her hand across the cold surface.

Above her, pots and pans of every size dangled from a metal frame protruding from the ceiling.

"So, what do you think?" Hugh emptied his satchel of firewood, adding it to the pile in the corner of the room. She suddenly realized that he had been watching her.

"What do I think? This kitchen is massive. It's beautiful. It's—" She wasn't quite sure what to say about a kitchen.

He laughed.

It was nice to hear laughter. It made her feel like she was visiting a friend, instead of being a prisoner.

"Not about the kitchen. What do you think about food? What are you hungry for?" He opened one of the steel doors. "I'm in the mood for a sandwich, how about you?"

Jeanette's stomach answered for her.

"I'll take that as a yes." He pulled the ingredients from the cold box and laid them out on the counter.

"I'm Jeanette, by the way."

He stood close to her. He raised his eyebrows. "I know."

She took a step back. "How? I never told you my name." She'd heard stories of beings who could enter the mind and search for information. No, that was unlikely. He probably knew her name because he's working with Larkus. She was his mark for the kidnapping and this, this *Hugh*, was part of that plan as well. Even though her mind told her to be wary of him, her heart told her to trust him.

"I can't tell you right now. I'm not— allowed." Pain flickered across his face. He shook his head. "Please, we can't talk about it."

She saw his pain, which hurt her heart. Somehow, telling her that seemed to have caused him pain. Her heart softened a tad. "Did you want to eat here?"

Tension left his eyebrows. He looked relieved that she changed the subject. It didn't matter how he knew her name. Not right now.

"Actually I thought we could eat in the library."

Wherever they ate was fine with her, as long as she could satisfy this hunger. Plus, she'd be able to see more of this place.

Hugh led her back out the same door they had entered.

As they passed the colored walls, Jeanette recalled the touch of Hugh's hand. It had a gentle roughness to it and she loved the little bit of hair on the side of it. She instinctively rubbed it, just as she had watched Beth rub Clint's hand. She had always longed for someone to do that with. He had surprised her when he grabbed hers to lead her away from the blue wall, but her hand now felt cold without the warmth of his.

Once in the library, Hugh gestured to two large chairs. They were exactly like the ones in that picture down the hall. She stroked the brown suede and imagined herself in that frame.

"There is more to this place than meets the eye," she whispered. More to herself than to Hugh.

"Yes. There is." His voice warned.

The warmth of his presence radiated behind her. She breathed in his scent. The woodsy heat that she smelled before, mixed with something else familiar to her. Closing her eyes, she took another deep breath, trying to place it. She enjoyed breathing him in, even though she knew she should remain hesitant of him, but she couldn't help it. Something about him felt familiar, comforting. There was a kindness about him.

Each bite of the sandwich reminded her of how hungry she was. She hadn't eaten anything since that soup her first night here. Her body wanted to devour it, but Hugh was sitting next to her. She wanted to be proper. He watched her with an unsure gaze, reminding her of the way she felt when trying to remember her mother's reflection. She looked away and turned her focus to the room around them as she took another bite.

A winding staircase led to a balcony overlooking the foyer. Overflowing bookshelves lined the walls. A dark hallway branched off to the unknown.

She let a contented sigh escape her. Her gut told her to trust the man beside her. In his presence, she felt safe, despite her circumstances. Next to him, with her belly full and books surrounding her, she felt a sense of comfort. Her mind turned sour on her and thought about what it would be like without him here. It would be just her and Larkus.

No. She didn't want to think about that.

Heavy footsteps jolted her out of her head. Her heart beat like a racehorse galloping through her body. Hugh was already looking down the dark hallway. Following his gaze, she saw the flickering of candlelight and a large shadow. Her mind flashed back to that night in the rain, caught in a muddy hole, her captor's flickering shadow standing above her.

She jumped out of the chair, her plate crashing to the floor. "Is that him? I thought you said he was out of the house." Her voice quivered.

Hugh stood behind her and wrapped a hand around her mouth. "I did, but obviously he's back, and he would've heard that crash. We need to leave. Now," he whispered in her ear.

They hurried back to her room. As they passed the picture, she wanted to see what was different, but they didn't have time for that. Hugh tightened his grip on her hand and pulled her away. His face was full of concern.

"I need to talk to Larkus about having you freely roam. Make him think it's his idea. I'll come back and let you know when I'm done." He stared at her. It was the same look he gave her on that first night when he brought her food. His eyes then moved to the desk.

"I— I didn't want Larkus coming in." Or him, to be honest, but she wasn't about to tell him that.

"It wouldn't matter." He looked down the hallway and hurried away. The door shut behind him.

So it wouldn't have mattered anyway. Great.

Her stomach sank at that new bit of knowledge, but fluttered at the memory of his touch. The way he stared at her. Every time. It was like he was trying to tell her something with his eyes. If only she could figure out what he was trying to say.

Maybe she should follow him; he might be headed to meet with Larkus. She needed to find her mother's necklace. It felt like a part of her she didn't realize was missing. She needed to get it back.

Jeanette hurried toward the door to slink out and follow Hugh.

Locked.

Of course it was locked.

She leaned back against the door, frustration rising in her chest.

Her eyes scanned the room for any ideas on what she could do.

Nothing out of the ordinary. Although there was the vent, she could try it again. Maybe it would help. There *was* more than one tunnel in the vents, one had to lead to her goal. The desire to retrieve her mother's pendant burned a raging fire in her chest.

She grabbed the champagne curtains and fastened them to the foot of the sitting chair. Now she could climb in and out of the pit.

She started crawling.

She knew that if she went straight, she would dead-end at the great hall. However, there was another route to try. The one that smelled of rotten meat.

"Larkus," Hugh said as he returned to the library with a broom and tray. Larkus stood over the broken plate. Just staring at it. "What are you doing back so soon? I thought you'd use the—"

"What happened here?" Larkus growled, interrupting Hugh.

"I was just eating a sandwich and—" Hugh couldn't think of a lie to tell him, but he knew that he couldn't tell Larkus that he had lunch with Jeanette. "And the plate slid off my lap." Hopefully that lie would be good enough.

Larkus eyed Hugh.

"Actually—" Hugh knew he needed to talk to Larkus about Jeanette. He had said that he wanted to observe her, and letting her roam around would definitely accomplish that. But he also knew that unless it was Larkus's order to unlock the door, he'd be the one who was punished.

Larkus growled again and stamped his staff.

Hugh was suddenly in his bedroom. A sigh escaped him. As much as he needed to figure out a way to make Larkus order him to let Jeanette roam, he really didn't want to be around him.

He paced his small bedroom. There was no use in trying to leave again. He didn't know where Larkus was at the moment, and if he caught him again, he'd just end up right back here. He'd have to wait long enough for Larkus's temper to cool down. That would be long enough until it was time for him to leave for his nightly chores, but maybe he could come up with a plan in the meantime.

T his new tunnel was full of curves. Jeanette felt like she was going in a large circle. As she got to a dead end, she let a moan escape. All that work for nothing. She wasn't sure how to turn around, darkness and dirt surrounded her. Her breathing tightened as the spaces closed in around her. She lay there for a moment, trying to calm down, the hair on top of her head tickled. She jumped in the small space; was there something crawling on her? Her hand brushed against her head, but didn't feel anything.

Nothing, not even the dirt. There was empty space above her.

Rolling onto her back and reaching her hands upward she felt air rising into the expanse. She slowly stood making sure to go slow enough that she wouldn't bump her head, as she didn't know how tall this cavity was. Her hands grazed the narrow walls as she stood. She couldn't spread her arms out fully, but the walls seemed packed enough that she could possibly climb them. There was only one way to find out. She pressed her body against one wall and her feet against the other. Slowly, she began her ascent.

Once at the top, she was relieved to find a ledge to climb onto. She wasn't sure how far she had climbed, but she knew she was no longer on the ground floor. She lay there on the new cliff, her legs shaking from exertion. Once she regained enough energy, she continued forward, now finding herself in yet another tunnel.

The stench of rotten meat filled her lungs and she fought the urge to cough. No one could know she was in here.

She continued her way closer to an opening, like the one by the great hall, and tried to peer through the slats.

It was dark.

She couldn't see anything, but the smell grew stronger. She heard the creaking of a door opening and then a candle gave off a dim glow while heavy footsteps shook the metal in front of her. It looked like the faceplate would fall off at any moment.

Jeanette froze in fear, trying hard to control her breathing. The stench made her eyes water. She spied through the slats again. A glow illuminated the outline of a bed frame, but that's all she saw.

There was a knock at the door.

"Enter."

"Larkus." It was Hugh's voice.

"What is it?" Larkus's low voice growled.

"I brought you your dinner." She heard Hugh take a deep breath. "Also, she's just been stuck in that room since you took her there. Maybe it would be good for her to leave her room. Be able to eat something when she gets hungry."

"Why should I care if she eats anything?" He snarled back to Hugh.

"I would think that you'd want her to keep up her strength," he replied.

"Look, boy! You don't make the rules!" Larkus shouted.

"Of course not." Hugh was quiet for a moment. "I just figured that if she could move around this place, you could observe her better. You said you wanted to keep an eye on her."

Larkus gave a huff, and then something gave a horrible wooden creak. He must have sat in an old chair because Jeanette heard him muttering something to himself and he sounded lower.

"Alright, boy. Make sure her door remains unlocked so she can wander around. I do need to know more about her. I need to know what she's capable of." Larkus chuckled.

Larkus's laugh made her blood run cold and sent shivers down her spine while nausea burned her throat.

The door clanked shut. Hugh must've left the room.

What she's capable of? She's capable of a lot. She now knows where Larkus's room was. A plan of her own started to form in her mind.

A plan to get back what was rightfully hers.

She waited.

Maybe she could find a weakness. She heard a pen scratching on paper. His chair creaked again, the door slammed shut, and his heavy footsteps got fainter and farther away.

She wiggled the grate. She remembered what Hugh had said when he saw her escape attempt. All it needed was to be pulled up and off. She lifted the grate; it gave a horrible, loud screech as the metal scraped against its home in the wall. She squeezed her eyes tight.

Hopefully no one heard that.

She lowered the grate back down. It was quieter this time. Maybe she just needed practice.

Yes! It hardly made a sound that time. She tried again. It was quieter. Once more.

Silence.

Her eyebrows furrowed trying to figure out how that happened. As she pulled it all the way out, her hands slipped, she dropped the grate and winced, waiting for the metal clattering on the stone floor. It never came. It truly was silent. Somehow, as if by her own will, it became soundless.

And now she had a way in.

Hugh knocked on Jeanette's door. No answer. That's strange, he told her to wait while he talked to Larkus. He rapped on the door again. Still nothing.

Opening the door, he poked his head in. "Jeanette?" He looked around the room.

Empty.

The bathroom door was wide open, she wouldn't be in there. He turned away from the bathroom and saw the grate to the vent laying on the ground.

She shouldn't go in there. It was dangerous.

He ran out of the room to the great hall. If she was trying another escape attempt— he didn't want to think of what would happen if Larkus caught her. His stomach dropped at the thoughts of the others Larkus had tortured.

He made it to the great hall at the same time Jeanette was exiting the library. He blinked away his surprise as she let out a quiet gasp.

"Oh, you scared me. I thought for a moment you were Larkus," she said.

"Yeah, well, it's a good thing you ran into me first. How did you get to the library?"

"The vent, another tunnel led to... um, Larkus's room."

"So, I guess I don't need to tell you that I talked to him." He cocked his head. "You can leave your room anytime. But, I don't understand, he was still in his room when I left."

"He left right after you did. I didn't want to crawl all the way back through the tunnels so I snuck out of his room. I walked toward the light and found myself in the library."

Hugh took a deep breath. How reckless, dangerous, foolish, and... brave. He wasn't sure he would've done the same if the places were switched. In fact, he knows he wouldn't have.

"Well, I'm not sure where he is right now, but you should probably stay in your room until tomorrow," Hugh said. He didn't want to think of what Larkus would do to her in his rage right now. Whatever happened while he was gone was obviously not what Larkus had hoped to have happened.

Hugh led her back to her room. He was trying to think of something to say... anything that would break the silence.

"I'm impressed that you're brave enough to go through the tunnels again. Those vents are so tight, and I'm not sure they won't just cave in," he said as he opened the bedroom door for her.

"Oh... Thanks."

"But, you really shouldn't go in there again." He didn't mean for it to sound like an order, but it came out that way.

Jeanette crossed her arms and moved to the window. She must be scared, not knowing what was going on. Maybe it was anger that flickered in her eyes.

"Why not? What is going on? I just want to go home," she said.

He looked away. How could he tell her what she wanted to know? It was simple. He couldn't. His curse made it excruciatingly painful for him to reveal almost anything to her.

He followed her to the window and looked out over the dark mist.

"I can't—"

"You can't tell me right now." Jeanette finished Hugh's sentence.

"Yeah." Hugh tucked one of Jeanette's curls behind her ear and skimmed a knuckle down her cheek. It was very brave of him.

Bold.

Maybe too bold. He needs to remember— that she doesn't.

Jeanette's breathing appeared to stop at his touch. Was she holding her breath out of fear, or something else?

He took a deep breath. She smelled of a mix of fruit and dirt. It made him think of picnics of the past.

"What is that dark mist?" She cleared her throat. "Let me guess, 'you can't tell me right now'." Her tone mocked him.

"You're right. I can't." Hugh straightened and took a step away. She obviously changed the subject because she felt uncomfortable.

"Please?" Jeanette looked at him with intrigue and desperation in her eyes.

He sighed. He knew he was going to regret this. "That mist acts as a barrier." He clenched his eyes shut as the taste of blood coated his mouth.

"A barrier?" Her gaze was fixed out the window.

He cleared his throat. "Jeanette, trust me. I can't say any more." He took both her hands in his.

She looked at them. Her expression was uneasy; her brows knit together, she clenched her jaw, and she was holding her breath again. She pulled away.

Of course she didn't trust him. For all she knew, he could be working with Larkus. As if he could work with such a vile creature.

"I'm sorry. I didn't mean to upset you." The look she then gave him stirred in him a desire to protect.

Her expression changed into something else. Her jaw softened, she let out her breath, and looked at him with wide brown eyes.

"I—" when she spoke, it was in a whisper, "I do trust you."

Chapter 7

Jeanette's realization shocked her. She did trust him. That was something new to her. Living by herself, she was used to being alone, but here, in an unfamiliar place, she hated the uneasy feelings that arose when Hugh was gone.

He had become a bright spot in the otherwise dark reality she was now living. Despite all the unanswered questions and unknowns, she felt safe in his presence.

"A barrier?" she repeated as she stared out among the black mist again. A barrier protects. She trusted that Hugh could protect her. He'd proved that already. Sneaking her some soup and taking her back to the bedroom before she got caught. But how could he be so loyal to that monster? There had to be more that he wasn't sharing. That he couldn't share. He kept telling her that himself. *I can't tell you right now.* His words echoed in her head.

She looked toward the door. He didn't say anything to her after she admitted that she trusts him. He just left. What was he thinking? What was she thinking? She barely knew him. How could she already trust him? Her mind paced with the unanswered questions.

She should've asked him for help. He would know how to get her mother's necklace back. But he doesn't know it's hers.

He's been with Larkus for who knows how long. To him, that pendant belonged to Larkus. What would Hugh think if she just asked him to help her steal it back? Sure, she trusted him, but she wasn't sure he would go against Larkus. He'd been keeping her out of trouble, but he also stopped her previous escape attempts. If he knew the truth, she wasn't sure if he'd try to help her, or try to stop her. Or worse— he might be bound to tell Larkus.

No.

That wasn't an option.

She couldn't include him in this. She needed to steal it back and find a way to get out. Or maybe she should find the escape first. Then she'd have time to figure out a plan to steal it.

But that would be an adventure for tomorrow. Her body threatened to collapse with every move. The lack of sleep from the night before was catching up with her.

Laying down in bed, the purple silk gown she'd been wearing all day was not the most comfortable thing to sleep in. Plus the dirt she accumulated on the bed was more than disgusting. She rolled out of bed, brushed as much dirt off the sheets as she could, and turned to the wardrobe. A light pink nightgown caught her eye.

She let the purple dress fall to the ground.

The nightgown slid down around her naked body, soft against her skin. Her every movement caused the lightweight fabric to flow around her.

She looked at herself in the mirror. The straps hugged her shoulders and hung gently against her body.

The fabric shimmered like sheer silk.

She blushed at her own reflection. Even though she had bags under her eyes, bruises on her knees and shoulders, and her wrists still had scratches along them, she couldn't remember the last time she looked or felt more beautiful.

"At least there are some good things in this place." She lay in bed and closed her eyes.

Hugh entered her mind. She smiled. She enjoyed thinking about him, his smile, his smell, his hands, the looks he'd given her...

She let her imagination take her away.

They walked near the lake, listening to the waves, looking at the mist. She felt like a kid again as she laughed in her fantasy.

Hugh stood next to her with a smile on his face. He looked happy, somehow younger though. He appeared the way Jeanette would picture him as a teenager. She felt weird about that; she made her fantasy shift to imagine him as she knows him now.

The handsome servant.

There, that's better. Now he looked right.

Hugh gestured for her to follow him as he ran to the side of the lake, took off his shirt, and jumped in to go swimming. He was handsome and muscular. Heat burned her chest thinking about him in that way. She imagined following him to the edge of the lake to swim with him.

Her captor's face popped into her head. She couldn't shake it out. All she saw was that grotesque monster. Her mind tried to rid itself of the sight, but his mouth started to smile; then she heard that evil laugh.

Her eyes opened wide and her whole body tensed up.

H ugh relaxed on his bed. She trusts him. It took everything he had to not lean down and kiss her. He had to remember, he's still a stranger to her.

If only he didn't have to leave her so quickly. If only he could tell her everything. But he couldn't hold the pain in any longer and had to leave. He felt better once he got to his room and drank some water. Somehow he would figure out a way to remind her of who he was. Who she was. Then maybe, she would be able to undo it. To turn this place back to the way it was before.

A smile spread across his face. He couldn't remember the last time he smiled. Actually— he could. It was twelve years ago.

So much had happened. He hadn't realized how much he truly missed her until she came back into his life. Even if it wasn't under the best circumstances.

He closed his eyes and thought about Jeanette. She looked beautiful in that dress.

In his mother's dress. Fit for a queen.

He always knew she would grow into a strong young woman. Stronger than Larkus anticipated. It could be the changing point.

But she doesn't know. There must be some way to help her figure it out.

To help her remember.

J eanette tossed and turned in bed. There was no sleeping after her
mind betrayed her and sent Larkus's face to interrupt her fantasy.
Larkus.

Just the thought of him caused her body to heat up, like throwing
gasoline on a fire. The fear she once felt toward him turned to anger.
How could he think that she would just sit by and put up with this?
He had her mother's necklace; she needed it back.

Now.

Throwing on a lightweight robe, she didn't hesitate to crawl
through the tunnel again. Her body may have been tired, but this was
more important.

The bitter cold bit her fingertips. Goosebumps broke across her
skin in waves. If there had been any light in the tunnel, she bet she
would've been able to see her breath. She should've wrapped up in
something warmer, her body was shivering.

By the time she got to the part in the tunnel where she needed to
climb, she couldn't feel her fingers or toes anymore. Her ears and nose
were numb. She braced herself against the wall and started climbing.

Even though she had been in this tunnel only hours ago, something
was different. The dirt felt— looser? It was colder, almost wet. She
made it to the ledge and as she climbed onto it, her foot scraped against
the wall.

The ground around her shook and shifted. Dirt fell behind her,
threatening to pull her down with it. No, it was pulling her down by
the slack of the robe. She needed to get it off. She wiggled her shoulders
until she was free from the force of the earth clawing at her.

She crawled away from the cave-in as fast as she could.

Panic throbbed in her ears. Hugh was right. There was only one
option now. She crawled the rest of the way to Larkus's room.

It was dark, with only a faint glow behind the slats. Hopefully the grate would still be silent. Otherwise, she'd be in big trouble. Placing her fingers against it, she took a deep breath and lifted it away from the wall.

Not a sound.

She crawled into his room, staying low. There was a large bulge under the blanket. He must be sleeping. Silence was key here. She must not get caught.

She slowly slid the grate back into its home. There, no one would be the wiser.

The room was musty. The stench of rotten flesh made Jeanette feel nauseous. She couldn't think about the smell; she only had one thing on her mind.

Her mother's necklace.

It had to be somewhere. As she slowly and carefully tiptoed around the room searching for his walking stick, the embers in the fireplace burned low, casting a red glow throughout the room. The dark furniture waved in the shadows. Larkus's desk had papers and bottles sprawled across it. Jeanette read unrecognizable words. Her vision blurred and her heart raced. A sharp pain stabbed the confines of her mind.

She turned her gaze away from the sickening pages. Thankfully, that helped clear her head again. Disappointment and fear crashed upon her when she realized her plan was failing and she was trapped in this ghastly room. The cave-in wouldn't let her get back to her room, and she wasn't sure if the door would wake him. Hugh was right again. She shouldn't have gone back through the tunnels.

Her eyes turned toward his bed.

There it was. His walking stick, clenched in his hands, with her mother's necklace still around the handle.

Jeanette held her breath as she dared to take a step closer to the sleeping monster. Her trembling hands reached out for the chain.

A low growl came from under the covers.

Her body recoiled and she dropped to the ground. Did he see her? He must have. Why else would he growl at her? She started trembling from fear of being caught.

Looking around, she tried to figure out what to do. She could go back in the vent, but that wouldn't help, it would just be a hiding place. She would need to escape through his bedroom door and hope she'd have time to escape before he reached her. She glanced behind her for motivation to move, to run, to leave... but something held her back, she couldn't just walk away.

Not without her mother's necklace. Determination burned in her chest.

Those evil black and red eyes met hers as she slowly rose from her crouched position. A slight squeal escaped her lips. Fear overtook the burning in her chest and she ran out the door.

Jeanette collided into a table and sent something crashing to the floor. Someone was bound to hear that. Her palms became sweaty, her vision swirled around her. She felt her heart shiver inside her chest as the thumping in her ears became louder. There was a dull groan coming from behind her. It sounded like her head was underwater. She couldn't focus.

Larkus must be getting up.

Light illuminated a door frame. She wasn't sure if that was the room she had just left. All she saw was the shadow of someone on the other side. Larkus was coming. She debated between holding as still as possible, or running as fast as she could.

The handle turned; she wanted to run, but her feet felt as if they were frozen to the floor. He must be using his magic to hold her in place, like he did in the dungeon. She held still and closed her eyes. If there was ever a time she'd wished she was invisible, it was now. The warmth of the light surrounded her as the door opened.

"Jeanette?" Hugh whispered, his voice sounded shocked.

Jeanette's eyes opened wide. Wave after wave of relief flooded her body. Her own fear must've been the one holding her in place.

He looked both directions in the darkened hallway, grabbed Jeanette's arm, and pulled her inside the room.

"What are you doing out in the middle of the night?"

Jeanette tried to calm down but her body was shaking from the inside out. She bent over, holding her chest with one hand, covering her eyes with another, and inhaling deeply. It was a technique Clint had taught her as a child when she would panic that her parents' murderer would come for her. He would remind her that she was safe, and to take deep breaths.

Her racing heart slowed with each exhale.

Hugh stared at her. He walked over, put his hand on her back, and waited for her to calm down.

She smelled Hugh, which, in some way, made her feel safe. The fire, wood, and that mysterious scent she'd been trying to place since they first met.

Her eyes burned with threatening tears. She wanted to tell Hugh that she snuck into Larkus's room to steal back what was rightfully hers— but he wouldn't understand.

"Are you going to open your eyes?" Hugh asked.

Jeanette shook her head. She felt as if keeping them closed would let her pretend it was a dream. That she wasn't caught by those dark eyes. She wondered if Larkus was still looking for her.

Once her breathing slowed, she straightened and looked at him. "I'm sorry." How could she tell him? Maybe he could help her after all. "I should have listened to you. But I was in Larkus's room. I went through the vent again."

"What? Why? That's dangerous. You shouldn't go in there!"

"I know. You were right. The tunnel caved in. But I needed to." She twisted the front of the nightgown in her fingers. "He has something that belongs to me. I tried to steal it back, but I think he saw me."

"What do you mean 'you think he saw you'?" Hugh's face was stern, his brows furrowed. A flexing muscle in his jaw made Jeanette's knees weaken.

"He growled and looked right at me." A tear escaped and rolled down her cheek.

"Oh." Hugh seemed to relax almost every muscle in his body. "He didn't see you." He wiped the tear from her face.

"How can you be so sure? He looked right at me." Jeanette shook her head to try to rid her mind of his face.

"That's his kind. He's a Triad-Elf. They don't close their eyes to sleep. And— he snores." Hugh groaned but gave her a half smile.

She let out a breath and let her mind relax, she was finally able to think clearly.

To see Hugh clearly.

His hair was tousled; she could tell he had been sleeping. He must have jumped out of bed when he heard the crash. His feet were bare and he wore gray flannel pants and a black robe that hung open over his bare chest. He bit his lower lip as his eyes swept across her body; one eyebrow raised. What was going on in his mind?

Blush flooded her cheeks and chest as she looked down at herself in her sheer silk nightgown. Goosebumps raised the hair on her arms as she awkwardly crossed them in front of her chest. She suddenly became aware of just how much Hugh could see of her. She slowly turned away from him.

"Oh, you must be freezing." He cleared his throat, looked around the room for something, and then started to take off his robe.

She peeked behind her, watching as the black robe slipped off his muscular chest and arms, caressing his skin. Jeanette realized she desperately wanted to be that robe. She swallowed as he held the robe open for her.

"Thank you." She dropped her arms and let him bring the soft, fuzzy fabric up and around her body. His hands squeezed her shoulders and slid down her arms. Everywhere his fingers brushed, her skin came alive with electricity.

"You're welcome." She felt his breath on her cheek.

She turned around to face him, but neither one moved away. They were almost touching. Her eyes met his, there seemed to be something behind them, something wanting. The intensity made her look away first and glance down.

He wasn't wearing a shirt.

His body was chiseled with a modest amount of hair that covered his chest and abs. She was impressed that her imagination painted him so accurately. Except for the scar on his body. He didn't have that in her mind.

"You're not supposed to have this," she whispered as one dainty fingertip grazed the scar on his left side. It was a clean cut, whatever had caused it must've been extremely sharp.

"What do you mean?" he whispered back. His breath felt hot against her skin.

"Um." She swallowed hard. What did she mean? It was just in her mind that he had perfect skin. She hadn't actually known what he looked like.

But something felt— wrong. Her fantasy was so real, and now seeing him like this in front of her, it felt familiar.

"Jeanette?" Hugh's eyes studied her. He probably thought she'd gone crazy.

She smiled, turning away and taking a step back. Embarrassment burned her cheeks. "Were you sleeping?" She looked at the blanket that was strewn across his bed.

"Well, yeah. But I don't sleep very well anyway. I heard a crash and thought it was Larkus," Hugh trailed off and rubbed his eyes. As he stretched his arms, he leaned backward. It made his muscles tight.

"Yeah," she started, but as she gazed upon Hugh's burly chest, she lost her train of thought. "That... that was me." She swallowed as her eyes traced the curves of his abs. A yearning burned in her chest and shot heat down through her stomach. "I, uh, I fell against a table in the hallway; whatever was on it crashed to the floor."

Hugh smirked as he watched Jeanette. "That must have been the vase. I'll walk you back to your room, but first let me get it cleaned up. We don't want Larkus to see it."

"Yes. I think I've explored enough for today," she chuckled.

Hugh carried a torch while they walked back to her room. They stopped at the broken vase and the knocked over table. He knelt down and stood the table back up, but it started falling over again. Flipping it over revealed a broken leg that must have happened when she tripped over it.

"I'll have to fix this as well," Hugh said it more to himself than to Jeanette as he leaned the table against the wall. He brought a hand broom and a tray and started sweeping the broken shards of the vase. Just then something clunked against the bristles.

"What's this?" He picked up a key and held it in the light. "Here, you keep it. Hide it somewhere safe. Larkus would be able to find it in my room." Hugh pushed the key into Jeanette's hand and she held it tightly.

"Isn't this Larkus's key? If he hid it in the vase then wouldn't he know it's gone?" Her eyebrows furrowed.

"No. That key is—" he paused, "mine." Hugh moaned slightly as if that hurt him to say. Jeanette felt a soreness in her own throat, although she wasn't sure what was causing Hugh's pain.

They walked in silence. She didn't know what to talk about.

As they passed the picture, Jeanette noticed that there was a slight glimmer. She couldn't tell if it was just the torch's reflection or something else.

"Don't you want to know what I was trying to steal back?" Jeanette finally asked when they got back to her room.

Hugh reached out and gave her hand a gentle squeeze. "Your mother's necklace."

Chapter 8

Hugh wasn't sure it was worth the pain that revelation had caused him. The look on her face, and the questions he couldn't answer afterward, she must think he's involved in Larkus's plot.

Hugh worked on his morning chores, reliving his momentary lapse in judgment from the night before. He shamed himself as he checked on Larkus's parchment supply; making sure he would have enough for the day.

"I need to go to that insufferable town today," Larkus said, breaking into Hugh's train of thoughts.

As he finished replacing the firewood in Larkus's room, a splinter from a log wedged itself into his ring finger. Larkus fastened a necklace around his neck. It had a yin-yang of faces; one laughing, one crying.

"Oh, I thought you said you were done going there now that we have her." Hugh regretted saying that as soon as the words left his mouth.

"I know what I said, boy. There is something I need to do there." Larkus stood with his staff and raised it above his head. Hugh flinched. He didn't mean to, but the years of abuse made it a reflex. "I should have made you mute," Larkus muttered as he left the room.

Hugh exited Larkus's quarters and slumped against the door. What did he do to deserve a life like this? He already knew the answer but he also knew he was destined for more. He wondered if he would ever reach his destiny.

He let out a sigh and went to finish his other chores. He needed to fix the table that Jeanette broke. He also hoped that he could search the painting. He went to fetch a hammer and get back to work.

His mind was elsewhere though. What good could have come from mentioning the necklace? What did he hope would happen?

He knew exactly what he had hoped for. He wanted her to remember. Because if she remembered, then maybe— No. He couldn't get his hopes up. Every time he thought about what happened, he felt dread in the pit of his stomach. He wished he could undo his mistakes. All of them. Even if she happened to fix it, Larkus would get exactly what he wanted. Not to mention Hugh would continue to be trapped. No good would come from that.

He shook his head. Focusing on that wouldn't help anything. He needed to get his morning chores done so he could figure out what he wanted to show Jeanette. Promising to show her something in the afternoon was the only thing he could think of to appease the situation last night. He only hoped it had calmed her down enough. He glanced around the library, the rows of books around him spurred an idea to form in the back of his mind.

The next morning, Jeanette decided to move the desk back in front of the window. If it wasn't going to keep Larkus out anyway, she didn't want it to block her running from the room if she needed to.

Now that it was back in its home by the window, she picked up the chair that she had thrown on her first night in the room. She hadn't cared about picking it up before. When she lifted the chair, she spotted a small box on the floor. That must've been what fell.

A beautiful little music box. It was white and had a red rose carved in the middle of the lid. She opened it, but there was no sound, and instead of a ballerina spinning like ones she had seen in the village, this one had a tightly closed rose bud. She looked under it to see if she could wind it up, but the bottom was smooth. She wasn't sure how it worked. Maybe it wasn't a music box after all.

Jeanette sat in the chair and looked out upon the grounds. The wall of dark mist moved like a flag waving in the wind. How did it manage to surround everything? An eerie pulsing thrummed from the murk. She could almost feel it. It was heavy and thick, like it could absorb her very being and smother her. A shiver crawled down her spine.

She looked toward the heavens. At least she could still see the sun and the clouds in the sky.

Leaning back in her chair, she realized she was still fiddling with the little box. She laid it on top of the desk.

A frustrated sigh escaped her. She just wanted to go home, but she was trapped. Even if she could leave, she wasn't sure how to get home from here. She wasn't sure where *here* was. Her mind went through the possibilities of escape. The tunnels were a no-go. The cave-in already made it impossible for her to sneak back to Larkus's room. Not that she really wanted to go back into his room, but she had to get that necklace back.

Her window wouldn't open. She wasn't sure how the glass was unbreakable.

She needed to talk to Hugh. Maybe they could come up with a plan. Although the lack of information she had gotten from him thus far hadn't been helpful. Larkus must be controlling him in some way.

He looked pained last night when she tried to ask him how he knew it was her mother's necklace she was seeking to recover. She felt that same burning in her throat every time she saw agony glimpse across his face.

Maybe Larkus told him it was her mother's. That could be why he kidnapped her. If only Hugh could have told her what was going on and why Larkus had it.

The only thing that Hugh said to her was that he wished he could tell her everything. She wished that was true, that would've been nice, to finally find out what Larkus wanted her for. Although, he did say that he wanted to show her something today, but he had his morning chores to do first. Maybe that would give her enough time to explore a little more. Maybe find a way out.

A sigh escaped her. There were too many unknowns about this place and her future. It scared her. Everything felt out of control. She tried to think of what helped her back at her little cottage when she felt like she was spiraling.

Nature.

Jeanette closed her eyes and envisioned her cottage, her lake, the crunchy autumn leaves, the wind whistling through the trees. She took a deep breath and smelled the dirt, she focused on the scent, she could actually smell the dirt. Her eyes flicked open and she looked down at herself.

Right.

It was her that she smelled— she was covered in dirt again from the tunnels.

After a bath and dressing in a beautiful, golden gown, she ran out the bedroom door to search for an escape route.

Jeanette was about to enter the portrait hallway when she saw Hugh around the corner. Something told her not to interrupt him. He was dusting her favorite picture. But something about the way he was acting was strange; he was extra close to the frame and kept glancing behind him.

"I'll come back later," he whispered, then turned and walked away. That was curious. He didn't dust any of the other paintings. Was he telling her that he'd come back later? She didn't think that he'd seen her, but maybe he did.

Her gaze was once again transfixed on the sitting room portrait. If only she could escape to that room. A steaming cup of what looked like hot cocoa sat on the table, a cozy blanket hung over the armchair, a warm fire crackling in the hearth.

Hugh's words echoed in her mind. It seemed like he was talking to the painting instead of her. Jeanette shook her head. Of course it was to her, it must have been. Why would he talk to the painting?

She forced herself away from the picture and continued on her way.

As soon as she got to the great hall, she saw Larkus coming out of the library. He was looking down at a book, his walking stick tucked under his arm.

Her stomach dropped and she hid behind one of the large couches. Peering out from her hiding spot, she watched Larkus skulk down the left hallway toward the kitchen.

No way would she follow him down there. Even if she did want to examine the shimmering blue wall. There had to be somewhere else that would lead to freedom. Jeanette looked around her hiding spot. She was in the corner of the room.

The same corner they had exited the dungeon from. Where was the entrance to the dungeon? She looked around the room, but the only doors were the double doors to the library. How was that possible?

Jeanette felt dazed. She felt the walls for a hidden latch. Anything to open that dungeon tunnel. There had to be a way out down there.

Nothing.

Frustration prickled the back of her neck. Could there have been a trap door in the floor? Probably not. Although, against her better judgement, she looked down at the plush rug, lifting one corner showed her how heavy it truly was. Her mind went back to that night. No. They definitely went through a full sized door.

The roaring fireplace fizzled and dimmed the entire room. The fire looked— pale. Footsteps echoed from where Larkus had gone and snapped her back to the present danger. She ran down the hallway next to her; the farthest toward the right of the room.

This hallway was bare. No paint, no decorative pictures, just stone floor and stone walls. The hallway got colder the further along she walked. It reminded her of the stone corridor in the dungeons. Maybe this was the way there.

But alas, there was only one door at the end of this hallway.

Sun rays danced across the stone floor through a window. Jeanette finally found it. The door to freedom.

There was only one question. She reached for the handle, her hand shaking. This was it, this was her chance for an escape. Her pulse echoed in her ears and her throat became dry, making it hard to swallow.

"Please," she whispered. She laid her hand on the cold handle and pushed against the golden metal.

It didn't budge.

Of course this door would be locked. There was no escape from this hell.

No. There had to be.

She banged her hands against the glass window in the door. Maybe if she could break it, she could open the door from the outside. She looked at her surroundings when her fists started to throb. There was nothing around.

Jeanette fell to her knees as hot tears threatened their escape. She took a deep breath and blinked through blurry eyes to try to get a hold of her emotions. That's when she saw it.

A small key hole in the doorknob. Could it be that simple?

She ran back to her bedroom and grabbed the bronze key they had found the night before. She held it in her hand. It looked as though it could fit that door. The head of the key was round, the shaft as long as her palm with two teeth at the end. It had to unlock the door downstairs. What else would it go to? But then, why would Hugh give it to her? No time to question it; she hurried back to the door.

Hugh leaned against the wall watching Jeanette. She was crouched by the back door. "Jeanette. What are you doing?"

She jumped up, her eyes wide, and her breathing quickened. "Oh, nothing." He watched as she rolled her eyes. "I just thought that I could unlock this door." Her head slumped, it looked like she was trying to hide the flush that spread across her cheeks.

"Hmm," he said and took another step closer to her. He saw that she was fidgeting with something in her hands. "Oh, that key doesn't go to that door."

All she did was nod and shove it in her pocket.

"Come on, I've finally finished my chores for today. It took a bit longer than I thought it would, but I want to show you something." He held his hand out for her to take.

"I just wanted to go outside," she finally admitted and placed her hand in his.

"I know. Maybe one day." He squeezed her hand. His ears felt hot knowing that he was being forward with her. He swallowed, trying to help his dry mouth as he glanced at her. She was still looking down. How he wished she would look at him. Hopefully his plan would work and help with her memories.

"I wanted to have a little picnic with you this afternoon," Hugh said as they walked into the library. He had laid a blanket and pillows out in the corner of the room, under the stairs. It was where they would picnic as children. He hoped that it would spur a memory.

Jeanette smiled. "How fun! I love picnics." She sat down on the pillow and waited for Hugh to join her.

"I thought you might enjoy it." He opened the basket and pulled out a roast chicken with a side of asparagus and rolls.

"How did you know this was my favorite meal?" Jeanette asked. "I remember making this with—" Her brow knitted together like she was confused at the memory.

"With?"

"Um," she paused. "I can't remember." She shook her head. "That's so strange. I have this cloudy image of making this before, but if I try to focus on the memory, it just swirls away." She laid a hand to her head.

"Oh," Hugh reminded himself not to say anything about their past. About the fact that he had that same memory; of the two of them making this together. "Well, it's one of my favorites too."

Jeanette smiled and bit into an asparagus stalk. "How did you get asparagus though? It's not in season!"

"I have my ways." Hugh winked.

"The only thing that would make this better is dessert," she chuckled. "I love dessert."

Hugh smiled to himself while he pulled out a plate of tartlets. Her favorite. He watched her eyes widen at the sight of the plate.

"How did you know?" Jeanette asked as she grabbed a tartlet. "Nevermind, you can't tell me anyway." She closed her eyes and leaned back on her arms as she ate the small pie.

Hugh's eyes traced down her face, her hair was in a large curl that caressed the slope of her neck, his eyes moved across her ample chest. He bit his bottom lip, imagining kissing down that waterfall of skin. Clearing his throat, he pulled his gaze. He shouldn't be looking at her like that, at least not without her consent.

"You're right. I can't tell you." Hugh wanted more than anything to have Jeanette remember. "If only there was a way."

Jeanette was quiet for a moment and then looked at all the food. What must she think? Hopefully, this will cause a memory to surface. Her favorite food in her favorite spot. He was sad that she couldn't remember him fully; that when the memory almost came back, she said it was cloudy.

"What if I ask you questions? I know there's a lot you can't share, but maybe you can answer a few?" She brushed the crumbs off her lap.

Hugh nodded. "Just don't be disappointed if I can't tell you anything. It's not easy for me to be—" he stopped talking before he said too much. He didn't want his curse to cause him unnecessary pain.

"Does he want me to be his slave too?" Her eyes looked moist. That must've been a question she'd worried about.

"No, he wants you for something else." Pain ripped at him. *I didn't say what!* The agony released its grip. He took a few steadying breaths and glanced at Jeanette. She didn't seem to notice his discomfort.

"Something else." Jeanette's eyes looked distressed. "And I'm guessing you can't tell me what that 'something else' is?" She raised an eyebrow.

"I'm not at liberty to say." Hugh closed his eyes. That damn curse.

They sat in silence for a few minutes. Hugh wasn't sure what to say, what he could say. Turned out he didn't need to say anything.

Jeanette stood. "There are so many books here. I would love to read some." She started for the stairs up to the balcony.

"Yes, let me show you around." Hugh held his arm out for her to take. In this moment, walking up the stairs, with Larkus gone, it felt as if everything was right. As if nothing had changed all those years ago. As if they could be together. But Larkus had captured them both, and Jeanette was a prisoner. Anger flared in his chest at the thought of her being subject to Larkus's terror.

He took a deep breath to try and clear his mind and focus on enjoying this time with Jeanette. "Fiction books are over there." He pointed toward the left wall. "If you want to see one of my favorites though—" He led her to the nonfiction section and pulled a book from the shelf. He held it in front of his chest so she could read the title. *The Art of Sword Fighting.*

"That scar I saw, it was from a sword?" She grimaced and grabbed her side as if it pained her.

"Yes," he started, "from a very long time ago. It doesn't hurt anymore." He wasn't sure what happened just then— she squeezed her eyes shut and started breathing heavily. "Are you okay?"

"I'm fine. It'll pass soon. I—" She took a deep breath. "I just feel others' pain sometimes. If I hear about an injury, or see it, I can feel it. It always happens. I don't know why," she said.

"Okay. If you're sure." It didn't always happen though. Not when they were kids. That must've been a repercussion. He was now more glad than ever that he had been hiding the pain the curse has caused him. "Would you like me to recommend some books for you?"

"Yes! I would love that." She followed close behind him.

"Here's something that might interest you." He pulled a couple of magic books from the shelf. One that she used to be familiar with. Maybe it would help her. "It's important to read up on magic. Be aware of what it can do. It might help you know what we're up against."

"That—" she hesitated. "That's a good point. Maybe it'll help me understand Larkus better."

"Yes. Larkus." That's not exactly what he meant.

Jeanette walked across the balcony with Hugh. There were all kinds of books. There were books about dragons, mermaids, travel, and history.

"There are more books in here than I could ever dream of." She stopped in front of a shelf and read a few of the covers.

Hugh handed her a book entitled "Trusting Briars." "Does this one look interesting to you?" He knew it was one of her favorites before— she had always longed for adventure.

The cover had a man and a woman with outstretched hands toward each other, but thorny vines separated them.

She opened a random page and read aloud.

"Charlotte called out his name. She reached for him. Johnathan howled in pain as he tried to run to her. The thorns twisted around him, choking him against the struggle, and eventually throwing him back. Charlotte swore that those vines would never keep them apart, but how could she get past the possessed soldiers?"

Jeanette closed the book and handed it back. "I don't think I want to read about being trapped in thorns, I feel like I am already living that," she admitted.

"I understand." Hugh stroked down her arm and squeezed her hand. All he wanted to do was cover her soft skin with kisses. He could tell her breathing quickened. He felt the most appealing urge to close the distance between them and press her against the bookshelves.

"Let me see if I can find another one." He cleared his throat and handed her "Flight or Fight." "This one has always been a favorite of mine." Ever since she was the one to introduce it to him.

The cover had a female warrior on it. With beat up armor, a bow and arrow in hand, and a bloody scratch on her cheek. She looked ready for battle.

Jeanette opened to a random page.

"Fiona knew she needed to get away from The Hunter. She had tried different ways to escape, but somehow, he always found her. She needed to take things into her own hands. She needed to fight. After days in the cave nursing her wounds, she was ready."

Jeanette closed the book and held it to her chest. "This, I can relate to," she whispered.

Chapter 9

Jeanette walked down the hall with the magic book Hugh had given her the previous week. It had been a long few days. Hugh had been given extra tasks and couldn't get away from his chores. She tried to explore, maybe find a way out, but every time she left her room, Larkus would watch her. His gaze burned against her skin, a dark aura wafting off him. She mostly stayed in her room, away from Larkus, grateful to have the books to keep her company.

When she got to the portrait hallway, she froze, then backtracked around the corner and pressed her body against the wall. Her pulse beat in her ears— she hadn't expected to see Hugh. He usually worked on the grounds in the morning. She knew because she would often watch from her second story window as he trimmed the rose bushes.

Her fingers found a snarl in her hair and she wished she had remembered to brush it before she left her room. She peeked around the corner, watching him for a few moments. He stood extremely close to the sitting room picture, his nose just a few inches from the canvas.

She hesitated, wondering if she should disturb him or stay quiet this time. Her mind went back to the week before when she caught him standing just as close to the picture. Her desire to be near him won out. Plus, she was intrigued by that picture as well. Its magical elements drew her in, but she wondered what drew Hugh to it. It seemed to be something more. After all, he was used to being around magic.

As she took a few steps toward him, her courage faltered and her nerves got the better of her, forcing the book to slide out of her hands. She frantically tried to grasp it again, but it slid across the floor and bumped into Hugh's shoes.

Hugh looked down, picked the book off the floor, and gave Jeanette a charming smile. Her heart fluttered inside her ribs.

"I... I like that canvas too," she stammered as she walked over and retrieved the book. The fire in the painting burned bright. Her eyes scanned the frame, searching for new changes, and caught on the corner of the rug that was flipped up under the mirror that she never noticed before in the far corner of the frame. There was a note stuck to the mirror, however, the note was too small to read any of the print.

"Oh... uh... yes." Hugh looked back and forth between her and the painting. "It's lovely, isn't it?"

Jeanette nodded. "Yes, I love the way it—"

"How are you liking that book?" Hugh interrupted her by pointing to the magic book in her arms.

"Um..." She looked down at the cover. "It was good. A little hard to follow, but some of the things made sense."

"That's good."

She assumed he wanted to hear more by the way he looked at her.

"I mean, I read it thinking about Larkus," she continued. "Like you said, it's good to know what we're up against." She liked saying "we." It made her feel like she and Hugh were a team against Larkus. When she thought about him like that, she felt— stronger, braver, safe.

They continued to talk about the book while they walked to the library so she could shelve it.

"Have you read any of the others? What about Flight or Fight?"

"No. I just focused on this one first. You said it was important to know what we're going to face."

"That's true. Did you enjoy it? Did you find it..." he hesitated, "useful?"

"Useful?" That was a weird thing to ask. She thought about the book for a moment. There were bits about the history of magic, a little about how to use spells, and a brief explanation of the light and dark side of magic. "I guess it was useful."

"Good!" Hugh said a bit too loudly as a smile spread across his face. Jeanette was confused by his reaction— he seemed too excited by her response.

"I..." she paused, "I figured out that Larkus is a dark sorcerer. I didn't even know there was such a thing."

Hugh grabbed her hands, stopping her from fiddling with her skirt again. "Was there anything else you figured out?"

Jeanette looked into his eyes. They were wild with... something. "Um..." Was there anything else? She tried replaying the chapters in her head. Nothing else popped out to her. "I don't think so."

Hugh took the book from her and scanned the shelves. "Here." He paused, pulling a new book off the shelf, his back still toward her. She attempted to look over his shoulder to see what was taking so long, but he had the book pressed against his chest, all she saw was the top corner of pages. Maybe he was trying to see if this was the right book he wanted her to read.

Jeanette shifted uncomfortably as she waited for Hugh to continue.

After a few long moments he spoke softly, "Maybe this one will help."

"Help? Help with what?" she said as she accepted the new book. The cover had a blue background with a golden sun across the front. Jeanette wasn't sure what Hugh was trying to tell her, but he seemed to be using the books to do so. The last book had mentioned a strong stench as a mark of dark magic; Larkus definitely had that. She understood now that Larkus was a dark sorcerer, but it seemed like there was still more Hugh wanted her to understand.

"I..." Hugh stared at her, his face defeated. "I just thought that these—"

"That these would what?" Larkus's rough growl made Jeanette jump. He was right behind her. It seemed like he appeared out of nowhere. His voice hit her ears before the smell hit her nose.

They both whirled around and saw Larkus. He had a disgusting smile across his face. His stringy white hair hung down in knots. It didn't look like he ever brushed it.

"Larkus—" Hugh took a step in front of Jeanette and squared his shoulders. She felt an overwhelming sense of protection.

"Silence," Larkus hissed. He stamped his walking stick on the ground. Jeanette learned from the book that it was his magical staff, used as a conductor to control magic. There were many such artifacts a sorcerer could acquire: a staff, a ring, a pendant, among others— each controlling a different aspect of magic. A blinding light forced Jeanette to shield her eyes. When she opened them, Hugh was gone.

"What just happened?" Jeanette looked around for Hugh.

"Don't play a fool," Larkus growled. "I know you've been reading up on magic."

"Yeah." That was true. Jeanette had acquired a limited understanding of magic. If Hugh was gone, it was clear Larkus used his staff to cast a location spell. Hugh disappeared from the room, sent off to a place of Larkus's desire.

Jeanette inched toward the stairs. Maybe, if she was fast enough, she could run down. There was that window in the back door; the book in her hand might work to break it before Larkus turned his staff on her.

Another blinding light.

Jeanette found herself sitting in the chair in the library. Her head started to spin. "You're right. I did read that magic book." It was the truth. "I know you're a dark wizard." She tried to be confident as she said it. It would've worked better if her voice didn't crack.

"That's not a secret." Larkus started pacing. "Why are you being so ignorant?"

"What do you mean? I'm not."

"Read this." He pulled a scroll out of his cloak and shoved it in Jeanette's face.

She looked at the paper. It was filled with the unrecognizable words she saw in his bedroom, the ones that made her dizzy. Just looking at the paper again made her see stars.

"I can't." She shook her head.

"What do you mean you can't?!" he spat.

"I..." she wiped some spit from her face. "I don't know how."

"You can't read?" Sarcasm dripped from his voice as he shook the papers in her face.

"No. Of course I can read." This wasn't getting her anywhere. "I just can't read *that*. I don't know those letters." She gestured. They were unlike any letters she'd ever seen.

He looked at her. Just stared, really.

"What do you want from me?" Something that she'd ask Hugh, but he wouldn't be able to tell her anyway.

"I don't have to tell you anything."

"I can't translate your scroll. I'm of no use to you. Just let me go." She hoped that he'd see reason. If he only kidnapped her to read that scroll, then she wouldn't be any help.

"No use? No use, you say? Oh I have plenty of use for you." He stopped pacing and took a couple of steps toward her. She scooted away. Everything in her body told her to run, and she listened to it.

Another blinding light.

She found herself on the couch in the great hall with Larkus looming over her. Nausea started to bubble up. "I'm getting sick of this," she mumbled.

"You're getting sick of this?" He shook his head. "I've been waiting for years! You have no idea what you've done."

"I haven't done anything."

"A child halted my plan years ago." He glared at her. "I'm much more powerful now, but I'm sure you are too."

"Me?" Jeanette's eyes widened. "Now I'm positive you have the wrong girl."

"Don't pretend you don't remember!" Larkus shouted. "You have to undo it! Undo it now!"

"Remember what? Undo what? I didn't do anything!" Hot tears prickled the back of her eyes.

He came close and stared into her face. His stench made her eyes water more. "You really don't remember." He straightened and took a deep breath. "What a pity." The room fell quiet. Too quiet. Like all the sound had been sucked out of it. Larkus was still— she had no idea what was going on in his mind. Her body started to shake at the unpredictability of what he might do.

Blinding light.

Jeanette found herself in her bedroom; her insides swirled as she caught her balance on the bedpost. She tried to make sense of what had just occurred, but the thoughts floating in her head were like a ship on rough seas. Instead of trying to organize them, she bent over as the contents of her stomach decorated the floor.

Hugh opened his eyes. The evening sun sent golden rays through his window. Larkus must've put a sleeping spell on him and sent him away. That would have left Jeanette alone with Larkus in the library. His mind spun with different scenarios of what Larkus would do if he found out she didn't remember. The thought of it made his fingers go numb. It was the only thing keeping her alive. He felt sick to his stomach knowing what Larkus was capable of. It was his job to clean up once Larkus was done with others in the past. He wasn't sure he would be able to clean up Jeanette's mangled body.

He wished Triad-Elves had restrictions on *all* their magic, not just the mortal danger kind. That would've made it so Hugh could've stayed with Jeanette. How many times had Larkus teleported him or cast that sleeping spell on him? If he had that restriction, he wouldn't be able to control him like that over and over again. He hated having no control over it.

Hugh made his way to Jeanette's room, his heart pounding as he hurried toward the great hall. His eyes glanced around the library as he passed through it. He took it as a good sign that there was no blood. But who knows what Larkus would attempt this time. His feet bolted up the stairs, skipping two at a time as he climbed. Arriving at Jeanette's door, he knocked— his knuckles aching from the force he put behind it. A cold sweat broke out across his brow when there was no answer. He knocked again. "Jeanette? It's me."

"Hi." She opened the door for him to enter just as he was about to call out again.

He resisted the urge to swoop her into his arms. Although he was relieved to see her standing in front of him, she seemed shaken. If only he could have protected her from Larkus. It tormented him knowing that she was now a prisoner as well.

"Are you okay?"

Jeanette looked pale, her hair frazzled, and there was a spot on the floor that was covered with a towel.

"What happened?"

"I'm fine." She nodded. "I'm not sure what happened." She was quiet for a moment. "He kept saying I needed to *undo* it. He kept asking why I don't remember."

"So, he knows you don't remember?" he asked. Fear turned his stomach into a knot. "What else happened?"

"He wanted me to translate some weird scroll." She looked exceedingly confused, her forehead creased as her eyebrows knit together.

"What scroll?" That was news to him.

"I don't know. It had some strange letters on it. I've never seen anything like it before." She shook her head. "Well, actually, I have. I saw it when I was in his room trying to get my mother's necklace."

Hugh nodded. "And you couldn't read it?"

"No." She looked down. "It made me dizzy when I looked at the letters."

Dizzy? It made her dizzy? Hugh knew those scrolls were Larkus's dark magic spells. He had seen them dozens of times but they never made him dizzy. Then again, he wasn't magical. "I wonder which one he wanted you to read." Hugh said it more to himself than to her.

"What is going on? You have to tell me." Jeanette begged him.

Hugh took a deep breath and started pacing across her room.

"Of course you can't tell me. I'm starting to get sick of all of this."

What am I to say to her? How much pain will it cause me to explain everything? I know it won't kill me, but the curse could cause so much pain I would wish I was dead. He argued with himself.

"Stop pacing!" Her fingers rubbed her temples. "Larkus was pacing too. You guys are making me feel sick."

She tossed a book on the bed. It was the magic book he'd given her right before Larkus interrupted.

"Have you opened that book yet?"

She shook her head. "No, I was busy regaining my balance to clean up my mess." She gestured towards the towel on the floor.

"I thought that these would help you," Hugh finally said as he gestured to the other magic books on her desk.

"Help me?" She looked at him. Her expression was unreadable. "Help me what? Remember?"

"Yes," he said. Hugh's frustration burst through and he groaned. What else could he do? He hoped that she *would* remember— even just one thing. He shook his head and looked at her. She sat on the bed and pulled her knees close to her. "Is there anything else? You look bothered by something."

"He said that a child ruined his plan," she started. "He thinks *I'm* that child. But that's impossible."

"Is it?" Hugh took a deep breath. "Open the book."

Jeanette hesitated for a moment but she picked up the book. Hugh watched as she rubbed her hand across the smooth cover. As she gently opened it, her eyes grew wide.

If this didn't help her remember, he wasn't sure what would.

Chapter 10

Jeanette's hands shook at what she saw. "How?" It was all she could muster to say. The book's pages had a hole carved in the center of them; dust from the cutting flaked off the edges of the hole. It was evident this hiding spot was new.

In the middle of it all was a necklace. Her mother's pendant sat amidst the chain. Jeanette's eyes burned with fresh tears as her thin fingers grasped hold of the chain and lifted the piece of jewelry.

How Hugh retrieved it didn't matter as much as the fact that he did. She laid the pendant in her palm and squeezed her fingers around it.

"Thank you," she whispered.

"You're welcome," Hugh said. Jeanette jumped off her bed and wrapped her arms around his neck, which caused him to stumble back a few steps.

Butterflies fluttered through her stomach as she hugged him like that. She couldn't help it. Just as she was about to let go, she felt his hands slide around her back and squeeze her tight. They stood in an embrace as their breathing synced together and became shallow.

They slowly broke apart and looked into each other's eyes. His were smoldering with fire. Her self-conscious fear got the better of her, and instead of staying pressed against his body and in his arms, she pulled herself away and started twirling her hair.

"I'm sorry," she sputtered. "Thank you for this. Really. It means so much to me. But how did you manage to get it from Larkus? Won't he be angry?"

"Only if he finds out," Hugh muttered and straightened his coat. Jeanette knew it was a mistake to hug him; he was just trying to be nice. She was sure he wasn't planning on getting mauled by her hug. Regret wrenched her stomach into a knot.

"What do you mean?" she asked.

"I know how much this means to you so I carved an identical pendant and switched them while I was doing my morning chores."

"So, he doesn't know that the one around his staff is a fake?"

"Not unless he tries to use the amulet." A grimace spread across his face.

"Right," Jeanette's throat burned, but it was the first time that he had said more to her about any of this; she didn't want him to stop talking. "Are you okay?"

He took a deep breath. "You remember the amulet has power?" He groaned in what seemed like pain.

"I..." she coughed, then paused as she looked at the amulet in her hands. Her mother's amulet had powers? A fuzzy feeling coated her mind as she tried to remember anything like that from her childhood. It was strange not being able to recall her memories.

The books, the amulet, even the sitting room portrait. All the things Hugh had shown her pointed toward one thing— magic. But when she tried to think about her past, it felt like something just out of reach. She feared if she admitted her shortcomings, Hugh would get frustrated and he would leave before she could get more answers from him. She couldn't let him stop talking yet.

"Think Jeanette," Hugh said. It seemed like he saw the struggle she was internalizing.

"I'm trying," she admitted.

"Here," he said and held out his hand. "Let me put it on you."

Looking down at the amulet, the four seasons felt familiar in a way that she couldn't quite touch. She laid the necklace in his outstretched palm and turned her back to Hugh.

He brushed the hair off the back of her neck. The gesture sent goosebumps down her body; his fingers were hot against her skin. He slipped the necklace around her and fastened it. His hands stroked down her arms; she felt his warmth behind her, his breath on her skin. She closed her eyes and arched her neck. She yearned for the touch of his lips, her mind creating a sensation of what that would feel like.

Hugh cleared his throat and took a step back. "Do you feel its power?"

Jeanette's eyes opened wide as his question snapped her back to reality. She felt a hot flush spread across her cheeks. "I'm not sure. What does 'power' feel like?" She turned to face him and placed a hand on her chest where the pendant sat.

Hugh sighed. "I wouldn't know." She could tell he became frustrated; he looked away and shook his head. His face turned hard, his expression was unreadable. "I have to go."

"No, please don't," she said and grabbed his arm to stop him. Her hand slid down his firm forearm and across his hand as she tried to hold onto his fingers. He flinched in pain at her attempt to stop him from leaving. Her eyes grew wide at the realization of what she had just done. "I'm sorry, I didn't mean to hurt you."

Hugh shook his head. "No, it's not you." He rolled his eyes and looked at his finger. "I have a splinter in my finger. I got it a couple of days ago; the day we had our picnic," he explained. "I haven't been able to get it out myself."

"A splinter?" Jeanette teased.

"Don't laugh, it hurts."

"I'm sorry, you've just been so stoic, I didn't think a little splinter would bother you."

"Well, some pain... you just get used to." Hugh stiffened.

"I'm sorry. I could try to get it out," she offered as she rubbed her own finger.

Hugh looked at his wound again and let out a deep breath. "I guess."

"I'll need some tweezers and a needle."

Hugh's eyes widened. "Uh..."

"Trust me."

Hugh nodded. "I have both in my room."

They walked in silence through the darkened house to Hugh's bedroom. She didn't realize how late it had grown. The stench from Larkus's room grew stronger as they continued down the hall. Panic set in. Her insides started shaking and her palms became slick. She reached for her necklace and tucked it inside of her dress, but still felt uneasy about it. Maybe she should've taken it off and slipped it into her pocket, but she didn't want to lose it either.

Hugh seemed to be able to guess her reaction to the smell. "Don't worry, he's bound to be asleep by now."

Jeanette nodded but the feeling didn't go away until they got into Hugh's chambers and he shut the door behind them. She let out the breath she didn't realize she'd been holding.

She looked around his room. The last time she was in here was after her failed attempt to get the pendant back from Larkus. She had been so worried about being caught that her adrenaline hadn't let her notice details about his room.

It was simple. Bed on one wall, desk in the corner of another, and the bathroom door was open. It was similar to hers, however his room had a fireplace in the wall while hers had that large mirror.

"Sit here, this will give us enough light." He motioned for her to sit on the bench that was in front of the fireplace while he placed another log on the fire. The dim flame crackled and sputtered at the weight of the log but soon enveloped the fresh food.

The warmth felt nice against her skin. She watched as he went to his desk and started rummaging through drawers.

"Found it." He sat down next to her holding a pair of tweezers and a needle.

Jeanette took both. "Now, which finger was it?"

"This one." He held out his left hand and pointed to his ring finger. Hugh took a few deep breaths.

"Don't worry. I'll be gentle," she said and gave him a smile. It was as if those words were magic; Hugh seemed to relax almost instantly.

She held his hand in hers; his rough fingertips from all the manual work he had done throughout the years grazed against her soft skin. The lack of a ring on his finger made her mind wander to the possibilities of a future that she never thought was possible in her tiny town with no prospects.

She worked on the splinter, her skills with a needle adapted well to this situation. Removing a sliver wasn't too different from taking a seam out of a dress. As soon as the piece of wood was uncovered, she pulled the rest out quickly with the tweezers. Hugh winced from the movement. Her heart fluttered like a bird as she kissed his injured finger.

"Thank you," Hugh said tenderly.

"You're welcome."

They sat in silence for a few moments, letting the fire illuminate them in a golden glow. "I guess I should get to bed. It's late," she finally said.

Hugh nodded. "I'll walk you back to your room."

"No, no, it's okay. I mean, you're already here. I'll be fine." She wanted to spend more time with Hugh, but she also wanted her mind to focus on what he had said. Her mother's pendant had powers.

She walked out of his room and hurried down the hall, away from Larkus's stench. She calmed her nerves as she reached the library. Her focus settled on the section of the bookshelves that contained the magic books. If Hugh was right, there had to be something about her mother's necklace being a conduit for magic.

She pulled magic book after magic book off the shelves, searching for more information about magical artifacts since the first book only briefly mentioned them.

Finally she found one. The inside cover had a handwritten note that read, *Chapter 4: artifacts, Chapter 9: sealing and unsealing spells.* She wasn't sure what that meant. The handwriting had a certain familiarity. It was too feminine to be Hugh's or Larkus's handwriting. She couldn't imagine either of them writing these neat, curvy lines. No, a woman definitely wrote this.

Jeanette skimmed the pages until she found Chapter Four. This one looked promising. She shelved the other books in their spots, scooped up the magic book, and hurried back to her room.

The chapter listed different types of artifacts and the spells that could be attached to them. She knew Larkus's staff could teleport— just the thought of it made her stomach feel queasy.

Among other powers, she found listings of artifacts that could change the wearer's physical appearance or control others' movements. Jeanette thought back to when Larkus showed her to her room. It was as though her feet moved against her own will, he must've been using a magical item to control her movements.

Toward the end of the chapter was a section about natural artifacts. She looked down at her amulet, it had the seasons on it. She wondered how Hugh would have been able to carve an identical piece, matching the detail of the autumn leaf, or the intricate snowflake for winter.

Jeanette had always been drawn to the outside world and its changes, maybe this pendant was why. She recalled the way the wind blew through the trees when she'd walk the path to gaze upon Rose Manor, or the way the breeze blew through the grass during her picnics. She had always felt the wind was trying to speak to her. Maybe it was. Maybe if she had been wearing the amulet, she could've understood what the wind was saying.

She wondered why Larkus had it though. That question had been burning in her mind ever since she saw it wrapped around his staff. Her mind turned to all the possibilities, torturing her into the unknown.

If her mother's necklace had magic, then maybe she used to have it as well. She wasn't sure if that was even possible. She shook the thought out of her mind and went to sleep.

The next morning, the sun was blindingly bright as it glared into her room. Jeanette walked to the window and saw Hugh working in the garden again. He wiped sweat from his brow despite it being almost winter.

Or maybe it was winter already; she had lost track of time since being captured. She wasn't sure if the Winter Slumber would occur here, wherever *here* was. It was possible this area didn't experience the changing of the seasons like her home of Mapleshire did.

An ache resonated throughout her chest at the thought of missing the time she would have spent celebrating with Beth and Clint. She loved it when they would snuggle under their heaviest blanket and watch the season turn from autumn to winter.

Jeanette started rubbing the necklace; it helped to distract her from her grief. It also gave her an idea.

She sat on her bed and skimmed the magic book again. It did have a chapter on spells! She found the one she was hoping for; to bring clouds to the sky. It seemed simple enough.

She went to the window and held her amulet. She took a deep breath and re-read the spell. If this worked, then that meant Larkus was right about her. That meant she did indeed have magic, and maybe if she could get better at it, then she would be able to use it to escape. She had her necklace back now. There was nothing stopping her. A pang shot through her as she glanced down at Hugh who was still working in the garden. Jeanette put her hands in the air above her head and chanted the spell.

Nothing happened.

Of course nothing happened. It was silly. She didn't have magic now and she never had it then either. They were both wrong. Larkus had the wrong girl and her mother's necklace didn't have any power.

Maybe someone else had a necklace that looked the same as this one. Maybe *that* girl is who Larkus needed. Shame and embarrassment swallowed her up like a monster swallowing its prey whole. It made her feel nauseated, weak, and dizzy. She needed to eat something to help settle her stomach.

As she got to the great hall, she ran into Hugh who had just come back from the garden. "Oh, hi."

"Hi," Hugh said. "Are you alright? You look pale."

Jeanette nodded. "Yes, I think I just need to eat something."

"I could eat too." He smiled. "Let's get some breakfast together." He escorted Jeanette down the hall, toward the kitchen. He kept glancing at Jeanette. "You might want to tuck that into your dress. We don't want Larkus to see that you have it."

Jeanette looked down and tucked the pendant into the bodice of her maroon gown. "There, is that better?"

She saw Hugh's cheeks turned pink as he glanced at her chest. "Uh, yeah," he said and turned away. "What would you like for breakfast? Do eggs sound good to you?"

"I think toast would help my stomach a little bit better than eggs."

Hugh nodded. He was quiet as they made toast, but looked like he was distracted by something. "Listen," he finally said. "I'm sorry I've been so pushy lately." He looked at Jeanette. Her confusion must've shown in her expression. "About remembering."

"Oh. I don't think you've been pushy. But I do think you guys have the wrong girl."

"'You guys'?" Hugh asked, his voice on edge.

"Yeah," she hated saying "you guys," it made her feel alone. "It makes sense that you're working together since you both wanted me to remember something that never happened."

"You think I'm working *with* him?!" His fists were clenched, his brow furrowed, his voice trembled with rage.

"What else am I supposed to think?" Jeanette didn't know why she was picking a fight with Hugh. She didn't *really* think that Hugh was working with Larkus. After everything that he had done for her. He'd even gotten her mother's necklace back for her. But none of this made sense to her. Maybe it would if she did have magic, but she just tried it and it didn't work. "You guys obviously have the wrong girl. You must be looking for some powerful enchantress, or some beautiful sorceress. I'm just a simple, lonely maiden who has nothing special about me other than being able to sew."

"You have no idea what's going on, why I'm trapped here with him," his voice was full of disgust.

"Because you can't ever tell me anything!" Her frustration was getting the better of her.

"That's right. I *can't*. You don't understand what would happen if I *did* say something."

Jeanette let out a disappointed sigh. She didn't want to fight.

"You are the right girl, you just have no memory because your spell backfired." Hugh yelled out in pain and fell to his knees. His breathing became labored and sweat broke out on his hairline.

"What is happening?" Jeanette asked and grimaced, she could see his pain. She could *feel* his pain.

Hugh jumped to his feet and ran out of the room.

Chapter 11

Hugh felt foolish for revealing so much in his anger; the punishment had started to tear his skin apart. It was the most pain he had ever felt from his curse. But his temper was fuming. *How dare she think that I'm working with Larkus! After everything I've done for her. I got her that necklace, I put my life on the line for her, and for what? For her to accuse me of working with him!* Disgust ran through his veins, steaming them up like his blood was boiling.

His anger flared with a burst as he threw his desk chair at the window. Instant regret replaced the release of anger as he saw the broken glass. He walked over to the shards scattered across the floor and started cleaning them up.

The pain had finally subsided now that he was farther away from Jeanette. When his attention turned toward the mess he made, he instantly noticed his bleeding had stopped. Even his cuts already looked better.

"What happened here?" Larkus's rough voice growled.

"I—" Hugh jumped and dropped a piece of glass, adding another slice down his hand. He wasn't sure what his master wanted. Larkus hardly ever came into his room. "I was trying to fix the curtain and... I fell off the chair and broke the window," he lied. He knew Larkus would recognize his wounds as punishment from the curse, hopefully this lie would be good enough.

Larkus moved his hands and muttered something.

Hugh watched the shards of glass rise from the floor and realign themselves into a new, perfect window.

"Get yourself cleaned up. You're in charge while I'm away."

"Away?" Hugh asked.

"Yes, I need to leave in the morning. I just learned of another artifact I need to track down, maybe two if I can find them." He muttered as he left the room.

Hugh's heart thumped in his chest. Larkus would be gone. Jeanette would be pleased to hear that. He went to his door to tell her, but then his hand paused at the handle. He saw his cuts. They were no longer bleeding, but they stood as a reminder of their fight. No, he needed to cool off more first. They both needed space.

He removed his bloody clothing while the tub filled with warm water. As he stepped into the bath, the water caressed his cuts. Each lash he got from his curse stung, though he knew they would heal eventually. He wasn't sure what happened to make Jeanette become so angry. He took the time soaking to go over everything.

When he gave her the necklace, it had almost seemed like she remembered, but when he placed it around her neck, nothing happened. He was expecting some big powerful moment for her. Either all of her memories would come back, or maybe she would feel a surge of power. Jeanette's words echoed into his head; *what does power feel like*? How was he supposed to know? Maybe she had felt something but didn't know what it was. He tried to see things from her perspective.

She doesn't remember him, or their past. He'd have to keep it to himself. That, along with his desire. Even though he remembers her, and his love for her had grown in the past couple of weeks, she still didn't remember him. He was a stranger to her. So that's what he would be from now on.

A stranger.

After all, how could she learn to love someone who'd made so many mistakes? Although, he had no idea how he was going to keep his distance. Every time he saw her, all he wanted to do was to sweep her up and kiss her.

He let his anger wash away, flowing down the drain with the rest of the water. Once dressed, he looked out the window, his head feeling clearer after his bath. He was surprised to see how much the weather had changed from this morning. The sky had quickly turned cloudy while he was working in the garden, and now it looked like it was about to snow.

Hugh knew he should apologize to Jeanette for his part in their fight. It made sense that she would think he was working with Larkus, but after all he had done for her, that stung worse than his wounds.

He wasn't sure where she would be. He had left her in the kitchen, maybe she'd still be there. He continued to remind himself to stay as distant as a stranger to her as he made his way downstairs and entered the kitchen.

She wasn't there.

He figured she probably went back to her room. As he arrived at her door, his fist hesitated a moment before he knocked. He wasn't sure if this was a good idea. They were both pretty upset. Maybe she still needed more time. He shook his head as his fist rapped on the door.

No answer.

"Jeanette?" His stomach dropped as he knocked again. "Can we talk?" He waited for her to answer the door. Still nothing. His mind raced around the house wondering where else she could be. There was no escape. Maybe she was trying to break through the back door again.

He turned on his heel and started down the hall when he heard a squeak. He turned back and saw Jeanette's door had opened just a crack. "Jeanette?"

Jeanette sat in her oversized chair, hugging her knees to her chest. She had rushed back to this position after opening the door in response to Hugh's knocking.

It had taken a moment for her to build up the courage to allow him in. She wasn't sure if she wanted to see him.

Her eyes burned from the tears she had been shedding, hating herself for the way she'd spoken to Hugh in the kitchen. She replayed the fight in her mind, she had started it for no reason.

But there was a reason— she was frustrated, and annoyed, and all she wanted to do was go home. If there had been a purpose for her being there, that would be one thing, but the spell failed her, she had no magic, and there really was no way out of this.

It was no wonder Hugh had run from her, he wanted to get away from her. She had broken the only good thing in this horrible place.

She buried her face into her knees as Hugh entered the room, his face soft as he slowly approached.

"What do you want?" Jeanette's voice caught in her throat.

"I came to apologize."

Jeanette shook her head. He had no reason to apologize, he didn't even have a reason to come check on her. She had started that fight. She was the one in the wrong. It should've been her to make the first move to mend the relationship. She sank even lower in her chair, not wanting him to see her in this state.

"No, I'm the one who should apologize," she sobbed as tears streamed down her face again. "I know you're not working with Larkus. I never should have said that."

Hugh let out a sigh. "Will you please look at me?"

She didn't.

Hugh placed a hand on her knee.

The scratches on his skin brought her out of her depressed slump. "What happened?" She grabbed his hand and finally unfolded herself from her cocoon. That's when she saw his arms, face, and neck were also covered in scratches.

Hugh didn't answer.

She thought about the pain they had shared earlier. "This is what happened in the kitchen. When you finally told me something about why I'm here." The puzzle pieces were beginning to fall into place. "That's why you can't tell me anything. Because you'll..." She couldn't bring herself to finish. That meant all those times she questioned and prodded Hugh, he was fighting against some horrific punishment. "I'm so sorry."

Hugh nodded. "At least now you know why I can't share, even though I want to."

Jeanette stood and faced Hugh. She grimaced as her eyes grazed the cuts covering his body. "This is all my fault."

"No," he shook his head. "I chose to say too much."

Jeanette understood, but it didn't help the discomfort she felt. He had said that she had no memory because her spell backfired. *Her* spell. It didn't make any sense. If only he could tell her more. Selfish guilt seized her as she glanced at his cuts once more.

Although it felt good to talk to him again, she wished the fight had never happened.

They had gotten to know each other in her time here and she felt comfortable with him, like they had known each other forever. A part of herself was complete, a part she hadn't realized was missing. She slowly wrapped her arms around his neck and gave him a hug. "I'm glad that I have a friend here," she whispered. "I'm sorry for saying that you were working with *him*."

"About *him*," Hugh echoed Jeanette. "I have some news."

"News that you can share?" One of Jeanette's eyebrows rose.

"Yes," he chuckled. "He's leaving for a while. I'm in charge."

Jeanette's heart skipped a beat. Larkus would be gone. Finally no more chills running down her spine. No more feeling like she was prey and he was hunting her. No more seeing his grotesque face since he never wore his hood inside the house.

"For how long?" If only it was permanent, and she could go back home and be with Hugh.

"I'm not sure."

"When is he leaving?"

"In the morning." Hugh cleared his throat. "I need to get some extra chores done for Larkus's trip, but maybe we can have dinner together? And then, I have a surprise for you tomorrow."

"Another one?" The last time he had a surprise for her was their picnic in the library.

"Yes." Hugh smiled and left the room.

The time she had spent crying had taken a toll on her; she felt drained and needed a nap. Talking with Hugh helped her guilt stop replaying the fight in her head. Tension gave way to relaxation. She moved to the bed and snuggled into her soft pillow. Her dreams took over her reality.

She awoke to hard knocking, her body jumped in response. How long had she been asleep for? She glanced at the dark window, the moon shone high in the sky. That must've been a long nap.

"Hi," she said as she opened the door for Hugh. He carried a tray of food and set it on her desk.

"Hello," he said. "Here's your dinner." He was being awfully short with her. She thought that since she apologized, things would go back to the way it was before, maybe he was still mad at her, or maybe the chores Larkus gave him were too much. She hoped it was the latter.

"Are you okay?" She looked over his scrapes on his arms, it looked like they were already healing. Her eyes traced the cuts on his face, down toward his neck, and landed on a necklace that she hadn't seen him wear before. It looked to have two faces engraved in the silver.

"I'm quite fine," he said. He gave a small bow and headed for the door. "I have more chores to do, I must leave you now."

"Wait," she paused. "Don't you want to eat with me?"

"No. I have work to do."

She nodded, but felt she had to do something to let Hugh know how grateful she was to him. "You... you make being here... not so bad." She blushed and looked away. She hoped telling Hugh that would help him forgive her.

He nodded, gave her another small bow and headed off without a word.

Jeanette stood in her doorway staring off in the direction he went.

The next morning, she heard a soft knock on the door. Jeanette was already awake, but still lying in bed, her guilt marinating in her mind. Hugh's short answers last night concerned her, she didn't want him to still be mad.

New tears threatened to fall at the thought that she ruined their relationship. She hadn't meant for him to get hurt, and she worried she might hurt him again if she continued to ask her questions. She would need to be more careful. But she needed to find a way for him to forgive her first.

Somehow.

There was another knock, this time harder. She closed her eyes and let out a deep sigh.

"Hi." Her voice was slightly groggy. She forced a smile as she opened the door, then her eyes grew wide as she saw Hugh's scratches were completely gone. "Wow, you're healed!"

"Yes," he smiled. "They never last very long." Hugh stood there in a red plaid overcoat and black slacks holding a picnic basket. The same basket from their first picnic in the library together.

"I'm glad you're better."

"You're not ready!" Hugh said when he saw Jeanette standing in the doorway with frazzled hair and wearing a white silk nightgown.

"For your surprise?" Jeanette asked.

Hugh had a quizzical brow. "Are you feeling alright?"

"Yeah. I was lost in thought." She placed a hand on her stomach. It did hurt a little.

"Well, Larkus left this morning for an indefinite time. I thought we could have a picnic for lunch," he said as he walked into the room and sat down on the bed, placing the basket beside him.

"It's already lunch time?" She didn't think she had slept that late, but apparently she had.

"Yep. I've finished all my morning chores."

Jeanette nodded as she glanced at the window. It was bright but there were clouds covering the sun. It made sense to her that she thought it was earlier. "Okay, just let me get dressed."

"Don't take too long," he said as he gave her a charming smile and a wink as he closed the door behind him. She was glad that he seemed to be himself again.

Hugh had another picnic planned and Larkus was gone. Her stomach churned. She wasn't sure if it was from the excitement she felt or something else.

Splashing some cool water on her face helped her wake up more and feel refreshed.

She looked through the dresses in the wardrobe deciding which one to pick; she wanted to match Hugh.

The sun glinted on something toward the back. She pushed a few dresses aside and saw a golden rose brooch pinned to a red and black plaid dress with black lace around the neckline and hem. The breastpin had the same rose shape that was found around her room. The gown had pointed gauntlet sleeves with finger loops. Whoever had made this dress, along with all the others, was quite talented. She had tried her hand at making sleeves like this, but could never get them quite right.

She put on the dress and looked at her hair in the mirror. She hadn't noticed how wild it had become. As she moved toward her desk, she remembered the drawer she found the night she used it to barricade the door. It was full of hairpins, which was exactly what she needed to tame her curls. She grabbed a few and pinned half of her hair up, letting the rest fall in ringlets. She was surprised at how long it had grown since being kidnapped.

Once she was satisfied with how she looked, she walked into the hallway.

"Alright, I'm ready," she said.

Hugh seemed like he didn't hear; he looked at her with that same expression she'd seen on him before. With his smile half-cocked to the right and his jaw clenched. She saw the muscles flex, which for some reason, made her take a deep breath; she smelled his familiar, mysterious scent. She never thought someone would look at her like that.

"Hugh?"

He blinked a couple of times. "You look beautiful!" She saw his cheeks and neck turn a pinkish hue as he smiled.

The butterflies in her stomach fluttered and she felt the heat in her own cheeks.

They stopped in front of a door down the hall from her bedroom. When Hugh opened it, Jeanette saw that it was a linen closet. He picked a heavy-looking red quilt.

They passed Jeanette's favorite painting. She took a quick look and noticed snowflakes fluttering into the scene. A door or window must've been open outside the scope of the frame.

Hugh paused in the middle of the room as they got to the great hall.

"Aren't we having a picnic in the library?"

"No." he smiled. "There's a light, fresh blanket of snow on the ground outside. There's not much, but it's still pretty. I was thinking we could go out and take a walk."

She just stared at Hugh.

He laughed, and it seemed like he could read the thoughts that were written all over her face.

"We're... we're going outside?" Jeanette's thoughts raced around her mind like a hummingbird; flitting from one idea to the next. From exploring the grounds, to having the picnic Hugh planned, to thinking she would be able to escape. If that happened, maybe Hugh would be able to go with her. Jeanette heard the pounding of her heart, she was sure it was loud enough that he could hear it too.

Her breathing was shallow as they stepped closer to freedom. Her heart threw itself against her ribs as Hugh opened the back door.

The cold air bit her cheeks as she took a deep breath; it made her chest tight. She smelled the snow and the ice in the air. It had been months since she had felt the wind on her face. Goosebumps prickled her skin from the excitement of being able to leave her prison.

Chapter 12

F resh snow crunched as Jeanette took her first steps outside in what felt like an eternity. She closed her eyes and breathed deeply, enjoying the sun's kiss upon her skin and the flutter of snowflakes dancing across her nose. After a moment, she twirled around to see the vast building that had been her prison, her eyes opening wide in surprise.

Rose Manor?

The salmon-colored walls looked familiar, but at the same time, she wasn't sure if her eyes were playing tricks on her. They'd exited the back of this mansion, a part of Rose Manor she'd never seen.

Her mind spun as she thought about the view from her bedroom; it didn't look like the grounds of Rose Manor. That could've been some form of Larkus's magic though. He could have an artifact that changed the grounds to look like somewhere else. She felt her insides flop around like a fish out of water. Her eyes stayed glued to the ivy covering the walls and the tall spires as she slowly walked toward the front of the building.

Sure enough, she'd been at Rose Manor all this time.

Her breathing quickened as she took a turn and ran toward the fence—to her favorite spot.

"Jeanette! Stop—" Hugh called after her but she didn't listen. Not when her home was so close. If she could just get the gate open, she could run home. It was within reach! She ran past the snow-covered remains of statues, which made them glisten and sparkle in the sunlight. Under any other circumstance, she would've thought they were beautiful, but she was too preoccupied.

As she got to the fence, she pulled on the large lock, shook the gate, and turned to Hugh who was still chasing after her. "Can you open it?"

Hugh panted to a stop. "Jeanette, you can't escape."

Jeanette huffed. "Why not? My home is right there." She gestured beyond the forest. "I want to go home." Her voice was full of desperation.

"I know, but—"

"You can come with me." Jeanette pulled his hand toward the gate. "We can run away from Larkus, start fresh."

"I can't."

He can't? Jeanette's heart dropped as she released Hugh's hand. She had often wondered what led Hugh to this place, to be stuck serving a master he clearly loathed. She sensed there was truth to his statement, that he truly couldn't leave, even if he wanted to.

She shook her head to focus on the now.

He can't leave, but I can. She thought as she turned back toward the gate, she'd climb over it if she had to. Her heart dropped to her stomach. Could she leave him? That was the question. She wanted more than anything to go back home, but the thought of living a life without Hugh seemed impossible. She was falling in love with him. She turned back to face him. His words popped into her head again.

Her spell.

"Please Jeanette. You can't leave even if you wanted to... and I *can't.*" He hung his head.

"You're..." she paused. "You're under a spell, aren't you?"

"A curse, really," he muttered and let out a moan.

A curse. A spell. The handwritten passage in that magic book passed across her vision. *Sealing and unsealing spells.* Maybe there was a way to break his curse.

"I—"

"Listen," he interrupted, "I wanted to experience the Winter Slumber with you. That's why I planned this picnic outside. It was just good luck that Larkus left when he did."

"The Winter Slumber?"

"You don't remember? It marks the beginning of winter."

Jeanette shook her head and gave a small chuckle. "I know what it is, I just didn't realize it was tonight."

Hugh nodded. So she hadn't missed it after all. Hugh planned this special picnic to experience it with her. And all she could think about was leaving, to go home. She turned back toward the fence, looking at the lock that seemed so impenetrable now. Her gaze turned to Hugh, his shoulders slumped, his eyes closed.

Her resolve shocked her. To stay with Hugh, to stay as a prisoner of Larkus, to try to figure out how to break his spell. She wasn't even sure if it was possible.

"Okay."

Hugh looked up, his eyes wide.

Jeanette nodded to reassure him. "I'll stay. We can have our picnic." She walked toward Hugh, away from the fence, away from her home. It strangely didn't feel as bad as she thought it would.

Hugh let out a sigh, his shoulders relaxed as a smile appeared on his face. "Shall we then?" He gestured toward the forest on the far edge of the backside of the property.

As they walked, Jeanette's heart skipped a beat at each new detail she could now see from the ground.

"Those really are beautiful," she said and pointed toward a snowy fountain. Icicles hung off each tier of the stone and each basin filled with sparkling snow. She looked at Rose Manor. The vast expanse of the building looked much larger up close versus from her spot at the gate.

"That must be my room there." She pointed toward a window high on the tower which rose above the rest of the mansion. It was strange to her that her window would be a focal point.

"Yeah, that's it," Hugh confirmed.

Jeanette had always yearned to explore the grounds. She longed to unbury the snow covered statues and fountains and see them in their full splendor, but Hugh kept walking. She followed him toward a darkened path through dense trees.

"Are we going in there?" Her voice quivered as her stomach did a somersault.

Hugh turned back and smiled, his eyes full of mystery. "It's still on the grounds. This mansion has a pretty big property surrounding it." He chuckled as if he told a joke that Jeanette didn't understand. "Come on." He headed through the trees.

"It doesn't seem that large from outside the gates," she admitted.

"Well, there's more to this place than meets the eye."

The path was narrow and dark, but beautiful. Shadows from the canopy overhead danced across the forest floor. As they traveled along the little path, she saw small ferns popping up through the snow. She took a deep breath and let the fresh air fill her lungs. She wasn't used to being outside, or walking this much anymore, her breathing was labored, and she hoped that Hugh didn't notice her distress.

A small bunny hopped across their path, landing in a deep patch of snow. Jeanette couldn't help letting a giggle escape as the animal disappeared into the powder.

It surprised her that it had already snowed before the full event of the Winter Slumber. That was a rare occurrence. It made her think of the strong breeze from the Fall Winds, a sign of big changes coming. The two could be related, she supposed. She glanced at Hugh as her mind traveled to thoughts of what it was going to be like to experience this event with him.

He walked next to her, carrying the heavy quilt and the basket, but not saying a word. Tension lined his features from the furrows on his brow, to the set of his chin. She wondered what he was thinking about.

She wanted to do something to bring him out of his thoughts, but she wasn't sure what she could do. Maybe he was staying quiet to keep himself from saying too much and getting punished again. She worried that if she started talking, she'd bring up questions that he couldn't answer. It didn't really matter now since she had decided to stay. There had to be a way for her to help him. Maybe he was still upset at her from their argument, but his mood seemed better this morning than it had last night.

As she glanced at him again, she noticed the crook of his elbow— it was inviting, almost as if he was silently asking for her arm to be there. Holding her breath, she slipped her arm through his. The gesture sent electricity through her veins as Hugh looked at her. His face relaxed but he didn't smile. His eyes met hers with a deep penetrating gaze that she felt could see into her soul. Blood rushed to her cheeks and chest before the intimacy of the moment made her look away.

Her stomach continued to flutter, but holding onto him made it easier for her to walk next to him without being so winded.

They finally got to a small, circular meadow lined with trees. The sun had melted all the snow that wasn't protected by the forest. Hugh led her into the middle of the clearing and set the picnic basket on the ground while he laid out the thick blanket that would protect them from the cold, wet earth. Jeanette sat, thankful for the dense velvet weight of the blanket. Meanwhile, Hugh retrieved the basket and sat next to her.

Jeanette wasn't sure what to talk about. *Does Hugh realize what I'm giving up by staying to be with him? Does he feel the same way?* Dread at the answers to those questions punched her in the stomach and she shifted her skirt, trying not to play with it. She noticed that Hugh had caught onto that whenever she was nervous.

"Do you want to see what I packed for us?" Hugh's words brought her back to the present, and she blinked away her troubling thoughts.

"Yes, what did you pack? I hope it's as good as last time."

Hugh chuckled and opened the basket. He pulled out two large rolls and a large cylindrical flask.

"I think you forgot the bowls."

Hugh shook his head. "No, here." He handed Jeanette a roll and took one for himself. He ripped the top off and emptied the fluffy bread from inside. "There, now we have our bowls."

Jeanette smiled and did the same. She watched as Hugh poured deep red liquid into their hollowed bread.

"Mmm." She smelled the soup. The steam coming off the surface heated her cold exposed skin and made her mouth water. She couldn't resist anymore. She brought the bread bowl to her lips and tasted the fresh tomatoes and herbs.

"You like it?" Hugh had been watching her.

She nodded. "I like everything you make." That earned her a smile. The hearty soup was delicious and helped her feel a little better. Maybe she should have told him that she had been feeling a bit off. They might've been able to have the picnic closer to the house rather than hiking through the forest.

"Good. I'm glad," he said as he dipped a piece of bread into his and ate it. Jeanette felt a shudder of embarrassment. She had just dug in without waiting for Hugh to show her how she was supposed to eat the soup. She copied him. It was a different experience. More bread, less soup. She watched as he continued to dip pieces of bread, but she preferred sipping it. She brought it back to her mouth and took a big gulp. The smooth, creamy bisque filled her mouth and coated her throat as it went down. The heat helped to warm her from the inside out.

As they finished their late lunch, Jeanette leaned back on her arms, closed her eyes, and gave a sigh of contentment.

"I hope you're not too full."

Her eyes flicked open, curiosity getting the better of her as she watched him pull out another flask.

"More soup?"

He laughed at her reaction. "Not quite," he said as he opened it and held it out for Jeanette. "I did forget the cups though."

She gave a hesitant chuckle as she took the container from Hugh. She peered into the small opening and took a quick whiff of the contents.

"Hot chocolate?"

"I hope you like it," Hugh said, prompting her to taste it.

Thick.

Creamy.

Rich.

The contents tasted just like the hot cocoa in town. Delicious. It made her happy, with a twinge of homesickness. It reminded her how close and how far away she was from her home. It made her think of Beth.

"It's wonderful," she finally said. "It reminds me of home. Beth and I would make a large pitcher of hot cocoa, and snuggle on a blanket right under this big oak tree during the Slumber."

"Beth?"

"Oh, yeah, she took care of me after my parents died. I was lucky that this newly married couple decided to take in this thirteen year old orphan. If it wasn't for her, I don't know what would've become of me. I owe everything to her." With tears threatening to fall, she changed the subject. "So, have you ever experienced the Winter Slumber before? How do you know about it?"

"Yes, I experienced it a long time ago," he said as he reached for the hot chocolate. She handed it back and felt butterflies as she watched him drink out of it. She had only ever seen Beth and Clint share drinks before. She wasn't sure what to think. It was more intimate than she had previously thought.

A sudden chill in the air sent goosebumps across her exposed neck and a shiver down her spine.

"I think it's starting," she said as she felt the temperature drop some more. The Slumber was beginning. "I love watching the changing of the seasons."

"Here, drink some more, it'll warm you." Hugh handed the flask back. She brought the mug to her lips and drank another sip of the decadent liquid.

"I should've brought another blanket," Hugh said as they both shivered. "I only thought about one to sit on."

"That's okay, we can just use each other." Heat burned her chest; she didn't mean to sound so forward. "And the hot chocolate."

Hugh smiled.

"Look." Jeanette pointed toward the edge of the trees. There was a small herd of deer foraging through some of the fallen leaves before the Winter Slumber fully hit. "I love seeing the animals during this time." They both watched as the frigid temperature hit the herd.

All the deer looked up at once and moved in unison to a low hanging tree. Seeking warmth, they snuggled under the branches together as they lay down to sleep.

"One time I saw a bear," Hugh started. "That's when I fully understood why it was called the *Slumber*. It wasn't a very big bear, I'm sure it was still trying to forage to get ready for hibernation, but the Slumber hit and he immediately collapsed."

"Oh no. I've always been told they're supposed to be in a cave by the time the Winter Slumber hits."

Hugh nodded. "Me too."

"What happened?"

"Well, it was my first winter with Larkus. He could tell how scared I was for this bear, so he used his magic to move him to a cave. At least, that's what he said he did, I don't know why he'd lie about that though."

Jeanette furrowed her brows. "How old were you?"

"I had just turned sixteen." Hugh grimaced.

"I'm sorry." She didn't dare ask more questions. She wasn't sure what his curse allowed him to tell her. Sometimes he could say things and seem fine, other times, she could see and feel his pain. It always burned her throat, she wondered how painful it was for him. Whenever she felt another's pain, it was much more muted than what the injured person felt.

"One of my favorite parts is watching the trees," he said as he relaxed back on the blanket propping his head with his hands.

Jeanette turned to watch the color fade from the foliage, but kept glancing back at Hugh. She wanted to be close to him, not to mention his warmth. She took a freezing deep breath, which stung her lungs, and rubbed her mother's necklace for courage. She let out that breath slowly as she laid down in the crook of Hugh's arm and placed her head on his chest; she hoped he couldn't feel her heart racing and her shallow breaths.

He shifted, and she thought she'd made him uncomfortable, until she felt his arm wrap around her and hold her tight. She relaxed into him, letting all the tension that her self-conscious fear brought melt away.

They stayed like that as they waited for the wind to cause the leaves to fall all at once, marking the end of the Winter Slumber. She closed her eyes as she listened to his heart. Being close to him felt good, it felt right. It helped her warm up, and her stomach to stop hurting. She kept her eyes closed as she stretched her arm across his body. She was nervous that she was being too forward with him, that maybe he didn't feel the same way about her. But he started stroking her arm that was across him.

He let out a contented sigh, which made her look up at him. His eyes were closed and a smile spread across his face. She felt as though she could stay in his arms forever.

The wind soon came, echoing through the trees. Jeanette closed her eyes as she always did, yearning to know what it said.

You're where you're supposed to be.

"What?" Jeanette whispered and looked at Hugh, he was now watching the trees. It startled her to think there was someone else around. But that wasn't possible. She brushed it off, hoping it was just her subconscious confirming that she had made the right choice.

Trust yourself.

"Who said that?" Jeanette sat up and looked around. Tree branches swayed with the pressure of the wind, leaning to the side as they tried to fight their way back. But she saw no one.

"What? What's happening?" Hugh asked.

"Did you say something?"

"No." Hugh also sat up and looked at Jeanette with creased brows.

Learn who you are.

Jeanette looked quizzically down at her necklace. "I think it's the wind."

We've been waiting.

"You can hear the wind?"

Jeanette huffed. "I'm not crazy, don't look at me like that," she said. "It had to be the wind, there's no one else around."

"Well what did it say?"

Jeanette knew he was curious, who wouldn't be? But she wasn't quite ready to reveal what the wind said. It would take time trying to figure it out for herself.

"Um..."

She turned back to Hugh, her eyes locked with his. A sudden loud crunch echoed through the meadow as the leaves in the distance behind Hugh's head fell to the ground in one swift drop. Instead of watching the leaves, he had been watching her.

"The Slumber's over," she said as she looked around. The wind was now gone. She felt guilty that she had made Hugh miss his favorite part. "We should probably head back, we have a while to walk." It was dark now, and the temperature continued to drop quicker with the sun's departure. The first night of the Winter Slumber usually brought a snowstorm; she didn't want to get stuck in that.

Hugh paused, but then agreed and packed up the picnic. "Listen, I'm sorry I wasn't able to have dinner with you last night."

Jeanette was grateful he changed the subject. "That's okay, it was still nice of you to bring me food. I know you were really busy with your chores," she said as they started walking through the darkened woodsy path. "Oh, by the way, I wanted to ask you about that necklace you had on. Why don't you wear it more often?"

Hugh froze.

His expression looked worried. "What necklace?" His voice sounded sharp.

"I'm not sure, it had an engraving of a face, or maybe two. I didn't get a good look at it." She looked at Hugh. His face was pale, almost as white as the snow around them. "What's going on?"

"A smiling face and a crying one?" His voice was shaky now.

"Yeah, I think so." Jeanette's stomach turned itself into a knot.

"Jeanette..." he started out slowly, "I didn't bring you food."

Realization struck Jeanette like a wave crashing upon the sand. Her head spun and she felt as if she was about to pass out. "If it wasn't you then..." She stumbled a few steps backward and inadvertently stepped off the path.

"No, stop!" Hugh reached for her.

There was a loud clash and she flew forward, landing hard on the ground. Frozen ice shards assaulted her chest and face as she landed. The soft powdery snow the bunny had hopped into had turned abrasive. She rolled over as Hugh ran to her.

"What was that?" she gasped as she tried to sit up but her stomach took control and she felt as if she was going to be sick. That was the last thing she wanted to do after her lovely lunch with Hugh.

Hugh took a deep breath. "I'm so sorry. We never should've come this far. It was just the best place for the Winter Slumber."

Jeanette looked at him without understanding.

"The black mist. We can't see it from the ground, but it's a force field around this place." As he fought to get the words out, cuts appeared on his skin. She felt each slice mirroring his, on her own body and wondered if they were actually cutting her too. It was the last thing she saw before everything went dark.

Chapter 13

"Jeanette!" Hugh shook her shoulders, but she remained unconscious. The cuts on his arms and hands started healing. The shock made Hugh jump back. If his slashes were healing already—

Hugh looked back at Jeanette, lying on the ground, pale and limp. Fear slithered into his mind; he knew the consequences of entering the edge of the force field.

"Jeanette?"

He inched closer to her, hoping he could see something that would indicate she was breathing. His mouth went dry at her still demeanor. There was only one thought in his mind: was she alive? He placed his ear to her chest.

A cold sweat broke across his temples as he heard the faint thump of her heart. He knew he needed to get her inside.

Hugh left the blanket and basket behind as he lifted Jeanette and ran toward Rose Manor. Sleet began to fall from the sky. By the time they finally arrived, they were both dripping wet and freezing.

He kicked open the back door and headed toward her room. As he laid her on the bed, she started shivering. He was glad she was still breathing, but she still wasn't awake. He wasn't sure if she would ever wake up. Fear continued to control his mind, never letting the dread go that his worst fear would come to light.

Hugh put one hand on her forehead, she was ice cold. Her lips were turning blue, and the little amount of color that was in her cheeks had drained out. She had scrapes on her face and chest. He didn't know if they were from the force field, or the snow.

Anger rose in his chest. Why hadn't he told her not to wander off the path? Even though she'd backed into the force field by accident, he still felt as though he should've done something to stop her.

Anything.

It was a miracle she was still alive to begin with. In the past, when he'd seen animals walk into the mist, they would get zapped and killed on contact. Hugh knew she had power inside her, maybe that inner strength had made the difference. He hadn't done enough to prevent her injury, but he would do everything in his power to save her. And to start, he needed to get her dry.

"Forgive me." He rolled her over and started taking off her wet things, which proved difficult. The velvet was sodden and heavy; it stuck to her skin. He pulled out his pocket knife and proceeded to cut the sopping dress off her. His hand accidentally grazed the side of the curves on her chest, immediately sending heat to his cheeks.

"Sorry, Jeanette."

With each cut, he saw more and more of her skin until she was lying naked on the bed. Never in his wildest dreams did she look like that. She was more perfect than he could've imagined.

If only he could've admired her body in a moment they shared together. Larkus would pay for this. Somehow, he would pay.

He covered her with the blanket and tucked it around her like a cocoon.

There, that should help. He stood there quietly watching her. It seemed being dry and tucked into bed helped her relax. Her shivering had stopped and her breathing became more regular. The only sound was the pitter-patter of his dripping clothes onto the wood floor.

Now that Jeanette was taken care of, Hugh realized how clingy and uncomfortable his own clothes were.

"I'll be back as soon as I can." As much as he didn't want to leave Jeanette, he also wanted to be dry.

He ran to his bedroom and undressed himself. His soggy clothes hit the floor with a thud. The air was cold against his bare skin, but he didn't let that bother him. The freezing temperatures helped numb the pain from his cuts. The ones under his clothes were healing just as quickly as the ones on his hands. He wondered if Jeanette passing out reversed some of the damage and not a sign of impending death.

If so, it wasn't worth it.

Once he was dressed in his warmest clothes, he hurried back to her bedroom. She looked peaceful, as if she was just sleeping on her bed. If only that's all it was. She hadn't come back into consciousness since getting struck. The wind howled outside— the snow had turned into a blizzard. He pulled her oversized chair next to her bed, nestled in, and waited.

The next morning came after a long night of restless sleep. Hugh tried to stay awake to keep watch over Jeanette, but he kept dozing off. Every time he awoke, he felt the need to check on her before returning to the chair.

The paleness of Jeanette's skin scared him and he felt her forehead to reassure himself that she had made it through the night. The coldness of her body had turned to a fever; he knew he needed to get it down, but what could he do? He was no doctor.

Jeanette was getting worse, he knew he needed to find someone who could help. There was one way, but Hugh had never traveled through it, only Larkus. He paced in her room.

He could probably do it.

For Jeanette.

"I'll be back, just hold on," he told her and closed the door.

As he walked down the hall, something in the sitting room picture caught his eye. There was an angry looking snowman built in the scene.

"I'm sorry. Jeanette is sick, she could die. I need to help her. I'll come back later, I promise," he said to the portrait as he headed toward the shimmering blue wall.

He stared at it. His insides squirmed like a snake caught in a trap. All he had to do was think of a place in the village that he'd been to before. But where? There weren't many options. Larkus hardly ever let Hugh out of the manor. Although, there was one place.

The bakery.

Larkus made him get a few loaves of bread one time; he would go there. *Bakery. Bakery. Bakery.* Closing his eyes, he took a few deep, calming breaths. He was about to walk into a wall, he could do this. This had to work, he knew it would work, he needed it to work. Once he had enough courage, he opened his eyes, held his breath, and ran toward the wall— through the wall.

He felt a rush of wind, and a tugging sensation. It made the queasiness his insides were feeling double, and the next thing he felt were his feet on solid ground.

When he opened his eyes, he stood in the corner of a basement. Nausea punched his stomach. He took a few more deep breaths and leaned against the wall of the stone room until it passed.

Finally being able to stand upright again, he searched the wall behind him to make sure there was a way back. He had to look close, but he saw the wall almost wave. He reached his hand out to touch it, but instead, the wall absorbed his hand. That was the way back home. Back to Jeanette. He shook his head to focus on his task and rushed upstairs.

"Where's the doctor?" He asked the baker.

"Hey, what were you doing down there?" The baker asked, shocked to see Hugh appear from the basement.

"The doctor!" Hugh yelled.

"He's in the center of town. That way."

He hurried out the door. Snow covered the ground, no one seemed to be out, there were very few footprints in the powder. The Winter Slumber's blizzard had died down in the night, and although it was still snowing, it was light.

Finally he found it, the small, tan building with a tiny sign on the door. He was breathing heavily as he walked up the three steps to read the sign.

Dr. Caldwell
All your healthcare needs
In one healthy place.

Hugh's hands shook as he reached for the handle. But before he could open it, the door swung inward, and a heavily pregnant woman exited the building.

"Thank you Dr. Caldwell, I'll see you in a few weeks." She turned and smiled at Hugh. "Oh, excuse me."

Hugh jumped back, making way for her round belly. She waddled past him, her brown hair swishing with each step. Once she passed, he entered.

"What can I help you with young man?" The elderly doctor asked as he placed some papers in a folder on his desk. He glanced up and his eyes grew wide. "Are you here about those cuts? They look a couple days old, you should've come right after that happened."

Hugh waited for the door to close before he spoke. "No, I'm fine. But I need you to come with me right now."

"Come with you? Can't you tell me what's wrong?" His eyes narrowed at Hugh.

"Not exactly. There's someone very sick back home. I need you to take a look at her. Please come."

"I need to know more about the sickness, so I can bring the right medicines and tools. Can you tell me anything?" The doctor sat in his chair behind his desk. He reclined and started swiveling back and forth.

Annoyance began to rise in Hugh's chest. He was scared for Jeanette's health and this doctor didn't seem to understand the urgency, he just wanted more information; information Hugh couldn't share.

He needed to get the doctor to Jeanette, he hoped that he would be able to bring Dr. Caldwell back through the portal with him. That is, if it didn't kill the doctor on contact. No, that wouldn't happen. The doctor wouldn't be staying long. He hoped.

Hugh closed his eyes. "She's sick, she's unconscious, I'm not sure what happened. She was fine during the day. We were on a walk, but the cold and the snow, it all was too much for her. Then she—" he took a deep breath, "she got struck." Pain gripped his throat and forced him to stop talking.

"I see," was all Dr. Caldwell said as he listened to him explain the situation. His forehead wrinkled as he swiftly packed his bag with bandages, a thermometer, a few medicinal bottles, and some notebooks. He wanted to leave right away.

Hugh felt relief as the doctor finally understood.

They walked to the bakery and Hugh entered, causing the little bell on the door to jingle.

"Is the patient in the bakery?" Dr. Caldwell asked.

The bakery was empty. Thank goodness. Hugh didn't want people to see him walk downstairs and wonder what he was doing or try to stop him.

"I'll be right out." The baker's voice boomed from the back room.

"You just need to trust me." Hugh took the doctor by the arm and silently moved toward the stairwell. As they went downstairs, the doctor looked around at the sacks of flour and sugar.

"I don't understand why we're here. Is this some kind of joke? I am a very busy man." He tried to break free from Hugh's grip but it wouldn't budge. Hugh ignored his objection and pushed Dr. Caldwell through the portal. Hugh looked around and made sure no one saw him as he stepped through the waving wall. Once he got through the portal, he saw Dr. Caldwell kneeling on the floor grabbing his stomach.

"Yeah, that tends to happen to first timers." He helped Dr. Caldwell to his feet and showed the doctor the way to Jeanette's room. He was relieved to see that she didn't seem to have gotten any worse while he was gone.

"Jeanette?" Dr. Caldwell hurried to her side. "I wasn't expecting her to be the patient."

Hugh needed to come clean to the doctor; it wasn't safe to let him treat her without the full story. He explained their picnic outside and the part about the force field.

Thankfully his curse didn't cause him pain, he hadn't been sure if the 'remember-me-not' spell on the portal would protect him since he, not Larkus, had brought the doctor. The lack of pain proved to him that the doctor wouldn't remember anything once he went back through. It didn't matter what Hugh told him now, although it still made him uneasy.

"I also think she might've gotten poisoned. She ate something last night that my master had brought her. And even though she was trying to hide her discomfort all day, I could tell she wasn't feeling well."

He watched as the doctor said nothing, but remained calm as he took Jeanette's temperature and pulse.

"I have to ask," Hugh started. "You seem very understanding about all of this. Going through a magic portal, learning about a force field. You don't even seem to have questions. Why?" He had never been around anyone so calm about magic.

"That is an excellent question, and one that I will answer and explain later. Right now, I just want to help Jeanette get better." Dr. Caldwell looked into Hugh's eyes as if he saw right through him. He didn't say anything else as he went back to examining Jeanette.

Hugh stood there watching him work.

"I haven't seen anything like this in years," Dr. Caldwell told Hugh. "It seems that whatever is ailing her won't let go."

"Do you think it's the force field or the poison? Can you help her?"

"It's hard to say, I need my notes; maybe I can remember what my old companion did for a gentleman he took care of years ago."

Dr. Caldwell went to his bag and flipped through notebook after notebook.

"What are you searching for?" Hugh asked anxiously as he watched.

"Got it." He nodded but ignored Hugh's question. His face began to fall slowly as his eyes darted back and forth down the page. "We need to make a medicinal remedy, but many of these plants are out of season."

"I can get them. There are ways for me. What are they?" Hugh was determined to save Jeanette. "I'll do anything for her."

The doctor began to write on an empty sheet in his notebook, looking back and forth between the pages and nodding. He then ripped the paper out and handed it to Hugh. "These are all the plants we need and their descriptions. The sooner you get them, the better."

Hugh stuck the paper in his coat pocket, ran to the kitchen wood pile, and started digging through it, searching for the gathering basket. Larkus had ordered Hugh to destroy it. Instead, he hid it.

After moving half the logs off the pile, he saw the braided handle. He moved a few more logs and pulled out the wooden basket. The basket had intricate floral designs carved into the side.

Hugh walked toward the great hall, past the shimmering blue portal and stopped in front of the dark green portion of the wall. He had never accessed this portal before and had only seen Larkus use it once in the past.

Hugh reached into the basket and grabbed a handful of dirt from the bottom. As he squeezed the soft, red soil, it kept its shape.

He looked back at the wall and rubbed the dirt across it— a red rainbow of clay covering the green. He watched as the wall accepted his offering, absorbing the dirt into its crevices as the wall started to glow.

He held the basket tight as he stepped through the portal.

The smell of fresh air filled his lungs as rushing wind encircled him. He felt weightless. Then, just as suddenly as the wind came, it was gone, and he found himself lying on his back gasping for breath.

Once his breathing slowed, he sat up and looked at his new surroundings.

He appeared to be inside a giant greenhouse. Trees towered around him, shading patches of flowers across the ground. The sound of running water alerted him to a stream nearby. The sun cast beams of light through the dome above him, which had invisible door outlines against the glass. One doorway glowed green; the same shade of the wall he had just walked through. That must be his way home. The distance that door now stood from him was daunting, he had no idea how he was going to get back up there. Even the tallest trees were still dwarfed by the distance.

Nervousness stung his extremities, he was afraid he'd be trapped here, and even more afraid for Jeanette. There was nothing else he could do; he pulled out the paper Dr. Caldwell had given him and started his search.

Most of the plants he passed were dormant, however, just ahead, he noticed one in full bloom. Its small, purple flowers, tubular in shape, matching the description of the first plant the doctor needed. So that was the key to finding what he needed— look for blossoming flowers.

But he was unsure how he was supposed to gather them. He tried to break the stem with his hands, but they were too fibrous. As he finally got one freed, he opened the gathering basket and found a pair of clippers. He rolled his eyes at himself and proceeded to clip a few more flowers. The doctor's note didn't say how many to collect.

He continued searching for the blooming plants, placing a bundle of orange flowers on top of the growing pile in his gathering basket. He checked his notes, making sure he was grabbing the right plants, which wasn't hard, they were the only ones in bloom. Only one was left on the list. He knelt by a spiky leafed plant and clipped a few branches.

He was about done clipping the last plant when an elegant looking flower bloomed right before his eyes. The petals of the flower were crimson and creamy white, the sweet scent penetrated his senses. He looked back at his notes. They didn't say anything about this plant.

He stood, staring at the blossoms. Then it occurred to him, if the plants he needed were in bloom, then what if someone else needed plants? He looked at the outlines against the dome. That's when he saw it, a black and gold door slowly appearing with a raven symbol— a symbol he'd seen before.

"I need to get out of here."

The pull of the wind seemed stronger than before; he closed his eyes and let the current carry him. It got colder as he felt his feet on solid ground. He opened his eyes and saw he was back in the manor, holding the gathering basket.

He rushed back to Jeanette.

Chapter 14

H ugh breathed heavily as he entered the room. "I have the plants you requested," he panted as he held the basket out for the doctor.

Once he'd made his delivery, he sat on the edge of Jeanette's bed, his heartbeat slowing to a normal pace. The blankets were new, as were the flannel pajamas Jeanette now wore. He had missed something while he was gone. Her skin burned as he held her hand.

"You managed to find them all?" the doctor asked as he opened the basket. "I'm not sure how you did it, but I'll get started on the remedy."

Hugh opened his mouth to explain, but realized the doctor didn't care for an explanation. He was already removing flowers from their stems as he looked at the notebook next to him. Hugh turned his attention back toward Jeanette.

"I see you dressed her in warm clothes." Hugh didn't take his eyes off her again.

"Yes, she vomited on herself and the covers while you were gone," Dr. Caldwell said mindlessly as he dealt with the plants.

"She woke up?"

Dr. Caldwell shook his head. "No, she started convulsing, It took me a little while to find a new blanket," he trailed off while searching through his bag. "I need a mortar and pestle."

"Mortar and pestle." Hugh paused trying to think of where one would be.

"Yes, it is a stone bowl—" Dr. Caldwell started to clarify but Hugh waved his hand to stop the doctor.

"I understand." Hugh left to retrieve the only one he knew of. He walked through the library, up the stairs, and down the hall to Larkus's doorway.

He paused.

He wasn't allowed inside when Larkus was gone. He took a few deep breaths before opening the door.

The stench of rotten meat filled his lungs. The mark of dark magic had spread from Larkus onto his belongings, like mold creeping its way across fruit. He found the mortar and pestle sitting in the middle of the desk. The porous stone vessel was large and heavy. Hugh finally managed to lift it off the desk by dragging it to the edge. He had to carry it with both hands, taking his time so as not to drop it.

At the doorway, he glanced back at Larkus's desk, the vacant spot where it once sat showed drag marks on the wood. Maybe he could fix that before Larkus returned. The thought of the punishment he would receive if Larkus found this missing made him shudder. But if it would help save Jeanette, it was worth it.

"Alright, just set it down there," Dr. Caldwell said and motioned next to his notebook as he took Jeanette's temperature again.

Hugh obeyed. "Should I get started? What am I supposed to do?"

"No, no. It'll be faster if I do it."

Hugh watched as the doctor carefully pulled each leaf off and ground them in the bowl. Then the doctor held the small, tube-like flowers and tilted them over the stone basin. To Hugh's surprise, purple liquid seeped out of the blossoms. The concoction resembled chunky paste, and the herbal scent permeated the room.

"There. That's everything."

"You're done? Can we feed it to her now?"

"Yes, she needs this as soon as possible." Dr. Caldwell pulled a spoon out of his medical bag. "Help her into a sitting position; I don't want her to choke on it."

Hugh slid behind her and cradled her in his arms. He wanted to be able to stay like this forever, but this was not the time. He wasn't sure if Jeanette would ever wake up— if they would ever get the future they were destined for.

"Now, hold her head up." Dr. Caldwell's words pulled Hugh from his thoughts.

"It's okay, I'm here," he whispered as he stroked the nape of her neck while the doctor gave her the remedy.

"Well, that's all of it. If this works she should get better."

"What do you mean *if* this works? You have done this before, right?"

The doctor took a deep breath. "Truth be told, I've never done this, but my cousin has. He told me about a case similar to this the last time we visited. These are his notes." He held up the notebook he'd been studying. "It worked for that patient. Let's hope it works for her as well."

Jeanette let out a soft moan.

"She's waking up!" Hugh's breath caught in anticipation.

The doctor's face didn't show the same enthusiasm. In fact, he looked concerned, his brows brought together with a frown painted across his face. He was slightly shaking his head.

Hugh looked down at Jeanette's face, her eyes were still closed and she looked ghostly pale. Hugh's excitement turned sour.

Jeanette's body jumped in his arms of its own accord.

"What's happening?" Hugh's voice barely came out.

"She's having another seizure. Tilt her head to the side." Dr. Caldwell checked his watch. Just as Hugh tried to steady Jeanette enough to move her head, he felt warm liquid across his skin.

"Oh no!" Hugh exclaimed.

Jeanette became calm in his arms. He gently laid her back on the bed as he got out from behind her.

"Will the remedy still work? I think I'm wearing most of it," he said as he examined the purple bile on himself.

"I hope so," Dr. Caldwell replied.

"Is this what happened to her while I was gathering the plants?"

The doctor nodded.

"Does she have a history with seizures?" Hugh hated asking that. He knew she didn't have any issues before, but he wouldn't know if she developed it after. He should have known. If he hadn't made that dreadful mistake, he would have.

"No, today is the first, well, and second time," the doctor explained. "Why don't you go get cleaned up, and I'll get her situated. It's also getting late, you should go to bed; there's no use in both of us staying up."

Hugh shook his head. "I'll get cleaned up, but I don't want to leave her."

Once Hugh arrived in his own room, he wiped himself down with a wet washcloth, which helped with the purple residue and a bit with the smell. He changed into clean, comfortable clothing.

As he walked back to Jeanettes room, the angry snowman was gone from the portrait, but a somber scene lay before him. "I'm sorry. For everything. If it wasn't for me—" Hugh's voice caught in his throat. "None of this would have happened." He placed a hand to the canvas and closed his eyes. He stood there, just for a moment.

Hugh heard movement from within Jeanette's room. He opened the door hoping to see she'd made it through her fever, but all he saw was Dr. Caldwell on the floor and Larkus standing over Jeanette's lifeless body. Larkus laughed and gave Hugh that maniacal smile.

"What have you done?" Hugh screamed at the monster before him.

"Now I can continue my plan," Larkus replied as he vanished in a cloud of smoke.

Hugh woke suddenly in a cold sweat. The morning rays streamed through the light curtains. He looked around to regain his surroundings. He had fallen asleep in the oversized chair next to Jeanette's bed.

"I'm glad you were able to sleep," Dr. Caldwell said as he stood next to Jeanette, checking her pulse again. After nodding his head with the beats, he let out a sigh and smiled. "Her pulse is back to normal and her fever broke in the night."

"Thank you, Dr. Caldwell." Hugh wiped the sweat from his face. He was grateful to the doctor. Jeanette made it through, but all was not well... she still hadn't come back to him.

"I must get home. I believe she'll be alright," Dr. Caldwell said as he closed his bag.

"Wait. She hasn't woken up yet." Hugh's voice cracked. He didn't mean to show his fear, but it broke though.

Dr. Caldwell nodded. "I know, but her vitals are all back to normal, and I do need to check on another patient back home, but I guess I could stay a little longer," he said as he checked his watch.

"Thank you. Besides, I'd like to know your story. Why does none of this seem to bother you?"

"Yes. I suppose I owe you an explanation. But first, I would like some tea." The doctor set down his things.

Hugh nodded and looked at Jeanette. The color had returned to her cheeks, she looked so peaceful. "I agree. Tea sounds nice."

Hugh brought a tray with two cups and a teapot. He poured the hot liquid and handed a cup to Dr. Caldwell. The scent of the peppermint and orange steam reached his face and gave him a sense of comfort.

"I had mentioned my cousin." The doctor started his story. "He lives in Aspen Glenn. Have you heard of it?"

Hugh nodded. He knew all too well of Aspen Glenn. The thought of the town made Hugh's stomach churn. He took a sip of tea which seemed to help.

"Well, he's the town doctor there. They had some issues with a nasty witch; made a habit of cursing people that crossed her and sent enslaved ravens to attack villagers. Also blew up quite a few buildings with just a glare from her malevolent eyes. I was lucky enough to get out of one of her targets before it became engulfed in flames. I'm still haunted by the image of her evil yellow eyes glaring behind those thick black frames." He shook his head as he took a sip of tea.

"I can understand how terrible that must've been." The details of the witch's power didn't faze Hugh; he'd been with Larkus long enough, going from town to town, reining chaos in his wake.

However, one detail stood out. Ravens. An image of the door in the greenhouse came to mind. He was now extra grateful he'd left before she arrived.

"Well, my cousin wrote to me asking for my help in treating patients. One of them had been injured in a similar way that Jeanette was." They both looked at her. "I arrived after he was healed of his poison, but my cousin had begged me to stay and help rid them of the town witch. We did months of research and finally found a ritual to cast evil beings away. The townsfolk couldn't wait to get started and proceeded to complete it. It was interesting for me to see non-magic beings able to complete something so..." he paused, his brows furrowed. Probably thinking of the right word to say.

"Magical?" Hugh filled in the word.

The doctor let out a sigh and nodded.

It made Hugh think about the portals. They're magical and he was able to use them. He thought about asking what the ritual was, maybe it could help him get away from Larkus.

Dr. Caldwell didn't seem to notice Hugh's internal struggle and continued, "The next day, that wicked witch was gone. I can't say if she died, or if she vanished, or what happened to her. As far as I know, no one has disturbed that village since, and I'm glad. My cousin can now practice in peace."

Hugh felt sick to his stomach. The tea no longer calmed his nerves. "That witch..." He wasn't sure how to tell Dr. Caldwell, but he knew one thing without a doubt. "That sorceress is still alive."

"How do you know?"

"When I got the plants, I went to a magic greenhouse. As I was leaving, her door materialized. It had a symbol of a raven on it."

The doctor looked at him with narrow eyes; Hugh knew what he said was difficult to believe. But now, he remembered where he'd seen the door before; it was the reason Larkus had been in such a hurry to leave Aspen Glenn, why he wanted the gathering basket destroyed; he didn't want to risk that witch finding him. A symbol like that could be tracked.

Larkus never used a symbol. He had always said it was careless to let people know where you were. Only now did it occur to Hugh that it might be turned the other way. He had always thought Larkus was the hunter, but what if he was the prey?

"Hugh," a small whisper said his name. Hugh jumped out of his chair so quickly that he knocked the teapot off the table and it shattered on the ground, spilling the orange and peppermint tea. The aroma filled the room. He didn't care about the mess— Jeanette was awake.

Jeanette's body jostled as Hugh sat down on the bed next to her. "I'm so glad you're awake."

"Hugh," she whispered again. She was happy to see him. She wasn't sure what had happened. Her mind felt foggy and a strange cloud surrounded her memory.

"How are you feeling?" Dr. Caldwell asked as he checked her pulse.

"Dr. Caldwell?" she asked, dazed. "What are you doing here? What happened?" Her head ached as she looked at her town doctor. Was she home?

"You don't remember?" Hugh's face looked tired. Lines creased his forehead and cheeks that she hadn't noticed before. She placed her hand to his cheek and stroked those lines. Hugh smiled and held her hand in place, kissing her palm.

"We think you were poisoned," the doctor answered. "And I'm sure that force field didn't help either."

"Wait." Jeanette pulled her hand away from Hugh and sat up in bed, her muscles protesting the movement. The ornate four poster bed and finely decorated walls told her she wasn't back in her cottage, but was still in her room at Rose Manor. Although her body ached, her confusion bothered her more... Dr. Caldwell was here, and he knew about the force field. "Why are you here? How are you here?"

"You got struck, I needed to get a doctor for you. I thought you were going to die," Hugh explained.

Her reaction came. A reaction she wasn't expecting to feel toward Hugh, or Dr. Caldwell.

Anger.

"You brought him here? And told him everything? I thought you said you couldn't leave! You could never tell *me* anything. Why him?" Jeanette's voice echoed the anger in her chest.

Hugh's eyes widened. "Jeanette—"

"And what about you?" She turned toward Dr. Caldwell. "What did you think happened to me? Did you think that I was just staying at home? For months? Has anyone looked for me, or even noticed I was gone? How dare you talk to me like nothing has changed, like any of this is normal!" She let her rage release, not realizing this layer of hurt she'd kept hidden. Seeing the doctor now brought on feelings of abandonment. She couldn't fathom that no one from her town had come for her before now. Beth? Clint? No one?

"My dear Jeanette, I'm sorry. But there was no reason to wonder where you were in the first place."

Jeanette looked at the doctor with disbelief. Is that what the town thought of her? No one cared in the first place? No sense of worry about her whereabouts?

"I see." Her voice became grave. All this time, her home, her town, her customers— no one cared.

"I don't think you do," he replied. "You see, the reason I didn't have to wonder, was that *you* came to the center of town and announced that you were going on a voyage." He held his hands in the air as if presenting a large masterpiece. "You kept fiddling with a necklace and said you were tired of this tiny town. That you were taking Beth's advice to travel and see the world."

Jeanette gaped at Dr. Caldwell.

"When was this?" Jeanette couldn't believe what she was hearing, although she should be used to it by now.

"About three months ago," Hugh finally spoke up, he had been awfully quiet. His face contorted into a grimace. "Jeanette..." his face softened as he looked into her eyes, a look of worry.

Her heart broke a little, but she was still angry. She felt the burning in her throat proving to her that he couldn't have told her before now. "That's right when I got taken."

"I'm so sorry you've had to go through this all alone," the doctor said as he patted her hand.

"Can you tell Beth I'm okay?"

"Um..." Dr. Caldwell and Hugh exchanged looks. "I won't remember any of this when I leave." Jeanette's shoulders dropped and she looked with questions between the two men.

"You can't tell me anything? Hugh must've told you information on why you're here. You know about the force field, you know about the poison... can't you tell me what's going on?" she begged the doctor.

"No, if he reveals anything to you, I will still get punished," Hugh said.

"And what do you have to say?" Jeanette turned toward Hugh. Something that looked like guilt painted across his expression.

"Jeanette, that necklace..." Hugh trailed off.

"I know..."

"It was Larkus."

She nodded. "He made sure that no one would miss me."

"Then he poisoned you." Hugh closed his eyes as a heavy sigh escaped. "I'm so glad you're alive. You were so sick, I thought you were going to die. Luckily, the good doctor here saved you."

"I'm sorry, dear. Now, that remedy seemed to do the trick. Your vitals are all normal. I must be going now." The doctor took one last sip of tea, grabbed his things, and smiled at Jeanette.

She nodded and thanked the doctor while Hugh left with him. Carefully, she walked to the window and stared out at the grounds, the black mist, the snow. She had experienced the best outing with Hugh until she got struck.

"Jeanette?" Hugh's voice came from right behind her. She turned around. Hugh stood close to her and stroked her arms, which felt good, but she was still angry and had questions. She closed her eyes, she didn't want to be distracted by his dimples or the way he kept glancing at her lips. She had a hard enough time with his scent penetrating her senses.

"Can I ask how you got the *good doctor* here?" She mimicked him. "How did you explain everything? About the force field, about Larkus, about *me?*"

"I was able to explain everything because he won't remember it. He has a past with magic, so it didn't seem to bother him. I brought him..." Hugh paused, which made her open her eyes and look into his. "I brought him through the portal." Hugh looked pained.

"A portal?" Jeanette's eyes widened and her heart quickened. "There's been a portal here the entire time? I could have gone home?"

"It's not that simple."

"Show me!" Jeanette yelled, anger building again. How could he not have told her about a portal before now?

"I can't. You don't understand, it wont work. I—" he shook his head.

"Show me," she demanded. This was something she needed to see with her own eyes. If Hugh was able to use it, to bring the doctor here, then she could use it too.

He led her down the hall, toward the kitchen, and stopped in front of the blue shimmering wall. He turned to her and let out a sigh.

"This is how I traveled to get Dr. Caldwell. I pictured a spot in the village that I'd been before and stepped through. All of these colorful walls have their own abilities. I have now used this blue wall and the green one."

Jeanette raised her hand toward the shimmering blue section, her hand hit the wall hard. She knocked on it, pushed it, and punched it.

Hugh let out a sigh. "Jeanette—"

"I don't understand. Why won't it work for me? I'm thinking of my home!" Jeanette yelled in frustration.

"You can only use this portal if your desire is to come back," Hugh explained. "I was able to travel to town to get the doctor because I wanted to come back here."

"Why would anyone want to come back here?" Jeanette asked, revulsion lacing her voice. How could anyone want to come back and be with a disgusting monster like Larkus? "This place is the worst possible place to want—"

Hugh's mouth crashed down on hers. His hands wrapped around her back, pulling her against him. His lips were soft, yet hot. Hers betrayed her anger and kissed him back. As he parted his lips slightly, she felt his tongue graze against hers, his breath was minty. Jeanette felt surprised when Hugh broke their kiss.

"To you!" Hugh's eyes stared into Jeanette's, as if urging her to understand the meaning behind his words. "I wanted to come back to you," he whispered as he released her.

She stood there, shocked at what just happened. Her mind spun, not knowing which point to focus on. He kissed her, he came back for her. She wanted to go home, but she wanted to kiss him again.

"Um..."

"'Um?' That's it? That's all you have to say?" Hugh huffed at Jeanette's lack of response and walked through the portal.

Jeanette watched the shimmering blue wall envelop Hugh as he disappeared.

Chapter 15

Wind rushed around Hugh as the portal transported him. To where? His stomach churned with the air around him. He hadn't thought of a specific place before walking through the shimmering wall. His emotions had gotten the better of him.

His skin itched, burning slashes wanting to come out. His punishment for revealing to Jeanette how the portals work. For revealing how he felt, her reaction to their kiss was punishment enough.

Their kiss.

He could still taste her soft, plump lips. How he thought, right at the end, she had started kissing him back, but he pulled away too soon. It wasn't how he envisioned their first kiss, but there were so many things different than how he envisioned them. Her reaction, or lack thereof, was definitely not expected. His whole life, having to be a servant to someone like Larkus was not how he had planned his future. He wished things were different. All this time, he and Jeanette had been growing closer. But in truth, the circumstances that plagued both of them also kept them apart.

Just as he thought the wind was taking a long time to deliver him, his feet landed on solid ground. He took a few steadying breaths and found himself somewhere he wasn't expecting. Somewhere he wasn't sure he wanted to be.

Jeanette's feet wouldn't move. The blue wall shimmered in mockery of the thoughts that troubled her.

Hugh left her. Meaning, he would come back at some point, but she wasn't sure when. Her anger subsided, and what felt like betrayal took its place as she thought about Hugh not telling her about this portal. She thought about her little cottage again, desperately wanting to go back home. To see Beth and Clint, to return to normal like none of this had happened.

"Let me go home, I'll come back. I will. I would come back and break Hugh's curse." The wall continued to shimmer. Jeanette held her hand just beyond the wall's reach. She let out a long breath and stepped forward.

Her hand hit the wall.

A shriek of anger escaped her lips. The wall seemed to know her truths. If she could go home, she'd never return. Who would?

Hugh.

Guilt slapped her as the realization hit. Hugh left this prison only because he truly would come back to her. He saved her. She promised that she'd break his spell, but she wasn't even sure how to do that. However, she knew where to start. The magic book in her bedroom had a chapter she wanted to explore.

On her way to her room, she passed her favorite portrait. Normally, the sitting room picture looked inviting, warm, and cozy. She loved how it changed. But this time was different. The gloom of the picture radiated past the frame. Jeanette felt sorrow in the subject matter.

Instead of a fire in the hearth and a blanket on the chair; a small stuffed toy dragon sat in the plush armchair and a pile of books lay open in a circle on the floor.

"I need to study my books too." She hesitantly placed her hand on the canvas, but instead of shocking her like last time, it felt... sad. How could a picture feel sad? She let out a sigh. Just the same as everything else in this house happens— magic.

Jeanette got back to her room and found the book on her desk, grabbed it, and got comfy in her bed. She opened the cover and saw the handwritten passage again. *Chapter 9: Sealing and unsealing spells.* That'd be a good place to begin. Her eyelids felt heavy all of a sudden, the pillow was cool and inviting, it was as if she couldn't keep her eyes open any longer.

Morning rays pierced her sleep and she awoke to the blinding sun. She felt disoriented, and looked at the book lying open next to her. She nodded, she needed to get back to work.

Sealing a spell forces it to become permanent. No other sorcerer can break that spell by ordinary, magical means, unless they have the one and only Serpent Gauntlet.

Note: see artifact in Chapter 6.

~ ~ ~ ~

If the sorcerer wishes to unseal a spell, the same words used in sealing the spell must be spoken and broken at the same time.

~ ~ ~ ~

If a spell has not been sealed, and the sorcerer dies, that spell is immediately broken.

~ ~ ~ ~

However, a sorcerer can place deterrents to stop anyone from unsealing a spell or breaking an unsealed spell; temporary blindness, temporary burns, onset sleepiness, among others.

Jeanette let out a yawn. That must be what was happening, she had just woken from a full night's sleep, but she felt her eyes growing heavy again. Her head spun at all the new information. There were notes in that same feminine handwriting in the margins of the book.

Where could the Serpent Gauntlet be? There's only one in the entire world.

Spoken and broken at the same time... how?

Check the Spellbook of Mangor to see if it has any spells that might help.

"The Spellbook of Mangor?" Jeanette closed her book and leapt off her bed. She repeated the name to herself as she raced toward the library, searching for this mysterious book that might be of use.

As she got to the library, everything seemed a bit too quiet, not to mention freezing. It seemed dark without the fires that were normally burning in the hearths.

"Hugh?" Jeanette wasn't sure if he had come back while she was asleep. No answer. She shook her head and decided to continue her search for this spellbook.

The magic books in the library consisted of history of magic, informational books, spellbooks galore, but not the one she was looking for.

Frustration thumped against her temples. She rubbed them as she let out a grunt. "I just need that book!" She closed her eyes for a few moments, wondering what else she could do.

A thud on the wooden floor made her jump. Was Larkus back? Did he magically appear behind her? She looked around and found she was still alone. However, a gray leather bound book lay on the floor near the corner of the bookshelves. Her curiosity made her forget the pounding headache that was brewing behind her eyes as she lifted the book to read the title.

The Spellbook of Mangor.

Did she do that? Or did the book sense her need? Either way, she was sure magic was behind this book appearing in front of her.

Jeanette lounged in the oversized chair in the library to read through the book. A shiver escaped as she looked at the cold hearth again. Her mind turned to think about how long Hugh would be gone. Just because he would come back doesn't mean it would have to be soon.

She shook her head as she turned back to the pages. She couldn't think about that right now, she needed to focus on the task in front of her. As she flipped through the book, she felt overwhelmed. There was so much information. It was full of spells to cast, sealing spells, and information on how to break curses.

"Finally!" Jeanette's heart fluttered when she read the title of that chapter.

"Finally what?" Hugh's calm voice came from the doorway. Jeanette's gasp made him laugh.

"Just something I was looking for. Where did you go?" She stood and ran to Hugh. "I'm sorry," she whispered as she wrapped her arms around his waist. For a split second she thought maybe this was Larkus in disguise again. It took a moment before she felt Hugh's arms return her hug. As soon as she felt that, any doubt that it wasn't actually Hugh vanished.

"I was so scared that Larkus was going to come back before you did."

"I'm sorry, too. I never should have left you like that," he said as he squeezed her tight. "And... I should've told you about the portal."

"You couldn't have," she said as she pulled away and laid her hands on his chest. "I understand that. I was just angry." The time alone gave her a new perspective— of course Hugh would've told her if he had been able to. Her homesickness had been a great weight on her shoulders that turned into bitterness when she found out about the portal. But it wasn't Hugh's fault; she realized that now.

"If I could've told you—"

"I know." She smiled. "Speaking of which," Jeanette went back to the chair and held out the spellbook to show Hugh. "I think this will help us to try to break your curse."

Hugh's eyes widened in response.

"There's just a few things that I need to know before we start." She opened the book to the chapter she had been studying. "This says there are different spells to break loyalty spells or servitude spells, slave spells or— I'm not even sure how to pronounce that word..."

"Um..." Hugh's voice trembled. "It's a servitude spell. I remember Larkus saying that I have to serve him until the day he frees me." Hugh was quiet for a moment. "I don't think that'll ever happen."

"'Until the day he frees you'?" Jeanette's shoulders fell. "That means it's sealed. Even if he dies, it won't break. You'd still be punished for revealing things. We'd never be free." She paused, grimacing as more cuts appeared on Hugh's face. "We need to figure out how to break it."

"What do we have to do?"

"Well, there are a handful of spells we can try, but I'm not quite sure how to test if it works," she said as she flipped a few pages.

"I have an idea…" Hugh let out a sigh. "The curse punishes me when I reveal too much."

Jeanette knew that would be his suggestion, but she had hoped there was another way. She didn't like being the cause of his pain, but since she would also feel the pain she sees, it would be her own punishment for hurting him. Besides, maybe this way, she would finally be able to learn more about why Larkus wanted her.

Hugh nodded. "Let's try it."

"Now?" Jeanette asked. When Hugh didn't reply, she looked at the page she was on. "I guess we could try this one." She read over it again and followed the spell. She read the strange words and mirrored the images of the hand movements. When she was done, she felt slightly lightheaded.

"Did it work?" Hugh's eyes had been tightly closed as if he was waiting for a blow to his face.

"How am I supposed to know? Tell me something."

Hugh looked at her and thought for a long time. He started pacing, kept opening his mouth to start, and then he'd change his mind. Jeanette wondered what was going through his head. He finally sighed as he nodded and turned to face her.

"We've known each other since we were children," he said as he fell to one of his knees and screamed out in pain.

"Oh no!" Jeanette cried out. She felt each of those cuts as if they appeared on her own body. She watched helplessly as Hugh ran out of the room.

I *hadn't even finished my sentence!* Hugh fumed as he lowered himself into a bath. His wounds protested as they entered the water, but were quickly soothed by the warmth. He hadn't been expecting his punishment to be that severe, but the curse seemed to know what he was about to reveal. He'd have to start smaller next time.

That is if there would be a next time. His cheeks burned as he thought of the way he had run out on Jeanette.

Again.

He just hoped she would be willing to keep trying. But he didn't want her to see how deep his cuts were getting. Maybe there was something they could do to prevent that from happening.

After his bath, he returned to the library. Jeanette was asleep in a chair, the spellbook laid open in her lap, she must have dozed off while studying. She had a blanket wrapped around her legs. It *was* rather cold. He looked at the dark fireplace. He felt bad he left her with no heat.

Once he built a fire, he turned back to Jeanette. She looked peaceful, sleeping on the chair. It was how he'd picture her if their lives had never gotten separated. He brushed a stray hair from her face and leaned down to kiss her forehead. "Jeanette?"

"Hmm?" Her eyes fluttered open and she smiled at him. "Oh, are you feeling better?"

He nodded. "I am. I'm sorry I ran out again."

"That's okay. I didn't mean for you to get hurt."

"Yeah... We'll need to figure out something for that. I don't want you to feel my punishment either," he said.

Jeanette looked at him with tears in her eyes. "I'm so sorry."

"It's okay, it's something that needs to happen if we're going to figure this out. I have full faith that you can break my curse. I trust you."

She gave him a small smile.

"Come, we can get some dinner," he said as he held his hand out for her. She took it and they walked hand in hand to the kitchen. "How are you feeling?"

"My body is a little sore, but other than that, I feel fine."

"That's good." He had noticed that she was moving around better. "I was worried that the poison mixed with you seeing my punishment would've taken too much of a toll on you."

"Yeah... no. Don't worry about that. I feel bad that I caused you pain to begin with. I don't have any memories of us as children though."

"You wouldn't."

She nodded. "Well, I don't feel any effects from the poison. It's as if it never happened."

Hugh nodded. "It must've been the remedy."

"The remedy?"

Hugh explained the remedy they made, the green portal he used, and how he took care of her. His stomach dropped when pain shot through his body. Thankfully she wasn't looking at him, and she didn't seem to notice his pain. Maybe they should've tried another spell before he explained everything, but it was too late now. After they finished eating, they sat in the library together. Jeanette stroked the cover of the magic book.

"So, you..." she paused. "You took care of me? You changed my clothes?"

"Well," it was his turn to pause. "I needed to get you dry, I cut you out of that dress."

Her eyes grew wide as her cheeks flamed pink. "That poor dress. It was such a masterpiece. Whoever made it was extremely talented."

Hugh smiled at the thought that Jeanette cared more about that dress than her modesty. "Your father made it."

"What? My father was the town's tailor, but I don't understand. We could never afford such fine fabrics. Velvet and lace. And how would it have gotten here?"

"Try another spell first but don't look at me."

She yawned as she looked through her book and found one that she thought could work. When she finished, she was breathing heavily.

"Your father wasn't just the town's tailor. Your father was the royal tailor. That's how he got such fine fabrics— the little shoppe in the village was his supplier," Hugh said as he grimaced. He wanted to tell her more but his throat burned and he tasted blood.

"So, that's how Kurt got the silk. But I don't understand, to be a royal tailor, he'd have had to live in a kingdom. This is just Mapleshire."

Hugh shook his head. "Another spell."

Jeanette hesitated and cleared her throat as she looked through the book again. "How about that one?" She rubbed her eyes.

"Mapleshire *is* a kingdom. It used to be, anyway. You split it into five small towns to protect it from going to war." Hugh tried to get it out all in one breath, but stopped as pain sent lightning across his eyes and thunder ringing in his ears.

"Five small towns?" Jeanette placed a hand to her head and clenched her eyes shut. "That would mean... all our neighboring towns! The farming town, Stennton? Our trading town, Hempsure? The mountain pass, Gravensburg? The Forest of Faiden Dell?"

Hugh just nodded, trying to deal with the pain. *Please no more cuts. Please no more cuts,* he begged his curse. He wanted more than anything to share this with Jeanette and not be punished. One of her spells would work, he knew it.

"I have no memory of Mapleshire being anything other than..." she shook her head. "Mapleshire." She stood and started pacing. "And how would I even have known how to do that? You say that I have this power, but every spell keeps failing. I'm not sure if I actually have any magic."

"You do." He placed his hands on her shoulders and brought her into a hug. "You got it from your mother."

"My..." Jeanette pulled away. "Mother?"

"Another spell first."

"I can't—" Jeanette hesitated. "Look what I'm doing to you. I can't keep hurting you."

"Does that mean..."

"Yes, I've been feeling the punishment too. It's my punishment for hurting you," she said and looked away. "I don't want to lose you."

"You can't lose me," Hugh said. "The curse punishes me, but it won't kill me. Larkus wouldn't let his servant die from a curse." He hoped that would appease Jeanette. It was true, Larkus's curse wouldn't kill him, but that didn't mean it wouldn't cause him enough pain that he wished he was dead. Hugh needed her to break his curse, he knew she'd be able to do it.

Jeanette blew out a long breath as she searched through the book of spells once more.

"Your mother was the king's sorceress. Most of these magic books were hers," he groaned as he pulled out the pocket watch from his pants pocket and handed it to Jeanette.

She turned it over in her hands. It had a long, thin golden chain attached to it.

"When I went through the portal earlier, I wasn't sure where I was going. I hadn't had a place in mind. But then you went through my head and I wished that we could've had different circumstances. When I arrived at Larkus's cabin, I was shocked. I definitely wasn't thinking of that place, but as I walked through the small, dark shack, I found my old pocket watch I hid."

"Larkus's cabin?"

Hugh nodded and waited while Jeanette read another spell.

"He killed my parents then kidnapped me. I knew if he killed me too, then hiding that pocket watch would help anyone who might've been looking for me. I put it on the bookshelf, near a book about dark magic. I hoped it would give enough clues to help a search party. But no one ever came."

"But," Jeanette paused, "he didn't kill you."

"No, he didn't. Sometimes I wish he had. The servitude spell forces me to follow his orders, and if I ask him any questions, he has to answer them. But what he's made me do..." he looked away, "I've done terrible things."

Jeanette was quiet for a long time. "You're a good person, Hugh. You saved me. The things you've had to do... It wasn't your choice."

"Maybe," his voice trailed off. "But I still did them. Anyway, when I woke up in the cabin, I got scared that Larkus might've returned before I did."

Jeanette looked back at the watch. "Well, how would they know this was yours? It's just a plain gold pocket watch? How do you even open it?"

"Oh, it's not plain," he said as he took the watch back from Jeanette. "Look, it has a secret. Although, now that you mention it, no one else would know how to open it, but I was a grieving sixteen year old, I didn't think that far ahead." He stroked the edge and tapped the top three times.

Jeanette watched as an engraving appeared in the smooth gold. Hugh's skin felt like he was sitting in fire, as if his words burned him. He wondered if Jeanette was feeling a similar punishment.

For Hugh.
My favorite little Prince.
You are precious.

Love Gloria

"Gloria. That's..." she paused, "that's my mother's name." She looked at Hugh with tears in her eyes.

"Yes," he replied and grabbed her hand. He was already in so much pain, what was a little more? He decided to push through and finish his story. "She made this special, just for me. I loved watching her work. Her magic was amazing to witness. One day, I was really sad. I was hiding in her tower, I think I broke something important, I don't even remember now. But she knelt down next to me and told me that everything would be okay. That she knew my parents loved me. She conjured this for me and told me that anytime I needed a reminder, to just stroke and tap it. I'll never forget her kindness."

Silent tears streamed down Jeanette's face. "What's inside?" She asked, wiping her cheeks and eyes.

Hugh twisted the cover of the timepiece a quarter turn clockwise and it glowed as the golden face sprung open. One side revealed a whimsical clock face, the other held a picture of a king and queen hugging a prince. "Those are my parents and that's me."

"But..." Jeanette furrowed her brows. "That's a picture of a royal family."

"That's right."

"That means..." She looked at Hugh. "You're a prince."

He nodded and looked back at his parents. His mother, whom he hadn't seen in twelve years, was beautiful with long blonde hair curled into an updo with a dazzling crown upon her head. Her arms wrapped around a young Hugh. He didn't even recognize his child self. And his father was tall and muscular. Hugh hadn't realized his own strong features mirrored that of his father's. His father had his arms wrapped around both his wife and his son.

Thankfully, sharing this memory only added a little pain to the throbbing his body was already experiencing. The added scratches were barely noticeable.

"That is quite enough talking!" Larkus snarled at the two while glaring at Jeanette, watching her every move. He stood in the doorway of the library, dressed in his black cloak. A strong stench, stronger than normal, radiated off of his body. Hugh could almost see it.

Chapter 16

Hugh lay in bed thinking of Jeanette. She reminded him of a timid mouse, squeaking in surprise at Larkus and scurrying out of the library, clutching the book. Hugh would've liked to stay by her side, but as soon as he started to follow Jeanette, Larkus stamped his staff and he was in his bedroom, with his door locked. Larkus hadn't locked him in his room in years.

He worried about Jeanette's safety. Larkus had already made one attempt on her life. He wondered when he would try again.

He jumped when he heard Larkus's rough growl reverberate through the wall followed by his heavy footsteps. Hugh stood beside the bed as he waited for him to enter.

The door slammed against the wall revealing Larkus hunched over and fuming. Literally fuming. A black aura emanating off of him. His overpowering stench made Hugh's eyes water.

"Where is it?" Larkus hissed.

"Where's what?" Hugh's heart sped as panic set in; did Larkus figure out that he had switched the amulet? "What did you do to Jeanette? Is she okay?" He hoped changing the subject would ease his mind.

Larkus growled. Hugh was lucky that he had learned to ask his questions fast enough to force Larkus to answer his questions.

"She's fine... for now. I need my mortar and pestle. What have you done with it?!"

"Uh..." Oh no, he forgot. How could he have forgotten to put it back, to fix Larkus's desk? How foolish did he have to be? "I needed to use it. It's in Jeanette's room. I can go get it right now."

"Stop!"

Hugh's body halted and Larkus moved closer.

"I know what you needed that for. How dare you interfere with my business! Now I have to come up with yet another new plan!" Larkus's slap stung Hugh's cheek. "Your punishment awaits." Larkus tapped his staff again and they were in the dungeons. The last time he was down here was when he had brought Jeanette soup when she first arrived.

Larkus pushed him through the doors of a cell. Hugh didn't argue as his wrists were bound in chains attached to the ceiling.

"I see your cuts, I know you've been revealing things to her. Just how much have you told her?"

Hugh didn't answer.

Larkus muttered something, and Hugh watched as a flogger appeared in his hands. "She won't be able to hear you scream down here," Larkus snarled.

As the whip met his skin, he felt the sting of a dozen cuts. The sting turned to burning as the cold air bit at the fresh wounds.

Hugh's screams echoed through the stone room. He didn't beg to end his punishment though. He knew he'd brought this upon himself. After ten lashes, his back felt like it was on fire. After twenty, he saw the pool of blood forming under him.

"You still won't tell me what you revealed to her?" Larkus panted as he came into view. "It won't matter; she'll be dead by morning and you will finally be able to fulfill your purpose." Larkus turned away.

"Wait," Hugh panted. "You don't have to kill her."

"I don't need her now. I have the last few artifacts that will help me with my revenge. She doesn't remember anyway; she's of no use to me. Once she's out of the way, the kingdom will be restored, and we can go to war."

Hugh let out a soft cry. He wished he could tell Larkus that she does remember. That he could use her instead. But his body was shutting down from the pain. He couldn't muster the ability to say anything else.

He was blinded by a bright light and then landed on his bed face first. He couldn't move, he couldn't think. The ache from his curse combined with the fresh bite of his lashes engulfed him in pain. His vision blurred as he succumbed to the darkness that crept through his senses.

Jeanette sat in her desk chair, gazing out the window. Larkus was back. Hugh's a prince. She wished she hadn't been unconscious for the majority of the time that Larkus was gone. Now their opportunity to be alone together had vanished in a moment.

She looked at the large stone bowl on her desk. Hugh said they'd made a remedy. Maybe that was how they made it. She wondered what all went into that remedy to require such a large bowl. Dwarfed in its shadow, the small music box glowed blue in the light.

As she opened the lid again, she was surprised to see that the previously tightly closed rose bud had bloomed in the full moon. A light tinkling tune came from the little trinket. It sounded familiar, but she couldn't place it.

She returned the music box to its spot on the table and turned her focus to the magic book; the one she had searched for information about her mother's necklace. But this time, she searched for a specific artifact. The Serpent Gauntlet. The note said Chapter Six. She flipped through the pages until she found the right spot.

The Serpent Gauntlet is one of the most powerful artifacts on the planet. There is only one in existence. The wearer may use the artifact to harness the central power of Mangor— the birthplace of magic.

Mangor?

Jeanette dropped the magic book and turned toward the Spellbook of Mangor. It only had spells, no information on this central power. She had never even heard of Mangor before; she thought it was a person, not a place. And she had no idea what this central power it talked about could be. Something else to study up on. But for now, she'd search more about Hugh's curse.

Her eyelids felt the weight of the deterrent just as she heard a far away scream. She didn't know who or what that was, but her fear told her to run as fast as she could... except there was only one problem. She had nowhere to run. There was nowhere to hide. She looked under the bed, it looked to have enough space for her, but if Larkus came in, he would be sure to find her there.

There was another place she thought might work. Although, if she tied the curtain to the chair again, Larkus would be able to see where she went. No, it would be better if she made no sign of where she was.

As she crawled through the tunnel once more, she made sure to prop the grate in front of the opening the best she could to try to make it look like nothing was amiss. She carefully crawled a few feet forward and felt the ledge that led to the drop off, just as she heard another shriek, the earth beneath her crumbled and she fell.

She lay there in the cold, dark hole. At least she wouldn't be seen. She couldn't keep her eyes open any longer, she curled into a ball next to the dirt wall and fell asleep.

The next morning came and she woke in the dark. Right. She was still in this pit. It wasn't the best sleep she's ever had, but at least she was away from Larkus's gaze.

She hoped Hugh had found relief from the pain of his curse in a good night's sleep. Her own pain subsided shortly after they were separated. It was only a fraction of what he must've felt. She didn't want to cause him anguish, but he seemed to be handling it well, and he kept telling her to try again. She'd have to thank him for sharing so much and telling her about her mother. She had mixed feelings about the things she had found out though. Hugh's a prince. How could they be together?

She brought her knees to her chest as feelings of fear, anxiety, and depression crashed upon her. Being in this hole, she wasn't sure what time of day it was. For all she knew, it could still be the middle of the night.

There was one thing she knew: Larkus had already tried to kill her, was unsuccessful, and now he was back. He was sure to try again. She would have to be extra cautious about what she ate from now on.

Once she stood, she regretted her impulsive decision. She had no way of getting out of this pit unless she crawled all the way to the great hall, as the other path had caved in. All she wanted was to get back in her room and stay there as much as possible so she wouldn't have to see Larkus. She wasn't sure if she'd run into him once she exited this tunnel, but she had no other option.

She crawled through the cold, dark vent once again. Finally reaching the exit without any delay, she paused at the grate. Listening for any sign or sound of Larkus or Hugh. Nothing came. Taking a deep breath, she slowly slipped the faceplate off and crawled out.

"Where do you think you're going?" Larkus's voice crawled its way inside her head. The stench burned her eyes before she could find him. "I should've known you were hiding in that vent when you weren't in your room."

Everywhere she looked, he was nowhere to be seen. Her mouth went dry and her breathing quickened. She felt dizzy and paralyzed. So, he *had* come for her.

"What do you want? Why did you try to kill me?!" She tried to sound brave, but her eyes teared up and her voice caught in her throat.

Larkus materialized in front of her with a flash. Her heart pounded in her ears. His scraggly hair hung down in front of his face, casting shadows on his sunken cheeks. It made him look skeletal. His breathing seemed labored, as if every movement was a bit too much for him.

"What has Hugh revealed to you?"

Confusion crashed over Jeanette at the abrupt question. "What do you mean?"

"I know his curse has been punishing him. That can only mean one thing— that he's been revealing things to you," Larkus said. The stench emanated off him caused Jeanette to recoil. "Why would he cause himself pain unless—"

Jeanette backed into the wall, she had no more room to move. Larkus disappeared in a flash. Jeanette started coughing, hoping to rid her lungs of the assault and replace it with a breath of fresh air. Larkus appeared in front of her in an instant, now holding a scroll, causing her to let out a small shriek.

"Let's try this one more time." Larkus shoved the scroll in her face.

"I can't. I told you before, I don't know that language." She tried not to look at the dizzying words.

"This is a different scroll." Larkus held it for her to take. "Open your mind. This is easier to use than the pure stuff." He pushed it toward her. "Let me put it this way. You don't have much of a choice. Do it, or die."

Jeanette grabbed the paper from Larkus with a glare. Her entire head felt the spin of a tornado, twirling the jumbled letters around in her head. She tried to clear her mind as she looked at the page.

"Breathe, and open your mind," Larkus was calm now, almost kind.

She looked again, trying to anchor her vision on the page in front of her. One word became visible in the jumble of letters.

"Sacrifice." She placed a hand to her head as the paper fluttered to the ground. "I can't do it anymore."

Larkus lifted the page from where it landed. "I've already been trying to do that!" he muttered under his breath and disappeared in a flash.

Jeanette felt dizzy and sick to her stomach. She wanted to rid both of them of Larkus's vile existence. She needed to break Hugh's curse now or never. She ran up the stairs to grab the spellbook and figure out how to free him.

As she got to her desk, she saw Hugh doing his morning chores. She wondered if he came looking for her when he woke up. But she doubted that since he probably would've called her name, or looked in the vent. He did none of that.

Hugh tended to the vegetables, although his movements looked labored. He must be out of practice since he had been busy taking care of her... although the screams from the night before came into her mind.

A tear fell down her cheek and she sniffed her worries away. Larkus's stench seemed to linger. She felt it on her. Disgust slithered down her spine. She needed a bath. She turned away from the window and headed for the bathroom. She turned the hot water tap and waited for the tub to fill.

As she relaxed, letting the stench wash away, the water turned itself back on. She tried to lean forward to shut it off, but she couldn't move. Her arms and legs felt heavy, as if something weighed her down. She tried to scream, but no sound came out.

The water began rising, continuing until it flowed out of the tub. Like a flash flood, it filled the corners of the small room. The torrent created waves as it rebounded off the walls. It looked like the lake in a strong storm. She tried to move any part of her body, but the only thing that seemed to work were her eyes. She watched, helpless, as the water continued to rise. And with it, so did her fear.

Once again, she tried to call for help, but her voice wouldn't work. With each blink, the water got higher. It now rested below her chin, just a few inches away from invading her airways.

She took a deep breath before her mouth and nose submerged. She tried wiggling, but her body refused to move. It remained pressed to the tub.

As the water rose above her head, her chest burned with pressure. She had no idea how it was filling the room so quickly. She wouldn't be able to hold on for much longer. She was running out of time.

Just then, she heard something from her bedroom. "Jeanette?" Hugh's muffled voice came from the other side of the door.

If only he could open it before she succumbed to this watery grave. She screamed, the sound escaped the confines of her body and reverberated through the water. Her desperation broke the barrier that had kept her silent, but she used every last ounce of air. The liquid stung her lungs and her body jerked in response. Her vision grew dark and her mind turned cloudy as she heard distant banging.

"Jeanette!"

The water disappeared as soon as Hugh kicked the door open. Like nothing was amiss.

"Are you okay?" He asked as he looked around. "Water was seeping out from the bottom of the door. What happened?"

Jeanette coughed and cried in the empty tub. She got out and ran into Hugh's arms. Her wet, naked body pressed against him, soaking his clothes.

"I don't—" Jeanette sputtered, "I don't understand what happened," she tried to explain between sobs, her breathing labored. "The water kept rising and I couldn't move. I thought I was going to drown." She buried her face in his chest.

Jeanette listened to the sound of Hugh's heart beating. It almost matched the intensity of hers. If he hadn't entered the bathroom when he did, she wouldn't be standing here now.

He was her hero, but he was also a prince. And he saved her. Again.

"I'm glad you're okay." Hugh slid his overcoat off and wrapped it around her. "I thought something like this might happen. I just had no idea it would be so soon."

"What do you mean?" Jeanette's words were muffled against Hugh's tunic.

"I knew Larkus would try again," he said. "I just didn't think he'd send me in to stop it."

"He sent you in here to stop it?" She looked at his face. He was surveying the room, his brows furrowed.

"Well, no. Not exactly. He sent me in here to grab the mortar and pestle."

He seemed to notice her staring. His eyes lowered to meet hers. She couldn't help but notice what looked like fear in his eyes. Fear and something else. He looked— alone.

A lonely prince.

She didn't want him to feel like that when he'd brought her such comfort.

As she noticed his lips, the feelings from their kiss at the portal came flooding back. She had been surprised and regretted her hesitant response. Now, she wanted him to know how she felt, to let him know he wasn't alone. She didn't want to think about what his princely duty entailed, she only wanted him. And she sensed he wanted her too as he brushed a stray hair from off her face.

"Thank you," she whispered as she wrapped her hands around his neck, pulled his face toward her, and stood on her tiptoes to kiss him. She didn't care that his jacket had fallen to the floor. She pressed her body to his as she slid her hands into his hair. His lips were soft but firm as he returned the kiss. She felt his hands wrap around her bare back and bring her even closer. His teeth grazed against her bottom lip.

"Oh, Jeanette," he whispered as he pressed her against the wall of the bathroom and kissed down her neck.

A soft moan escaped her lips. She had never felt so comfortable with anyone before, there was no one she ever thought she could be intimate with. Reaching her arms around him, she pulled him close.

He arched his back and screamed out in pain as he backed away. "I'm sorry, I need to go."

"Hugh! Wait," she called after him. "What's wrong? What did I do?"

Hugh shook his head. "It's not you." He sighed as he took his tunic off and turned his back toward her.

Her eyes widened. She felt the pain of each of those cuts as if it happened to her. She couldn't breathe, tears fell freely. "What happened? Is that from the curse? Or from me?"

"It was my punishment for saving you. And for not returning that." He pointed at the large stone bowl.

"He did this to you?!" she screamed. Anger replaced the pain in her back. He couldn't get away with this. There had to be something she could do.

Hugh nodded.

"I'm sorry," she said. "He'll pay for this. I'll make sure of it."

Hugh was quiet for a moment, then shook his head. "It's okay, I don't want you to stoop to his level. It's not worth it. I need to get back to my chores." He dressed himself, hefted the large stone bowl, and left her standing naked in her bedroom.

Jeanette spent most of the day studying in her room, more determined than ever to find a way to help Hugh. She made one trip to the library to grab another book, hopeful it would have a spell that would work.

While there, she ran into Larkus, the heat of anger burned through her veins like a wildfire rampaging through a forest.

"How dare you!" She wanted to go off on him; scream, yell, punch. She didn't know what, but she felt she had to do something. She grabbed a random book off the shelf and threw it at him. He stamped his staff on the ground and the book vanished.

"Are you finished?"

"You tried to kill me! Again!" She balled her hands into fists, ready to start hitting him if he moved closer. "You hurt Hugh!"

He, once again, pushed the same paper as before in her face. Calmness swept over her. She was surprised at how gently he asked her to try reading it, he even expressed gratitude that Hugh saved her. This time the only word she could read was 'obtain'.

She felt his stench on her, but since her bath fiasco earlier, she didn't want to take another one.

Instead, she turned back to her magic books, desperate to help Hugh. After a couple hours, she came across something that looked promising. There had been no word from him since earlier; it seemed late enough that Larkus would be asleep by now.

What was she thinking, kissing him earlier? And naked, to boot. Embarrassment burned her cheeks as she thought about the vulnerability that she showed him. It was useless. He's a prince. They could never be together. She was just a peasant girl.

Her hunch was right, there was no one around as she made her way toward the library. She arrived at Hugh's bedroom and softly knocked on the door.

"Come in."

Jeanette opened the door and peered inside. Hugh was shirtless, laying on the bed face down. She grimaced at the look of his shredded back and took a deep breath to try to ignore the pain she saw. She walked in and shut the door behind her.

"I'm sorry for earlier," she said as she walked to the bed and sat next to Hugh. "But I think I found something that might help." She held the spellbook.

"I don't think my body can take any more punishment right now. We'll have to try a different night."

"It's not that," she said as she turned to the bookmarked page. Her hand hovered over his cuts as she read a spell. She hoped it would work.

This would help him, not to mention prove to her that she did, in fact, have magic. She waited and watched as his back healed itself.

Goosebumps covered her skin as she felt this warmth inside of her.

She had magic.

"What's that tingling?" Hugh stiffened.

That took a lot of energy, more than she had expected. "I hope that feels better."

Hugh relaxed and let out a sigh. Jeanette watched as the pain and tension melted out of his expression as he closed his eyes. "Thank you."

"That's a healing spell, although it says your body will still be sore afterward," she explained as she reached for his hand, but pulled back. She knew she needed to restrain herself. Even if what she wanted more than anything was to continue their kiss from earlier and to be with Hugh. But he was a prince and she needed to remember that. Even if that meant all her hopes and dreams for the future shattered right in front of her.

Over the next week, they'd visit each other at night and try to break Hugh's curse. With the healing spell now under her belt, she was able to heal him if his curse caused him too much pain. The only downside was the effect it had on her. She'd get so tired.

During the days, Larkus would find her and ask her to read more words from the paper; *ritual, circle, strength.* Each time she felt more and more comfortable doing so. She didn't mind helping Larkus. In fact, she almost wanted to. The last word she translated was *power.*

A knock on her door brought her back to the present. Hugh stood in a loose tunic, instead of his full suit of servants' clothing. A prince in servants' clothing, she shook her head at the absurdity.

"Ready for our next attempt?" he asked

Knowing his true identity, she saw his status. Even though Larkus took him when he was a child, he still moved as royalty. The way he held his head, his demeanor, the way he turned a phrase. She wished so much that they could've had a future together.

"I guess so."

Hugh cleared his throat. "Why does it smell like Larkus in here?"

"Because he was here earlier." Jeanette sighed. "I feel like it's on me." She sniffed her arms and a shiver escaped. "Ugh."

Hugh studied Jeanette for a moment. "It is on you," he paused, "well, it's coming *from* you."

"What do you mean?"

"Why was Larkus in here earlier?"

"I've been helping him translate a scroll. He told me that I had no choice, 'read it or die'. I can really only ever get one word before my head feels like it's about to explode."

"Why have you been doing that?" His eyes widened.

She shrugged. "I didn't really have much of a choice. I don't want to die, but I didn't mind, honestly. He was actually... a little bit... kind. He told me to relax and open my mind, he always tells me good job after."

"He's not being kind." Hugh pressed his fingers against the bridge of his nose. "It's a persuasive spell. It makes the victim perceive him as someone they would trust. They'd do anything for him during that time."

Guilt, regret, and disgust turned to a lump in her throat. "I feel so foolish."

"There's more."

"More?"

Hugh nodded. "His scrolls are full of dark magic. Just translating it has marked you."

"What do I do?"

"Next time he wants you to read it— lie. Say you've read a word, try not to even look at it. I think you'll be okay."

Jeanette felt sick to her stomach. She had no idea what she was doing, she felt like a child being tricked.

"Are you ready to try another spell, or not tonight?" Hugh tried to comfort her by rubbing her arm.

Jeanette nodded. She found a spell and started reading, but stopped at a small snake symbol she hadn't noticed before. "Wait..."

"What?"

She flipped through her magic book to Chapter Six. "The Serpent Gauntlet."

"What about it?"

"We need it." She stared at Hugh with a sense of discouragement. "There's only one in the entire world." She shook her head.

"When Larkus came back..." Hugh paused for a moment, "he said he had the last artifact he needed to fulfill his plan."

"Do you think it's The Serpent Gauntlet?"

"I'm not sure, but I know how we can find out."

Chapter 17

As the two stood in front of the gold portion of the wall, Jeanette wondered what they were doing. Hugh had said that Larkus might have The Serpent Gauntlet, so then why weren't they going to his room to search for it?

"What are we doing here?" she asked.

Hugh didn't answer her question, but instead asked one of his own, "You have your mother's necklace?"

She pulled the chain and pendant from under her décolletage and handed it to Hugh, whose eyes hovered hesitantly over her bosom before he took it.

Hugh pressed the pendant to the middle of the wall. A glow burst from the necklace and transformed the gold painted wall to a golden wooden door.

He walked behind Jeanette and returned the necklace by anchoring it back around her neck. Then, reaching around, he patted the pendant as it sat on her chest and whispered in her ear, "There, now it's back where it belongs."

She wobbled where she stood as her knees weakened and heat pulsed in her chest. "What do we do now?" she whispered. She shouldn't be having these feelings for Hugh, she had been doing well at combating the urge to kiss him every time she saw him. She swallowed and regained her composure as she tried to hide her feelings, knowing they shouldn't be there. *He's a prince,* she reminded herself once more.

Hugh cleared his throat as he pulled open the door. "This is where Larkus keeps magical artifacts. That's why I needed your amulet— only something magical can open this room."

She walked into the small space and looked around. It was filled with pouches hanging on hooks lining the walls. Desks held a variety of different trinkets. Hope filled her. If Larkus did indeed have The Serpent Gauntlet, it would be here.

"What are we looking for?" he asked.

"I'm not sure exactly. Something with a snake."

Hugh started at the far end table, pulling open drawer after drawer. They went through every bag and found necklaces, bracelets, belts, dragon scales, headpieces... but nothing with a snake. Jeanette closed her eyes and hoped with all her might that they'd find it. As she opened her eyes, she thought she saw something shimmer on the back wall.

She slowly moved toward the spot and lowered the few pouches that were in the way. The wall didn't look different from any other spot, but when she placed her hand where she saw the shimmering, it felt warm.

"Hugh," she called.

He arrived by her side. "What is it?"

"Here." She placed his hand on the spot. "Does it feel warm to you?"

"Not really."

"There has to be a way to open it," she whispered. Just as if by her will, the spot on the wall melted away, revealing a small, darkened space. She felt around the hole and grabbed something cold. Drawing her hand back revealed a small obsidian serpent, curled into a coil.

"Do you think that's it?" Hugh asked.

"I'm not sure. It's supposed to be some type of gauntlet," she said. "But it's the only snake-like object around."

She held it in the palm of her left hand. The black scales shimmered as the ruby eyes glowed. It was beautiful.

The serpent wriggled in her hand, almost as if it knew her thoughts of admiration. She almost dropped it, but tried to stay still as the snake unfurled itself and wrapped its tail around her wrist. The body slithered to the back of her hand and curved toward her fingers while the head of the snake wove around and bit her middle finger to form a ring. Jeanette jumped as the obsidian teeth dug into her flesh. She brought it close to her face as she examined her new wound. She could feel the teeth inside her finger as the power the gauntlet possessed passed through her.

"Well, that definitely looks like a gauntlet now," Hugh said. "Are you ready to try?"

Jeanette nodded and they headed back to her room.

She read the spell aloud and waited for Hugh to reveal something to her.

"There's one thing that I really want to tell you. We've known each other since we were children."

"I know, you said that the other day, but then you got hurt..."

"Hmm." Hugh paused. "Do you think it worked since I'm not in pain? Or do you think I'm not in pain because I've already revealed that part to you?"

"I'm not sure, I guess you'll have to reveal more and see."

Hugh nodded. "Well, you know that I'm a prince."

Jeanette nodded this time. She was repeatedly reminding herself of that fact in an attempt to stifle her feelings for him.

"And with royalty, we are betrothed to someone," Hugh started out slow.

Jeanette's stomach dropped. Her biggest fear confirmed. "So..." she let out a breath. "You're destined to marry some far off princess?"

Hugh's eyebrows came together. "That's not really how it works," he cleared his throat. "A prince or princess would be betrothed to a sorcerer in order to bring magic to the kingdom."

Jeanette's confusion must've shown on her face because Hugh kept talking.

"My father and your mother were betrothed, but they both fell in love with other people. They made an arrangement that they would work together but have families of their own."

It took a moment for Hugh's words to sink in.

"So, my mother was your father's sorceress?"

"Yes, and you were destined to follow in her footsteps."

"That would mean..."

"That's right." Hugh smiled. "We were betrothed to each other. You, being the next sorcerer and I, being next in line for the throne."

Jeanette couldn't believe what she heard. Her love for Hugh hadn't been in vain. Her heartache at the thought of losing him forever though, had been. She couldn't control herself anymore, she lunged at him, her lips landing on his as they fell to the bed. They started laughing, surprised by the force of her jump. She wanted to keep kissing Hugh, to spend the rest of her life with him, but something stood in their way.

"Wait, there's something I need to know first. Tell me what Larkus's plan is."

Hugh nodded. "Larkus wants to go to war with his old kingdom. His daughter was betrothed to their prince."

"He has a daughter?"

"Well, that prince didn't want to marry her, so instead of making an arrangement like our parents did... he killed her."

Jeanette gasped.

"Larkus was furious and wanted revenge. He started dabbling in the dark arts, and when the king found out about it, he banished him."

"But why us?"

"Mapleshire is the neighboring kingdom. Larkus figured that if he could take over the throne, then he could go to war and avenge his daughter."

"That's terrible."

"Now you know. And..." Hugh straightened as he stood. "I'm not in pain."

Jeanette smiled and stood to hug him. "We did it!"

"You did it. You saved me," he said as he cupped her cheek with his hand. They embraced in a long hug. Neither one of them could stop smiling. She felt relief for Hugh, that he would no longer be punished when they would talk. He could tell her anything he wanted now. And best of all, they could finally be together, and not be tied to Larkus.

Larkus.

He was still in their way. "What do we do now?" she asked.

"I'm not sure. We still can't leave, there's the force field, and we wouldn't be able to use the blue portal; there's not much we can do."

They both stood in silence as their triumph seemed to falter slightly. She tried to think of an option. "I have The Serpent Gauntlet now, although I'm not sure how to take it off... but maybe we could use it against Larkus, or to get away?"

"That is a very good point."

"But it would take time to figure out how to truly harness it... and find a spell that could work."

Hugh nodded. "Well, we can figure it out together, but for now, it's late. I should get to bed."

"Wait." Jeantte grabbed his arm to stop him from leaving, her fingers grazed down to his wrist. "You could stay here." Heat flushed her face and chest. She wasn't used to being forward, but this is what she wanted.

Hugh turned to face her with a smoldering expression. His eyes burned into her own before moving down to her lips.

No words needed to be spoken.

He lowered his head and pressed his lips to hers.

They kissed softly at first. She breathed in that mysterious, familiar scent she had grown to love. His teeth found her bottom lip and the gesture shot desire to her extremities. She gasped and moved closer to him, pressing her breast to his. He feathered kisses along her jawline while she tilted her head and extended her neck. He took the invitation and kissed down her skin, stopping to nibble at her collar bone, while his hands pressed against the hollow of her back. He lifted her, laid her in bed, and slowly unbuttoned her dress to let it fall open on either side of her body. He stood and pulled off his tunic.

Her eyes roved over his body with wild admiration. A modest amount of hair accentuating each curve of his firm muscles. His shoulders broad, his princely stature showing in every movement. His eyes held a look of love she'd never seen before. He climbed in the bed, his strong arms on either side of her.

They forgot their worries as passion electrified their night.

Jeanette found herself at the base of Mount Gravensburg. A cloaked man stood over two bodies in the distance.

"So long, little one... for now. I'll come back for you," the man snarled and vanished in a flash.

As she knelt beside her parents, she pleaded through sobs for them to stay. She tried saving them, but they were barely breathing. Just before they left the thirteen year old girl to become an orphan, they told her to be strong and brave, that they loved her. Always.

Jeanette woke in a cold sweat trying to forget the horrors of her past. Throughout the years, that same nightmare plagued her sleep over and over again. But this time, she wasn't alone when she awoke. She turned and smiled at Hugh's sleeping face. She was glad that he was with her, but she knew she'd never be able to get back to sleep, no matter how long she tried. Every time she closed her eyes, she'd see her parents' bodies. It would torment and torture her. So instead, she got out of bed, slipped into her silk nightgown, and softly padded to the window.

The moonlit grounds looked peaceful. The stars and the moon, which had always given her comfort, shimmered in the black night sky. The obsidian snake remained as a gauntlet on her hand.

"Little one," she whispered. It reminded her of how Beth called her unborn child *little one*. Why would her parents' murderer call her something so endearing? Shivers ran across her body as she thought about the man in her dream again. Jeanette gave a quiet shriek of terror as she realized the monster from her childhood.

"It's Larkus!"

She heard a rotten laugh. "Of course it's me."

Jeanette gripped her mother's necklace and shoved it under her dress as she spun around, but couldn't see anyone in her room.

"Now, I need you to read this scroll one more time." His voice was gentle now as he appeared out of the shadows.

Her fear melted away. All she wanted to do was please the man in front of her. The Serpent Gauntlet writhed against her wrist, its obsidian teeth quivered in her flesh. There was almost a hissing sound coming from it. She took the scroll. Hugh's words echoed in her head. *Lie.*

"Just relax and open your mind. You can do this."

"I don't..." she tried to think of a word to tell him, but nothing came to mind. Nothing except for the word she saw on the scroll. She looked toward Hugh. He was still asleep.

"Focus," Larkus reminded.

"Um..." She looked at Larkus. His pale skin looked a bit pinker, she didn't see those dark patches anymore, and his cheeks didn't look so hollow. The three points on his ears turned downward— it reminded her of a hungry puppy. His eyes were wide, the red and black twinkled in the moonlight, and his normally stringy gray hair looked a bit fuller. He looked so kind and wanting. He needed her, and of course she would help him.

"You can do it."

"Sacred," she read the word on the scroll. Once she handed the scroll back, the Serpent Gauntlet calmed against her skin.

"Good girl," he held his hands in front of her face, whispering a chant in some language unknown. A sudden rush of faintness made her mind turn to darkness.

Pink flashes of light passed across Jeanette's eyelids. She blinked against the brightness and saw scenery rushing past. The sun shone through the little window. They were in a carriage, going fast, but she had no idea where they were going. She straightened and looked around the small coach. Fear filled her chest and made her tremble.

"Oh, I see my enchantment has worn off. I'm guessing Hugh's probably awake as well, and wondering why you aren't lying next to him." Larkus sat across from her. He stopped to give a laugh that made Jeanette's stomach churn. "The enchantments are useful, except they don't last very long."

Heat stung her cheeks as she looked out the window at the snow-covered trees. Had Larkus watched them last night? She looked down at her shivering body and realized she was still in her nightgown, the necklace still hidden under the cloth.

"What are you going to do with me?"

"I'm going to use you, of course," Larkus spat.

"Use me for what?"

"Don't be daft." He inched closer. "You remember. You have grown strong in your magic in such a short amount of time. And to be wearing that," he pointed at The Serpent Gauntlet, "yes, you are strong indeed. To be able to break my servitude spell on Hugh. That takes some magnificent power."

"How did you know?"

"You think I didn't feel it when my own spell broke?" He leaned against the black cushion of the carriage.

"I hadn't thought about that," she admitted. She had just started studying magic. Breaking Hugh's curse took priority. She hadn't studied casting spells or what happens when a spell is broken. "I just wanted to help him."

"Well, now you can help me."

"How?" she asked. "With your daughter?"

Larkus growled and looked out the window.

"Hugh told me that she died. I'm sorry."

"She didn't just die, she was slaughtered by that impudent—" Larkus couldn't finish his sentence. It seemed talking about his daughter made him vulnerable. Maybe that was a good way to connect with him. Maybe then, he'd let her go.

"What was her name?"

Larkus didn't answer.

"I know how you feel. My parents died and it still hurts. It's something that will never go away. But even if I avenged their deaths, it wouldn't bring them back."

He scoffed, but his face softened. "Angela Valone was her name. She was a beautiful Triad-Elf; long, flowing blonde hair, stunning eyes so blue they were nearly purple." Larkus almost looked happy as he recalled the mental image of his daughter. "And with my magic, I can bring her back. I can bring back my little one," he said as he shook his staff.

Little one. He called her that in her dream, her memory. "Would Angela want you to do that?"

"Do not speak of her." Larkus pounded his staff and silenced Jeanette. He muttered something under his breath.

Jeanette resumed looking out the window.

Larkus huffed and muttered that same phrase again. A phrase she recognized. She had said it when she first got her mothers amulet, when she tried to summon clouds.

She glanced at Larkus from the corner of her eye, making sure to keep her face toward the window. He was fiddling with the fake necklace Hugh had switched. Closing her eyes, she repeated that phrase in her mind. Hoping it would bring the clouds and appease Larkus.

As her eyes opened, she saw clouds roll in and cover the sun. A breath of relief escaped. She wasn't used to summoning these unfamiliar powers, each time taking a toll on her. She wondered if Larkus felt energy taken from him when he did magic. Did he notice the clouds weren't from him? She shook her head at the troubling thoughts.

"Where are we going?"

Larkus continued to ignore her. She wasn't sure if the silence was better than hearing his scratchy voice.

"If I'm going to help you, you might as well answer me!"

Larkus looked at her. His black and red eyes, normally dead inside, held a small amount of... grief?

"We're going to The Sanctum."

"The Sanctum?" she asked. "Why don't you just stamp your staff and transport us there?"

Larkus sighed. "Because The Sanctum is a sacred circle that one cannot enter by magical means."

A sacred circle? Jeanette wondered what that meant and why they were going there. Something about it seemed familiar to her— a sacred circle.

At dusk, the carriage finally pulled off the road to a small clearing.

"We have to stay here tonight," Larkus told her as she exited the carriage. She watched as he pulled something from one of his hanging pouches and recited strange words. Two small tents appeared. "I've put a concealment charm on them, so they can't find us."

"Wait, so who can't find us?" she asked. She knew that he didn't want Hugh to find them, but Larkus said "they."

Larkus never answered, just gestured angrily at the smaller tent and disappeared inside the bigger one.

She thought about running, escaping, getting away from him. But it was getting dark and she had no idea where she was. Besides, he said that he put a concealment charm on them. It made her think of the black mist back at Rose Manor. She definitely didn't want to get struck again, so she ducked into her tent and found a sleeping pad, pillow, and an extra blanket. She wondered for a moment whether she should've thanked him.

Later, unable to sleep, she tried the zipper of her tent when she had heard Larkus's snores; it wouldn't budge.

As she lay there awake, howling echoed through the dark of the night. Wolves. Her breathing quickened, adrenaline pumping through her veins, making her heartbeat ring in her ears. She'd never be able to sleep now.

The rustling of leaves almost covered the sound of her tent unzipping itself. She held her breath, ready to scream, when a dark figure stood at the opening.

"I told you to get some sleep!" Larkus growled. "No one can find us here, my concealment charm is also protective." He extended his arm and whispered his sleeping chant; Jeanette was no longer aware of the worldly dangers that lurked in every hidden place.

The next morning she woke in the carriage once more. They traveled most of the day in silence. Her stomach growled and she groaned. She didn't want to expose any sort of weakness to Larkus.

"Oh, you're hungry?" He chuckled. "Do you trust me to conjure you some food, or are you still bitter about that whole poison thing? You can trust me on this, I don't try anything twice. You will need your health when we get to The Sanctum."

"No, thank you. I'm fine," she said.

He grunted and pulled out a bracelet. In the language unknown to Jeanette, he held his hand out, and she watched as a plate with a sandwich appeared out of thin air. She turned away, not wanting to touch anything Larkus had made.

"Here." He handed her the plate. She ignored his request. "Eat," he commanded, and she forcefully, reluctantly obeyed.

It was dusk again when the carriage came to a sudden halt. Jeanette lurched forward, landing on Larkus's lap. "Ugh, I'm sorry." It came out as a reflex. Beth had taught her manners. It was Larkus who owed her a million apologies though. She didn't care if she never got them. She didn't want anything to do with him.

"We're here." Larkus stamped his staff and the carriage disappeared. He ended up landing on his feet in one smooth motion— Jeanette landed on her rear end.

"Come." Larkus left her sitting there and stalked into the forest.

She sat there for a moment watching him get farther away from her, and when the shadows fully enveloped him, she made her move. She ran as fast as she could away from where he was, toward the direction they had come, but quickly realized she wasn't going anywhere. Then she heard his evil laugh. As she looked at her feet, she noticed that she was in some type of orb. She looked around and realized she hadn't moved an inch.

"I said 'come'," he snapped his fingers, which held a new ring, and the orb was gone, her bare feet now involuntarily following Larkus.

He jingled as they walked through the snow, his abundant amount of artifacts swaying with each labored step. She recognized the bundles as the ones that hung in the golden room. She made sure that her mother's amulet was still tucked into her dress.

Jeanette stumbled as darkness engulfed the forest floor. A heavy weight permeated the woods tonight. It smelled different than her woods back home; sour, moldy.

Larkus huffed every time Jeanette fell over a log, or walked into a low hanging branch. It wasn't as though she could help it; she wasn't a bat or an owl.

"How are you doing this? It's so dark." Jeanette complained that Larkus hadn't tripped once.

He looked down at her on the ground. That's when she saw it. He wore a pair of glowing goggles. "Just stay near me, step where I step."

As much as she didn't want to be near Larkus, at least she would stop falling in the snow. Her silk nightgown held no protection against the frigid cold, and she couldn't stop her teeth from chattering.

Larkus stopped in his tracks, causing her to run into him. "We're here."

Moonlit clouds illuminated the forest around her through a break in the dense canopy. Jeanette could finally see her surroundings. This place didn't seem special— just more snow-covered trees. These had white trunks striped with black. Well, maybe that was a bit unusual.

Larkus got down on one knee, Jeanette thought he might be praying. As he finished, she watched as snowflakes lifted from the ground, swirled in a mist, and then settled again. There— where nothing had been previously— stood a marble plinth with a stone book perched on top. Circling the plinth were orbs of glass.

"This is The Sanctum?"

"It might not look like much, but this place is sacred. Some of the most powerful magic has been done in this circle," he said as he stood behind Jeanette. She squirmed as his filthy breath touched the back of her neck.

He grabbed her arms and dragged her to the marble statue. She tried to fight back, to kick at him, to wriggle free, but he was too strong. The woods echoed her screams back to her. Pulling rope from a pouch in his cloak, he bound her hands onto the stone book.

"Does this look familiar?" He pulled a scroll out and waved it in front of her face. It looked like the one she had been translating, but at the same time— different. The parchment had turned yellow, and the words weren't in that dizzying language.

"It's the scroll."

"Yes, but it's not just any scroll. This is a Gull Scroll. It tricks the victim into telling the owner how to get what they want from them." He laughed. "It took me a while to track one down, but I ended up finding it the same time I found The Serpent Gauntlet."

"I thought you wanted me to 'undo' it," she seethed as she wrenched against the rope.

"I don't need you to undo anything now. I need to obtain your power and strength by sacrificing you during a ritual in the sacred circle." He read from the scroll. The words she had translated stood out to her. "And once I drain your power, I can retrieve my gauntlet from your lifeless body. It's a good thing I realized there was more to this scroll that needed translating before you drowned." He let out a cackle.

He tapped each orb with his staff, once they started glowing, he returned to where he'd knelt and started chanting.

Jeanette knew she needed to think of something. The clouds she had summoned were still in the sky. She hadn't studied the spells to cause other natural events, but she knew she had power. She thought about rain. She *willed* it to rain. Only when she felt a raindrop on her nose did she realize it worked.

Larkus stopped chanting and looked toward the heavens. "What's this?" He picked up his staff and studied the fake amulet again.

Jeanette had bought herself some time. The orbs dimmed out. He got up, tapped each orb again, returned to his spot once more, and started chanting again.

She needed to break her bindings. But how? There weren't any sharp edges. Her fear caused the rain to start pounding harder. An idea came to her mind.

A lightning bolt struck the plinth right between her bindings.

Chapter 18

Hugh rolled to his side expecting to find Jeanette laying next to him. He had just spent a beautiful night with her and was excited to figure out their next move together. Reaching his arm toward her, he felt around, patting Jeanette's side of the bed. Finally, he opened his eyes to find it empty.

"Jeanette?" he called for her. His head spun and his eyes turned blurry. He remembered this feeling; his stomach dropped at the reason— Larkus had cast the sleep enchantment on him.

That could only mean one thing. He was going to fulfill his plan for Jeanette. Fear caused the hair on the back of Hugh's neck to rise. Dread filled his stomach like he was sinking in the depths of the ocean. He didn't want to think of what Larkus would do to her. Hugh jumped to his feet, then paused and bent over as another wave of dizziness dropped him to his knees. As soon as it passed, he rushed from the room, calling Jeanette's name.

Hugh opened door after door searching for her. He went to the great hall, the kitchen, the library, even to Larkus's quarters. Nothing. He checked his own room, maybe there was a sign that Larkus had needed him the night before.

If Larkus had come looking for him, he would've been angry when he didn't find him and would've gone after Jeanette. He knew Larkus wanted to use her for his plan, but he was terrified that he'd torture her first.

Hugh searched everywhere. As he stood in the center of his bedroom, his nerves got the better of him and his mind went frantic. There was only one place left to search: the dungeons.

He went to the corner of the great hall, to the hidden door, invisible until the correct stone was released. He found the right one that popped out slightly, gave it a half turn, and pulled until it refused to come any further. He held that position until he heard a click and the door swung open. As Hugh let go of it, he watched as it slowly rotated back into its slot in the wall.

"Jeanette?" Echoes followed behind him as he raced down the long stone corridor. He searched each prison cell, but found no sign of her. Finally, he reached the wooden door that Larkus had used to bring Jeanette into the dungeons. Into Rose Manor.

She was gone.

They both were.

How could he have let this happen?

He needed to get out of the mansion, to get to her, but he wasn't sure how. He couldn't leave. He looked at the door next to him, and remembered how odd that night had been. Larkus went out without his staff. In fact, he'd left all of his magical items in the golden room. Which was confusing because Larkus never went anywhere without at least one of his magical artifacts.

Then he'd come back with an unconscious Jeanette. He must have knocked her out somehow. But it always confused him why he hadn't just used magic to kidnap her. There was no point in taking her without magic.

Unless...

Hugh knew Larkus couldn't cause any harm to the same person the same way twice. It was part of being a Triad-Elf. Their magic would never take the same shape twice. Even though Hugh's curse caused him pain over and over again, it was still due to the original spell. If he tried one way of doing things, and it failed, he could never try that same spell again. That was one reason why he had so many artifacts, why it took so long for him to make another plan. So if Larkus had used non-magical means of taking her, that would mean that he had tried to harm her with magic before.

He remembered being with Larkus since the day Jeanette transformed the kingdom, the terror he had felt when Larkus turned on him. Hugh's guilt crashed on him like a wave on rough seas. If it wasn't for his mistake... none of this would've happened in the first place.

Closing his eyes, he tried to remember that dreadful day so long ago. Larkus had been ranting about raising Jeanette in the dark arts. He had been so angry when he was unable to capture her. Hugh shuddered as he thought of the years of pain and agony he'd experienced under Larkus. Thank goodness her spell had protected her.

If only he'd been able to protect his family.

Shaking his head helped him refocus. He needed a plan, he needed to escape. He looked at the wooden door again.

It was a possibility.

Hugh quickly went to the wood pile in the kitchen, grabbed the ax, and hurried back to the dungeon door. The sound of the metal hitting the wooden door rang through the stone corridor. He pounded for what seemed like an hour.

Nothing happened.

Not even a dent.

He put the head of the ax on the ground and leaned against the handle, panting. This seemed hopeless. It was clear to him that Larkus had made sure he couldn't escape by that route. Or Jeanette, if she ever found her way to the dungeons.

Making his way to the great hall, he collapsed on the long sofa. His mind swam with questions. Where had he taken her? Was she okay? Why did he want her to read that scroll?

Hugh never did find out what the full extent of Larkus's plan was. All he knew was that he wanted Jeanette to turn Mapleshire back into a kingdom so he could go to war. To avenge his daughter. Maybe Hugh should've pushed Jeanette to undo it as well, maybe then she'd still be here.

It was too late for that; there was no use in fretting over the past. He needed to do something now, something that would help him get to her.

He sat up straight as a thought popped into his head. There was another option, but would it work for him now?

As he approached the wall, it just looked blue. Plain. There was no shimmer, no glow, nothing magical about it. He touched it, pushed on it, he even ran into it.

Nothing happened.

Just as he thought. The lack of shimmer proved that Larkus closed it before he took Jeanette. Hugh doubted it would've worked for him anyway though. He didn't want to come back. He just wanted Jeanette.

His eyes moved to the dark red wall. The only one he had yet to try. He thought about what the doctor had said— non-magic beings that were able to use magic. Maybe this was that type of magic.

As he stood in front of it, nerves made his stomach tighten. Taking a deep breath, he pulled out his pocket knife and held his palm in front of him. He placed the blade against his skin and with one swift motion, he sliced his hand to bleed.

Hugh marked the wall in a bloody arch. The colors matched perfectly. His sacrifice absorbed into the wall and it began to pulse. He touched the wall, to see if the portal opened. It felt warm but unwilling.

"What am I supposed to do?" he asked.

The portal pulsed and bloody words appeared. *What is it you want?*

Hugh jumped away from the seemingly alive wall. "Um... I want to find Jeanette."

If you enter, you will find what you seek, but it may not be what you think.

"Okay!" Hugh didn't care to try to figure out the portal's puzzle, his mind just thought of Jeanette.

You may enter.

The wall still felt reluctant, but he forced himself in and managed to push through the thick boundary.

The flesh of the wall encompassed him. It was a struggle to move through the portal, it felt as if he were being digested. Everywhere he looked, he saw the red pulsing muscle. He closed his eyes as his heartbeat harmonized with the pulsating all around him. He gulped down nausea that burned his throat and continued, step after step, through the throbbing passageway.

Suddenly, he felt cold, crisp air, and heard the crunch of snow.

Hugh opened his eyes and found himself on the cliffside of Mount Gravensburg. Hot red mist swirled around him as he exited the portal. Mapleshire was far in the distance, down in the valley. The afternoon sun reflected against the snow. Heavy breathing and heat came from behind him.

He jumped and turned to look. There before him lay a dark cave entrance. Out of its depths, he heard the scratching of something sharp scraping against rock coming toward him.

What emerged from the cave was something he'd only dreamed of seeing, never believing he'd be able to witness with his own eyes.

Stretching to its full height, a dragon towered above him. The red scales of the dragon's body glowed as it stood on all fours. Great brown talons extending from its paws. Scarlet wings protruded out of the beast's shoulders; in between laid a spine of horns that traveled down to his tail with smaller thorns at the base of each one. Tendrils of spikes surrounded its head.

Hugh had heard stories of these beings. Everything in his body was telling him to run. Dragons were dangerous, and Hugh had just appeared on its front door. But he had nowhere to go. His breathing quickened as he stared into the golden eyes.

The beast crouched low to the ground and extended a wing toward Hugh, as if it were waiting for him to mount.

"Am I supposed to ride you?" he asked the dragon.

The dragon bowed his head lower and huffed out a puff of hot air toward Hugh as if saying "yes."

Hugh didn't move.

How could this be real?

This must be the work of the portal. He knew he needed to activate it with blood, and it was supposed to deliver him somewhere that would help, or at least that's what he assumed. Larkus had said he'd use this portal himself as a backup if his plan didn't work.

He'd hoped it would deliver him right next to Jeanette, not this dragon.

With no other choice, he climbed onto the massive creature. He sat right in front of its wings, stradling the spikes that extended from the creature's neck. The tendrils that fell near Hugh were surprisingly rigid, which helped him hold on.

Hugh knew this dragon was male, the sheer size of this beast and the amount of spikes he had. He'd seen old drawings of dragons. The female ones were quite smooth and beautiful, but the males looked like they were born for the battlefield.

"I guess I'm ready," he said once he felt comfortable. As comfortable as he could feel on a dragon. He wasn't sure what to expect. Dragon slowly moved to the edge of the cliff and spread both wings wide and tall. He crouched and waited for a moment. Hugh wasn't sure what he was waiting for, but just as he was about to ask the majestic being, he felt strong winds blow through his hair. Dragon shook his head, his scales and spikes tinkled together like the rustling of leaves. Then, he leapt off the cliffside.

The two coasted down the mountain. Their surroundings passed by Hugh in a blur. Icy blasts of wind forced his eyes closed. He leaned close to the creature. A scent of fire and earth penetrated his senses. Dragon's Breath. Strangely, it helped calm his nerves. He tried peeking out to see if they were still free falling and saw the mountainside coming to meet them. He braced for impact. Maybe Dragon wasn't used to carrying anyone. Just as he was sure the beast was about to crash, Hugh felt his stomach drop as Dragon flapped his enormous wings and headed toward the clouds. They were now soaring in the heavens, Hugh was finally able to sit up, spread his arms wide, and feel the wind in his hair. The clouds around him were ice cold, but he didn't mind. This experience was awe-inspiring.

He was flying.

On a dragon.

The stories he had heard when he was little, he'd thought, were those of myths. His grandfather would tell him of the olden kings who owned dragons and would intimidate other kingdoms into doing their bidding. Hugh had never thought it was anything more than stories, but this... this dragon was definitely real.

As Hugh admired Dragon's glimmering red scales, he noticed that each was surrounded by black at the very edge— something he hadn't noticed when he first appeared. The spikes and thorns looked sharp, but as Hugh stroked one, it gave way under his hand. The soft shell of this dragon gave Hugh a new appreciation for the creature.

"Where are we going, Dragon?" he called out. Clouds thickened around them, blocking his view of the ground. Hugh wasn't sure if it was the work of Dragon that brought the clouds, providing them cover. However, it made it impossible for Hugh to know where they were.

They'd been flying for a while. The setting sun cast a golden glow across them. Hugh yawned, he had no idea that riding a dragon would take so much energy.

As if Dragon knew about Hugh's ailment, he descended through the blanketed sky and landed in a clearing near a darkened copse.

"Why did we land?" Hugh asked as he climbed down Dragon and peered through the trees. "Is Jeanette nearby?"

Dragon gave a huff and Hugh looked back at the creature. In the dusky sky, the center of his chest continued to glow, creating a shimmer that rippled through his scales, illuminating the almost all black color they had turned. He breathed heavily.

"Oh, ok. I understand, Dragon." He felt bad for the beast to have used so much energy. "We can rest."

Just as Hugh finished speaking, Dragon curled himself into a semi-circle and fell asleep. Hugh looked toward the darkened trees again.

"If Jeanette is here, I doubt I'd be able to find her by myself— in the dark." He decided to rest as well; he could check in the morning.

He stepped over the blackened tail and lay against Dragon's ribcage. The glow from his chest warmed Hugh and kept him from freezing on the snow-covered ground.

Hugh awoke to the morning sun beaming in the sky. He blinked against the brightness.

Dragon was gone.

Hugh jumped to his feet when he realized he was alone. "Dragon?" He felt foolish calling out for a dragon, but wondered where he went. Without any clue, one thing was certain— he was on his own now. He looked around to consider which way to go and decided to head through the trees. He thought that was the direction they were heading and, hopefully, if he continued that way, he would find a clue that led to Jeanette.

Hugh hiked until he found a trail. He tried following the path as it was smoother than the ground between the trees, but swiftly regretted his decision as it wound around a ridge instead of continuing in a straight line.

This would definitely be the long way, and he considered hiking back down and trekking through the woods again, but he needed to know which direction to go. He decided to keep climbing and get a view from the top.

Sweat coated his skin as he ascended the steep incline up the side of the mountain. Even though there was snow on the ground, the sun beat down on him out of a cloudless sky. There was no shade on this rocky ridge

When he reached the summit, he found a cave entrance, which brought a huge sigh of relief. At least he would have a respite from the blazing sun. He got into the shadow of the mountain, closer to the cave, when a low growl echoed from the darkness.

Then another.

"Dragon?"

He froze in his tracks.

"Yep, definitely a mistake," he told himself as a pack of wolves emerged from the mountainside. He took a few steps back as the wolves advanced; their teeth bared as they continued to growl. He knew he shouldn't make a run for it, he could never outrun a wolf. He'd quickly become that animal's lunch.

He took another step back.

And again.

More wolves exited the den. Yips and howls of pups resonated behind them. No wonder they acted this way. They were protecting their kin.

"I'm not gonna harm them," he said, hoping the wolves understood. One of the beasts leapt toward him; he lurched backward and just missed the attack, but his retreat had brought him to the edge of the cliff. He had nowhere else to run.

Then a loud, thunderous roar filled the sky. The wolves cowered at the announcement and a large shadow appeared overhead.

Hugh looked toward the heavens when another roar released. A dragon approached, silhouetted by the sun, flapping its wings hard toward the wolves. They scurried back into their cave. He held his arm in front of his face against the abrasive wind, unsure if it was his dragon or a different one.

He clamped his eyes shut against the flurry of snow, but the strength of the wind caused him to lose his balance, and as he stumbled, his feet met nothing but air. He managed to throw his body forward and land hard on his stomach with his legs dangling over the side of the cliff.

Slowly, he started sliding off the edge of the mountain. He groped the ground with his arms, trying anything to stop from slipping, but it was no use. There was nothing to hold onto. For a brief moment, he held himself by his fingertips on the edge of the cliff, until they, too, slipped over the side and he fell.

It felt like slow motion.

Like he was out of his body.

He saw himself falling back first, his arms and legs flailing about while he descended further toward the treetops. This was the end. He was going to die without ever telling Jeanette how he felt about her; never saying the words. Now, she'd never know.

"I love you, Jeanette," he whispered to the wind, hoping it would deliver his declaration.

Just as he was about to close his eyes and accept his death, he saw a red torpedo dive toward him. Strong talons caught him, the soft pad of the dragon's foot wrapping around his waist. It flew as silently as an owl. The red, glowing scales on his chest rising and falling with the exertion of carrying Hugh's weight.

This was his dragon.

"Thank you," he called to Dragon, who merely let out a puff of smoke from his large nostrils. He didn't even care anymore that Dragon had disappeared that morning, he was just glad he had returned in time to save him now.

They landed near a stream; Dragon set Hugh down gently and nudged him toward the stream with his muzzle.

"What's this?" he asked. Dragon blasted him with hot breath and nudged him again. "I don't understand, do I need a bath?"

He hoped that was not Dragon's plan. The edge of the stream was frozen, but the water in the middle was still running over rocks and logs.

His stomach growled and he thought maybe there were fish in the river. But how was he supposed to fish? He had nothing— no net, no pole, no hook, not even bait.

"I don't know what you want me to do, Dragon." Hugh looked around, he didn't want to waste time. "We need to get going. We need to find Jeanette."

Dragon huffed again and walked to the edge of the stream. Hugh watched as Dragon breathed on the river— the water stilled. Another exhale, the water rising into a vortex, coming away from the rest like a tiny tornado.

Hugh saw Dragon's golden eye glance at him, and he took a few slow steps closer. Dragon lifted his head away from the stream and the vortex followed. He thrust his head toward Hugh and the whirlpool wove a path toward him, dissipating right before he got soaked.

Half-a-dozen fish flopped onto the snow and Dragon nodded with a puff of smoke from his nose.

Hugh's stomach growled and distracted him. He needed to keep searching for Jeanette, but he also needed to keep up his strength to be able to help her when they found her. The fish were out of the water now anyway, better not let them go to waste. He looked around for anything that would help him build a fire to cook them. He gathered the fish and dug a hole in the snow to store them.

After Hugh went into the trees and gathered some wood, he headed back to Dragon.

It seemed Dragon summoned more fish while Hugh was gone and was happily eating them.

"I'm not sure how I'm going to make a fire out of these logs, they're pretty wet," he muttered as he dropped his armful in the snow. He stacked the logs into a campfire before he pulled out his pocket knife and started cleaning the fish.

Dragon took a long, deep breath in, and on his exhale, breathed fire onto the wood. Hugh jumped back as the campfire lit— he was standing fairly close and didn't want to get burned.

"Thank you, Dragon."

Dragon bowed his head in response, then went back to his half eaten fish.

Hugh cooked two whole fish and was glad his stomach was full. He let Dragon eat the rest, since he preferred them raw.

"Thanks again for saving me from the wolves." He leaned against Dragon's warm side as he waited for him to finish eating. "It just occurred to me that you don't have a name."

Dragon bristled; all of its spikes stood on end and he huffed a puff of hot air at Hugh.

"I'm sorry, you do have a name?"

Dragon nodded.

"I wish you could tell me, then I'd stop calling you 'Dragon'."

Dragon looked down at the snow and exhaled a heavy breath. Hugh followed Dragon's gaze, the word "Phyre" was written in the snow.

"Alright Phyre, nice to meet you." Hugh shook one of Phyre's horns on his head. "It's time to keep going."

Phyre nodded and let Hugh mount him before he rose to his full height, pushed off with his hind legs, and soared toward the sky.

Chapter 19

B ranches and leaves whipped Jeanette's face as she ran, not looking back. Larkus had stumbled backward as soon as the lightning struck the plinth, severing her bindings. While he shielded his face from the blast, she took the opportunity to run from The Sanctum as fast as she could.

She came to the edge of a clearing and stopped, staying hidden in the trees as she watched the sky. The thick, stormy air made it hard for her to breathe.

"I will find you!" The rumbling vibrations of Larkus's anger made the trees quake.

Fear froze Jeanette where she stood. The storm clouds opened and let out the stinging icy rain. The air's freezing temperature mirrored how she felt on the inside.

Standing at the edge of this opening made her feel scared and exposed. She wasn't sure which way to go. Into the clearing and try to reach the other side before being seen, or stay under the darkened canopy and slowly make her way through the trees. She wasn't even sure if she was going in the right direction, she just wanted to get away from Larkus.

Wolves howled in the near distance and her heart sped to a pounding in her ears, the beasts sounded close. If she continued on her path, she might run straight into them. She looked around to see if there was any movement, but it was too dark. She closed her eyes and tried to listen; the rain through the leaves, the hooting of an owl, the snapping of a branch behind her.

Her eyes flicked open as she twirled around to see what was advancing. Between the storm and the dense trees, she could barely see two feet in front of her. The icy rain turned to hail as it pounded against her skin.

Another crack of a twig and rustling leaves echoed around her. She wasn't sure which way it came from. She backed away from the sound and bumped into something hard. A scream escaped her lips— she wished she had better control of her emotions. Larkus was bound to hear that, it would lead him straight to her. Unless the hard object she bumped into was Larkus. At that thought, she turned around ready to fight against her captor.

A towering aspen tree stood before her, a large split down the middle of the trunk. She climbed into the split and shimmied up toward the branches, the same way she did in the tunnels. It shielded her somewhat from the frigid wind. Relief washed over her. At least she was hidden from the dangers on the forest floor.

Jeanette placed a hand over her eyes and another hand over her heart, forcing herself to take deep breaths like Clint had taught her. Hot tears came once the adrenaline wore off. She silently cried in the tree and felt her emotions. She was scared. Larkus had ripped her from her intimate night with Hugh and the relative safety of her room. She hadn't even had time to process everything. Her body ached; she hadn't realized how sore she was until this moment. The hail subsided and the rain became a dull drizzle.

There were so many questions running through her mind. First off, how could she be so stupid? She had told Larkus exactly how to defeat her. Hugh had told her to lie, but she couldn't.

Hugh.

She hoped she would see him again. He was her prince; she wouldn't give up without a fight. She was hell-bent to survive so she could be with Hugh and see Beth and Clint again. She had thought her life was empty, but now she realized she had so much worth fighting for.

Determination burned in her chest as the rain stopped and the clouds disappeared. The night sky didn't seem so dark with the full moon illuminating everything around her.

The air was quiet, even the water dripping off the leaves didn't seem to make a sound. She felt confident that she had run far enough from Larkus. Maybe she could try to find her way to a village; there had to be one nearby. Once there, she could ask for help and make her way back toward Mapleshire.

Jeanette climbed out of her tree and looked around. In her panic, she had gotten disoriented. She took a few footsteps away from her hiding spot, and then a few more. Suddenly, the still around her stopped feeling peaceful and the unnatural silence gave her a pit in her stomach. Like something bad was going to happen, but she didn't know what.

She placed a hand on her chest and reached for her mother's pendant. It was gone. It must have fallen off when she was running. It could be anywhere in the forest. Sorrow washed over her and she fell to her knees. New tears streamed down her cheeks. The only thing she had left of her mother was gone.

"Are you looking for this?" Larkus's rough voice echoed around her. He appeared in front of her in an instant and squeezed her mother's amulet so hard it shattered in his hands.

"No!" Thunder echoed around her, reflecting the pain in her heart.

"Did you really think you could run from me?" He let out a laugh that shook her bones. "I knew there was something strange about this one," he pulled the fake necklace off his staff, "I have to admit, it is a very convincing replacement."

"That pendant was my mother's. It belonged to me! You stole it!"

"That's right. Your mother was no match for me. Her life fell as easily as the rain coming down. She never should have tried to stop me. But one good thing did come from her death— I had gained yet another artifact." He laughed again.

Jeanette was determined not to be afraid anymore. She just wished her body had gotten the memo— she couldn't control her shaking. "You won't win, I'll never fall. I'll continue to run and fight as long as I live."

"That won't be very long," he muttered. "Is it a game of cat and mouse you want to play? I'll be the cat!" he laughed and vanished again.

The woods around her changed, the white and black trees turned thick and heavy with dark brown bark. Pine needles littered the ground and hung in the air far above her head.

"Run, little mouse," Larkus's voice echoed. "Run!"

Jeanette didn't hesitate. The forest floor here was smoother than the previous forest, ferns growing everywhere with a constant mist of rain. The pine needles were the problem now. Pain shot through her each time one pierced the tender skin of her feet, but she wouldn't stop. She couldn't.

"Little mouse!" Larkus taunted.

A future awaited her. A future she wanted more than she had ever wanted anything. She tripped over a moss-covered rock and landed against a pine tree. Needles and water fell on her, and she tried to brace against the incoming attack.

"Oh, come now, that wasn't nearly as fun as the last one..." Larkus materialized in front of her. "Shall we go again?"

Before she could speak, she found herself on her feet in yet another forest. This one had tall trees with leaves that fanned out in all directions. It was not snow-covered here, nor was it cold. The ground was flat and barren. Dry, cracked dirt stretched as far as her eye could see. She had no idea where she was now, but one thing she did know— she was far away from home.

"Come, come, little mouse," Larkus's voice sounded through the trees. "Don't keep the cat waiting."

His echo slithered down her spine like a snake slithering down one of the tall palms. If only she had her mother's necklace still. Maybe she could've used it to help herself, but without it, she felt helpless.

She wanted to get away from Larkus's voice, but with no idea where he was, she ran over the dirt and rocks. She tripped in a crack and bumped into the trunk of one of the trees. The rough bark scratched her arm and snagged the silk of her nightgown, tearing a large slit down the leg. She stumbled onward and only stopped when she broke through the forested palm trees and reached a beach.

Ocean waves crashed upon white sands, but she had no time to admire the beauty of it. She ran into the ocean and started swimming. Her foot got tangled in kelp and she was dragged under the surf. As she tried to free her leg from the seaweed, another blade wrapped around her arms, then her neck. She struggled against the kelp forest.

"You can't escape." Larkus appeared amid the seaweed. A string of pearls created a necklace holding a large, iridescent, turquoise scale on his chest. He had no problem breathing or talking underwater, he seemed to be controlling the kelp with his wishes.

Air escaped from her lungs as Jeanette fought harder against the tangles. She knew she needed to do something, but her struggles were only weakening her. She knew Larkus wanted to drain her power. If she was dead, he wouldn't be able to. She closed her eyes and let her body go limp.

"No!" Larkus's anger made the kelp recoil. She held still a moment longer, she needed to know where he was. When she felt his arms around her, she grabbed hold of his staff and envisioned Mapleshire. She wasn't sure how his artifact worked, but it was worth a try. Hugh had said that was the way the blue portal worked, maybe it was the same with this. She felt herself being flipped and spun and couldn't hold on any longer.

She found herself on her back looking up at the aspen forest again. It wasn't Mapleshire, but at least she was on dry land.

Larkus was coughing next to her. "Damn you, girl! What were you trying to do?"

She clambered to her feet and started running away from him again. She ran through the dense trees and didn't care which direction she was heading.

Suddenly a crackled high pitched laugh pierced the air, bouncing off the trees around her. It was joined by a shriek of terror that echoed through all the darkness of the night.

She froze.

That wasn't Larkus's laugh.

"We can't play our game anymore. Let's go." Larkus grabbed her arm so tight she felt his long nails dig into her skin.

As he dragged her through the forest, she started to recognize some of the scenery around them. He was taking her back to The Sanctum.

"No!" She fought against him. They were almost to the clearing when he stopped mid-step. She struggled against his grip, but when she looked at his face, it was even whiter than normal.

He looked afraid.

She scanned the forest trying to find out what would scare Larkus, and between the trees, she could see the plinth. It looked taller to Jeanette this time, but maybe it was just because they were farther away.

Another scream rang out, and this time, Jeanette could see who it came from. She watched as a young woman was tied to the plinth, her arms and legs each bound to a corner. They were too far away to hear what was being said, but the young woman shook her head and cried.

An old hag staggered toward the same spot that Larkus had been chanting, she held an artifact of some kind toward the heavens.

A flash of light blinded Jeanette and she found herself sitting on a small couch in a tiny cabin. A dizzying sickness washed over her.

"Where are we?"

"My cabin. We'll have to go to The Sanctum tomorrow and try again," he replied.

"Who was that back there?" Jeanette clutched her stomach, hoping the contents would stay put.

"There are worse things in this world than me, little one."

Hours passed and Jeanette continued to shiver in her soaking wet, frozen nightgown. She looked at the fireplace, it was stone cold. There was no hint of warmth anywhere in the cabin. Larkus paced near the windows. Whoever was at The Sanctum definitely made him nervous. He was quiet during this time but Jeanette's mind was busy. There was no way she could sit back and wait for her death at the plinth the next day.

"You don't have to do this."

"Ugh, this again," Larkus scowled.

"I understand you're angry. But there has to be a better way. I took the time to grieve for my parents. Beth and Clint showed me how, they taught me, they raised me. I can help you overcome this grief as well."

"I don't need to overcome it," he snarled. He stopped pacing and turned toward Jeanette. "Don't you understand? When I have enough power, I can turn Mapleshire back into a kingdom. I can kill that unruly nuisance and finally bring my daughter back."

Jeanette sat there, freezing and confused. "I don't understand," she whispered. "Angela's gone."

"Don't speak her name!"

"How can you bring her back?" She shook her head. There was no way to bring anyone back from the dead... was there?

A book bound in black leather dropped onto the seat next to her. She jumped in response. She hadn't noticed that Larkus had made his way from the window to the bookshelf behind her.

"Open to the bookmarked page."

She picked up the tome and noticed that it was quite a bit heavier than it looked. A great weight was inside this book. She let the book fall open to where the large carved bookmark lay. The letters swirled inside her mind, grabbing a hold of the edges and making her dizzy.

"I can't..."

"Relax your mind. This isn't hard."

As much as she didn't want any part of Larkus's plan, she was curious if there was a way to bring someone back— to bring her parents back. Hope prickled the back of her neck. So, she tried again. She looked at the book, it felt like the strange words were attacking her. Something pinched her hand.

She took a deep breath and tried to relax her mind. Once she stopped fighting against the book, the words fell into place. She felt movement on her hand and looked down to see the Serpent Gauntlet unwind and coil itself back into a tight obsidian spiral. Strange that the snake would release Jeanette when she tried to look at Larkus's book.

His dark magic book. Maybe that was the key in using the snake. It needed to be pure magic. That meant Larkus would never have been able to use it. Her curiosity got the better of her and she looked back at the book in her lap.

"Necromancer spell?" Jeanette asked and looked at Larkus. That's when she really saw him for what he truly was. His grief turned him toward the dark arts. Dark magic had corrupted him from the inside out. He was literally rotting away, causing the stench that emanated off of him. How much had he actually used over the past decade? "To become a necromancer, one must succumb to the inner battle," she read a passage from the book.

Larkus nodded as he continued to pace.

"Don't you understand what that means?"

Larkus paused. "And you think you do? You read a few magic books back at Rosemont Castle, and now you think you understand the meanings of spells?"

"You mean Rose Manor?"

"Ha!" Larkus scoffed. "You still don't remember?" Larkus repeated a chant three times and Jeanette's vision spun into a whirlwind of color.

Jeanette ran through the gardens with a small boy. "Hugh! You can't catch me!"

"Oh yeah? Well, you don't know my shortcut!"

She looked behind her, and Hugh was gone. She slowly turned in a circle peering through the tall plants.

"Gotcha!" Hugh jumped out from behind a large sunflower, tagged her, then continued to run.

"No fair! That's cheating," little Jeanette called after him. She chased him toward the front of a majestic castle and stopped when he looked back at her. "Wait!"

It was too late, he ran head first into his father, and caused him to stumble. A king does not stumble, Jeanette knew it would be a lecture for both of them.

"Hugh Rosemont! What is the meaning of this?"

"I'm sorry Father, we were playing tag." Hugh bowed to his king.

"Go to your room, and as for you Jeanette," her king turned toward her, "shouldn't you be studying with your mother?"

Jeanette's mind swirled back to the present. Larkus was staring out the window now. She placed a hand to her head.

"Why do I have no memory of that?"

"When you changed Mapleshire into a small town and promptly ruined my plans," he paused to glare at her, "your spell was too strong for you. In a way, it backfired and caused your memory to know nothing from before, just like the rest of the town."

Like the rest of the town? She had caused the entire town to forget who they were? What about the other surrounding towns? Hugh had said they were once part of the kingdom as well. Did they also forget? This was all her fault. Without a castle and a kingdom to come home to, she knew Hugh couldn't fulfill his princely destiny. He was supposed to become a king.

And her beautiful, neglected Rose Manor was meant to be the magnificent Rosemont Castle.

Jeanette closed her eyes and pictured the vision again. It was as if everything was frozen in time. The grounds looked similar, although the ruins were in their full splendor. The fountain she had always admired was full of pink water with birds chirping as they hopped on the edge of the marble. The statues were not overrun with weeds and vines, but stood as emblems of the honor that embodied the royal family. And the castle was breathtaking. It was much taller than Rose Manor, with stained glass windows and granite columns.

The room she had been staying in at Rose Manor seemed to be the focal point of the castle, on the southernmost tower. She'd seen pictures of castles from other kingdoms, that was always the room that would've been reserved for the royal monarch. It just occurred to her that she had been staying in the royal bedroom at one point.

Her mind focused on the king and his son. The king stood tall, proud, the heaviness of responsibilities on his shoulders. Hugh looked like his father, he had grown into such a strong, handsome man. But she'd ruined his chance at being the ruler she saw in him. What must he think of her? Little Hugh was a cute boy, full of life and wonder; how different would he have grown up if she hadn't turned his kingdom into a small town?

Tears fell onto the book she was still holding. Wiping away the drops brought her mind back to the issue at hand.

"To become a necromancer, one must succumb to the inner battle," she repeated. "It's true, I don't know the meanings to most of the spells, I'm still learning. But this one seems pretty straightforward. You're too close to it, you don't see what's happening."

"And, what, pray tell, is happening?"

"Dark magic has marked you. You're dying from the inside out and you have to succumb to this decay in order to become a necromancer."

"If I can bring my daughter back, then so be it."

"But..." Jeanette paused, "even if you are able to bring her back, she doesn't belong here anymore. And you won't be *you* either." Larkus was the most cruel being she'd ever met, and becoming a necromancer would make him much worse.

He had to be stopped. Somehow.

Jeanette looked at her surroundings. This must've been the cabin Hugh had talked about. There was a portrait on the far wall that held a small family. She couldn't see it very well from the couch. She was so cold, she felt as if her limbs had turned to ice, which made it hard for her to move, but she managed to make her way to the picture. Larkus didn't turn away from the window.

Her body moved slowly, but as she gazed at the family, she saw the joy on their faces. A handsome Triad-Elf with thick black hair and joy in his red and black eyes. The smile on his face made his cheeks full and his dimples pronounced. He had an arm wrapped around a beautiful female Triad-Elf, each point on her ears held an earring. Her purple hair was braided into a crown on her head, her eyes were brilliantly gold and happy. The couple held a young girl. Blonde curls fell every which way, untamable. Her eyes were closed in a grand open smile.

"Was this your family?"

Larkus sighed.

"They're beautiful."

Larkus stood beside Jeanette. "Thank you."

"What happened to her?" She pointed to the woman. "Was she your wife?"

Larkus nodded and stroked the painting of his family. "She died shortly after this was taken. I raised Angela on my own. She started showing magic that very day. She had a promising future," he talked about his family with joy.

"I'm sorry."

"She was taken too soon." Larkus's countenance changed; he became angry again. Seeing Larkus talk about his family was so different than any other time she'd interacted with him. She could tell he used to be a man of honor, pride, and respect. One tragedy changed him forever. She felt heartsick for this broken shell of a man.

A thunderous roar shook the small cottage. Jeanette lost her balance and fell to the floor. She watched Larkus's eyes widen as he made his way toward the window. A large gasp escaped his lips. She rolled out of the way as pieces of the ceiling fell to the floor.

"What's happening?" she cried out.

Larkus's growl almost rivaled that of the roar outside. He ripped open the door and disappeared into the night. The shaking didn't stop; Jeanette dodged out of the way again when a beam fell. She followed Larkus out of the cabin.

What she saw made her eyes widen and her heart race. She had never seen anything so ferocious or majestic in her entire life.

A dragon!

Chapter 20

A thunderous roar shook the ground beneath Jeanette and caused the branches above her to thrash wildly. The dragon soared above the treetops. Its wings spread as wide as it was long. It swooped at the cabin again, using its talons to cause more damage to the roof.

Larkus hollered at the creature. He used his staff to send a spark in the dragon's direction. The beast retaliated by breathing fire at Larkus.

Jeanette gasped at the incoming flame. She cowered behind him as he shielded himself with his staff, causing the flame to disperse.

The dragon landed at the edge of the treeline, pacing until it curled itself into a half circle. Jeanette looked between the large dragon and her captor. The darkness of midnight made it hard for her to see, but the dragon's wings were still outspread in a display of strength. Larkus stood his ground against the massive creature.

The night sky turned stormy once again, mirroring the storm she felt inside. Snow began to fall from the sky and moonlight reflected off the clouds, illuminating the ground around the cabin. Jeanette could now see the dragon clearly; its black scales were striking against the white snow. Dragon breath wafted around them, stirring the powder on the ground.

Larkus was visibly angry, his shoulders moved up and down, a scowl on his face. "How did you find us?"

Confused, Jeanette looked back at the dragon. Only when she moved to the side of Larkus did she see who he was yelling at.

Hugh stood on the forest floor next to the dragon.

Her heart leapt in her chest as she ran to embrace him. He caught her hug and only stumbled back a step.

"I thought I'd never see you again," she cried into his tunic. She didn't want the hug to end. The heat radiating off Hugh provided warmth and comfort, and his strong arms around her gave her peace.

But it did end. "I have to finish this once and for all," he whispered and kissed her as he pushed her toward the dragon's abdomen. The glow inside its chest warmed her to the core, as if she stood next to a fire.

Hugh turned to face Larkus.

"I repeat, how did you find us? I put an enchantment on the cabin," Larkus growled.

"Apparently Phyre wasn't affected by your little enchantment." Hugh's taunt made Larkus shudder. "Let's finish this."

"You think you can defeat me?"

"I know I can." The confidence emanating off Hugh made him even more attractive to her. There was a determination in his stance, his strong arms and chest ready to fight. His face showed unwavering dedication to the daunting task in front of him.

A gentle breeze brushed through his hair and Jeanette thought about all that Hugh had been through. He was her prince, but his worth was so much more than his royal bloodline. At this moment, his inner strength was on full display.

Larkus stamped his staff twice. A sword appeared at Hugh's feet, and Larkus's staff turned into a sword in his hands.

Hugh placed his foot under the long blade and kicked the sword into the air. He caught it by the hilt and swung the sword side to side. Jeanette never realized how talented he really was. She didn't want to lose Hugh to the monster in front of him.

Larkus laughed. "I guess you took advantage of the library books on sword craft."

"You're right." Hugh started pacing. "Did you think all those times you were away I just sat back and twiddled my thumbs?"

"Did you practice as well? With no one to spar against? You couldn't have gotten very good."

"I practiced enough to kill you!" Hugh exclaimed.

Larkus gave a short huff. "We shall see." He lunged forward.

Hugh blocked with his sword and swiped at him in return.

Larkus dodged the attack and laughed.

Hugh raised his sword and aimed for Larkus's neck. The sound of blades crashing together echoed through the trees. Jeanette watched the two opponents take careful steps waiting for the next attack. Hugh spun the sword in his hand, ready for Larkus to make his next move.

Larkus thrust his blade toward Hugh's abdomen, but Hugh blocked with another swift parry. Their swords clanked edge to edge, both leaning against the other trying to get the upper-hand and wound their opponent.

Larkus' eyes widened. "You've learned much while I was away," he growled as he pushed Hugh hard enough to disengage their swords and take another slash at his arms.

He missed.

"Please, stop!" Jeanette called. She didn't like this.

Hugh lunged and slashed Larkus's chest, forcing him to stumble backward.

Larkus shrieked in pain and grabbed his chest. Jeanette saw a giant gash in the fabric as blood started to seep through his clothing. She grabbed her own chest bracing for the pain, but nothing came. Larkus was muttering words that Jeanette recognized. It was the healing spell. Once he finished healing, he growled at Hugh. He pulled a leather gauntlet from one of his pouches and started chanting. Jeanette didn't see anything change, it was strange Larkus would take the time to cast a spell that did nothing.

Hugh advanced again, raising his arms to put his force behind the attack. Only when he came down upon Larkus did Jeanette understand. Hugh's blade hit a force field causing the blow to miss. Hugh tried again, and while Larkus stayed perfectly still, the barrier held. Jeanette remembered reading about spells that could only be in effect if the sorcerer held completely still.

Larkus took this opportunity to slash Hugh's right side.

"No!" Jeanette screamed. She saw his shirt turn red with blood as Hugh cried out in pain. This time she felt the wound as it happened. She grabbed her side and even looked down at her hand to make sure there wasn't any blood.

"Ah, you're not as good as you think you are!" Larkus shouted, still fighting.

Hugh grabbed his right side while he blocked Larkus's sword. Hugh's blood continued to soak through his shirt and drip onto the snow, but Jeanette knew he wouldn't give up.

There were flashes of blade and skin. Hugh struck Larkus against his cheek, drops of blood ran down his face. He took a few steps away from Hugh and healed himself again.

Jeanette started crying, she saw how Hugh's injury caused his movements to become labored.

"Can't you do something?" she asked the dragon beside her. If he was able to damage the cabin, he was surely strong enough to stop Larkus.

All the dragon did was exhale.

"Please," she cried. Snow fell from the clouds above them. Tiny ice drops made their swords slick.

Larkus lunged again.

Their swords crashed against each other, the scraping of blades echoed around Jeanette. She felt the reverberations through her entire body. Hugh got the upper-hand and Larkus fell to the ground. He raised his sword, ready to strike as he stood above Larkus. As Jeanette watched, Larkus put one hand behind his back and summoned a dagger.

"Watch out!" Jeanette screamed, but it was too late. Larkus whipped his arm forward and stabbed Hugh through the leg.

Hugh stumbled backward falling to his knee. She knelt, matching Hugh's pose, he was in a vulnerable position. He grabbed the dagger and pulled it out of his thigh. He flipped it around to wield both the dagger and sword. Larkus huffed and said an incantation. Jeanette watched the handle of the dagger turn red hot causing Hugh to throw it to the ground.

Her hand mirrored the pain of the burn on Hugh's palm. She rubbed it, trying to rub the sting away. She knew it would only last a moment for her, but the pain would continue for him. Hot tears fell from her eyes just as blood dripped from Hugh's leg, forming a crimson puddle in the snow.

Larkus advanced on the kneeling Hugh.

"Get up! Please," Jeanette begged. She didn't want to watch him get hurt anymore, but there wasn't much she could do.

Hugh swung at Larkus, even from a kneeling stance, he managed to injure Larkus's leg. Larkus screamed and grabbed his wound; immediately healing it by his touch.

"When we first met, you were this little sixteen year old boy, unfamiliar with the skills of swordsmanship." Larkus stood above Hugh. "Does this look familiar? Those injuries I gave you back then, I'm giving you now."

"You won't win this time," Hugh replied. "I am stronger now than when we first fought."

"You're no match for me. Not then, not now." Larkus taunted. "Your injuries will hold you back, just like they did last time. You've always wanted a rematch, so here we are, in the same situation we were back then."

"I won't back down," Hugh panted hard.

"Last time?" Jeanette said. Was that how Hugh got that scar on his side, and the one on his leg? They'd fought before. No wonder he took the time to study those books.

Hugh tried to stand, but fell to his knee again. He still managed to slash Larkus across his chest once more. There was now a bloody 'x' on his shirt. Scarlet blood dripped onto the white snow. Larkus stepped back and looked down at his chest, healing himself again.

They were both breathing heavily as the adrenaline pumped through their veins. With how things were going, Jeanette knew it wouldn't end well. Larkus kept healing himself, while Hugh continued to get injured. If only she still had her mother's necklace, she could try the healing spell. Maybe it would heal Hugh. But Larkus destroyed it. There was nothing she could do.

"Please, get up! Keep fighting!" she called to Hugh.

Hugh's eyes glanced at Jeanette, they looked helpless, tired. Her pain mirrored the pain he must be feeling. His clothing was saturated with blood and he looked pale.

"Don't give up!"

"Yes, Hugh, don't give up." Larkus laughed. "Then all my fun will end. You have been a fairly decent slave. I could use you when I take over your kingdom."

"There must be something you can do," she turned toward the beast. "You're a dragon!"

Phyre's eyes narrowed and looked at the scene before them. A low growl reverberated through his chest as he nudged Jeanette.

"Me?" Jeanette questioned. "I can't do anything. I don't have my mother's amulet anymore."

Another rumble through his chest. Jeanette got the feeling that the beast was trying to tell her something. He nudged her again, then laid his head down on his massive paws.

Confused, she turned back to the duel.

Hugh had managed to stand and swing at Larkus. They were in another block of blades and anger. Hugh twisted his sword with such force that he caused Larkus's sword to break free from his grasp and fly across the snow. As soon as it left Larkus's hands, it turned back into his staff. Larkus made an attempt to reach for it, but Hugh sliced his wrist.

Larkus recoiled in pain and punched Hugh causing him to stumble back. Then, he reached his staff and healed himself. Instead of turning it back into a sword, he started chanting. Larkus gained an aura around him.

A dark black aura. The stench grew and was overpowering.

Jeanette started coughing, her vision turned blurry as her eyes watered and burned. Phyre bristled his neck and raised his head, his horns stood on edge. She knew something bad was about to happen.

Hugh screamed in pain.

Jeanette's gaze darted to where he stood. His contorted body fell to the snowy earth beneath him. He writhed on the ground and continued to scream until no more sound came out of his mouth.

"No! Stop. Please," she begged. She couldn't stand seeing Hugh in silent torture.

But Larkus didn't hear her, or he just didn't listen. The aura turned to a black fire as he continually chanted. She couldn't take it anymore and ran in front of Hugh with her arms spread wide.

"I said stop!"

Larkus blinked against the interruption. The black fire disappeared, and he turned his focus on Jeanette, his face held a slightly amused look. "And what are you going to do? You have no weapon."

"I don't need a weapon to defeat you," she argued. Hugh lay panting on the ground behind her, his eyes closed and his body curled up. Blood-red snow surrounded him.

"You have no artifact, nothing to defeat me, you have no power." Larkus laughed.

"I have more power than you could ever dream of," she said. Finally, she understood this feeling inside of her. It was her magic. Something that had been buried and hidden for a long time. But she knew herself now, something that had always troubled her. She knew she was meant for more than just being a small town tailor. She was meant to be a great sorceress, and she didn't need her mother's amulet to prove it.

Larkus glared at her. "You don't even remember your past, how can you think you have any chance in defeating someone who has gained so many artifacts?"

"That doesn't matter, I don't need one."

Larkus laughed. "You don't understand. You can't harness any power without artifacts. The owners of these couldn't defeat me, why do you think you can with nothing?"

Jeanette didn't answer. She glanced at the many pouches hanging off his belt. Each of them containing one he stole from other sorcerers.

"Jeanette," Hugh whispered from behind her.

She didn't turn.

"You alone stole those from others, they don't belong to you," she challenged.

"Alone?" Larkus laughed again. "Who do you think helped capture those poor souls? Who do you think helped lock them in the dungeon? Who do you think helped trick them into giving up their power and telling me how to defeat them?"

"I—"

"Your dearest Hugh. That's who!" Larkus laughed again. "He's not as perfect as you think he is."

"You forced him to do those things." Jeanette knew Hugh. She knew he regretted his previous actions. "You couldn't have defeated them without his help. You're weak."

Larkus glowered at Jeanette and started muttering under his breath. As he chanted, Jeanette felt the earth rumble beneath her feet. Looking down, she had just enough time to dodge the deep crack that was meant to separate her from Hugh.

She glanced at Hugh to make sure he was okay and turned to watch Larkus dig through his pouches and don another artifact. She wished she had enough time to close her eyes, look inside herself, and figure out this power she had. But Larkus sent a fireball directly at her. She leapt away, but the fire caught on her nightgown. She knelt in the snow and put out the charred fabric.

Fire, earth, wind... How could she tap into the elements without her mother's necklace?

Her necklace.

Her mother was gone. She had to start thinking about the magic as her inheritance, and to stop thinking of the magic as her mother's— it was hers too. She was destined to be a royal sorceress. To be Hugh's wife. And she wouldn't let anyone get in the way of that.

Larkus turned his attention back to Hugh. That black fire surrounded him again, she knew he was using dark magic to harm Hugh. If she didn't do something soon, she would fail at protecting him.

The snow around Hugh melted and steamed. He was too weak to move away from the boiling water, only his screams would escape.

Anger burned in her chest. There was no way she would let this monster hurt anyone else. A warmth radiated from the fire inside of her.

"That's quite enough." She moved in front of Hugh again. Her fire burned bright white, encapsulating her in a heatless flame, she felt as bright as the flame itself. Larkus's reign of terror needed to end. Magic swirled in her chest as the snow swirled at her feet.

Larkus stopped chanting and stared wide-eyed at Jeanette.

She felt powerful.

As she raised her arms, the swirling snow rose from the ground, encircling her and lifting her into the air.

"So, you've made a tiny whirlwind of snow," Larkus taunted. "What are you going to do with that?"

Jeanette didn't answer. Her anger provided the fuel that pointed her magic at Larkus. Each snowflake turned hard, elongated, and sharp. She was now hovering, surrounded by icicles.

A glimpse of fear flashed across Larkus's face, which quickly turned to anger as he scowled at her. She wouldn't let him reach for any more artifacts. Each icicle pointed at Larkus. With one swift thought, every single dagger of ice shot directly at him.

Impaling him to death.

Chapter 21

Each icicle stabbed him quicker than he could heal himself. Once his dying breath left his body, he collapsed to the ground. Dark magic had taken over Larkus a long time ago. The fumes from his rotting body told the tale to anyone who came near. It only took a few moments after his death for his body to disintegrate into black sludge. The ground trembled as the sludge melted into the earth, causing a hissing sound to echo around Jeanette. When the sound stopped, and the earth stilled, there was no trace of Larkus anymore. The only evidence that there was once someone there were the pouches of artifacts that lay in a pile.

They were finally free.

Jeanette's feet found the ground again as the fire around her slowly dissipated. She swayed where she stood. Her mind fogged over in a daze. She couldn't comprehend what had just happened.

She had used magic.

Without an artifact.

She didn't know if it was her anger toward Larkus for hurting Hugh that enabled her to tap into the magic within, or if it was something else entirely.

Her feet gave out from under her, and she fell to the ground, weak and dizzy. Breathing heavily, she turned her head toward Hugh. A pool of blood surrounded him, she couldn't tell if he was breathing or not. His body was limp and his skin was pale.

"Hugh," she whispered with her last ounce of energy. Her eyelids turned heavy and she surrendered to the darkness.

H ugh squinted as Phyre exhaled over him. The dragon's breath was warm and soothing. He blinked against the large black snout that hovered close to his face. Letting out a groan, he closed his eyes. He placed a hand to his side. His eyes flicked back open when he realized he wasn't in pain. He felt no wound.

"What happened?"

Phyre puffed another wisp of smoke in Hugh's face.

Hugh coughed and slowly sat up. He looked at his body— there were no cuts, no burns, no blood.

"Did you heal me?"

Phyre nodded. His eyes were focused on something else though. Hugh followed his gaze and saw Jeanette laying on the ground.

"Jeanette!" He wasn't sure what happened to her, he only remembered his own injuries and passing out from the pain.

No.

He remembered Jeanette running in front of him to stop Larkus.

Larkus!

He looked around and saw the pile of pouches. He closed his eyes and tried to remember, but he couldn't recall what happened.

His head spun as visions flashed in his mind. The last thing he saw was Jeanette floating in white flames. Her hair was wild and her face held an unwavering stare.

Despite being healed, his body still protested each movement as he crawled to where she lay.

"Jeanette?" He brushed a strand of hair off her face. She wasn't moving.

"Can you hear me?" She wasn't breathing. Fear crashed upon him, suckerpunching him in his stomach, taking his breath away. A tightness clutched his chest and crushed his heart. She couldn't be dead. After all this time, they were finally able to be together, she just couldn't be dead.

Phyre took a few earth-shaking steps toward Jeanette.

"She's not waking up," Hugh said. "You healed me, can you heal her too?"

Phyre moved close to her and exhaled inches from her face. The Dragon's Breath steamed and glowed in the cold weather. Hugh watched as it went into Jeanette's mouth. He saw her chest rise and, as it fell, the Dragon's Breath left her lips.

Jeanette coughed and her eyes fluttered open.

Relief flooded his veins as he pulled her close and wept into her hair and neck.

"I'm so glad you're okay." His heart sped as he leaned down and brushed his lips against hers. That earned him a smile and he helped her to a sitting position.

Her eyes studied him. She looked down at his chest and his leg. Her brows furrowed as she pulled the rip in his shirt open. Her fingers grazed his old scar, it sent tingles through his body.

"You're healed," she said.

He smiled at this beautiful woman in front of him, just awakened from death's door and more concerned about his injuries than her own.

"Phyre did that. He healed you too."

"He's magnificent." She looked at the towering beast with wonder in her eyes. Hugh couldn't help but think just how beautiful and magnificent she was.

Hugh pulled Jeanette close and cradled her. She relaxed in his arms, relaxing her head against his chest. He felt content, although there was something that he needed to say.

Out loud.

"Jeanette," he whispered.

She looked into his eyes.

"You are my one true love. I've waited half my life for you to come back to me." His undying love shone through in his eyes as well as his words.

She grinned. "I love you too."

Hugh's heart had never felt as full as it did in that moment, the love of his life nestled in his arms. He was hers— always had been and always would be. And she was his.

A slight snoring interrupted their moment. Hugh turned and looked at Phyre. He was fast asleep.

"We need to let him rest," Hugh said. "Look at his scales."

"What about them?"

"They're black. It means he's out of energy," he explained. "When I first met him, he was bright red. His scales darken and turn black as he flies."

"Oh, I see."

"Yeah, it took a while to get here."

"Poor thing." Jeanette walked to the dragon, leaned down, and kissed the scales on his head. "Thank you, Phyre."

Hugh saw Jeanette's body start shivering. She was only in her nightdress, and it was nearly ripped to shreds. She must be freezing.

"Let's get you inside," he said as they leaned on each other, entering the cabin.

"I'm not sure how much warmer it'll be inside. Phyre damaged the roof pretty well."

"Yeah... sorry 'bout that." Hugh laughed. "When we landed, I was aiming for the clearing, but Phyre went for the roof. Then, when I saw Larkus, all I wanted to do was destroy something of his, so I let Phyre cut loose. After all, this was his family's cabin."

Jeanette just laughed. "The partial shelter will still be better than nothing."

Hugh nodded. As they entered the cabin, he saw the wake of destruction that he and Phyre had caused. With the now open roof, snow had coated everything in the front room.

"Well, I guess it doesn't really matter. It's still freezing in here." Jeanette rubbed her arms and hands.

Hugh walked to the bookshelf and looked for the one he and Larkus had used so many times. It was small and tan. Extraordinarily plain, without any of the golden filigree on the edges that the surrounding magic books had. Pulling it out by the top, Hugh tilted it to an angle and waited for a click. That portion of the bookshelves swung inward and revealed another room.

"This one will be warmer," he said.

Jeanette squinted into the dark space, hesitant to enter, but when another shiver escaped, she ran into the room without delay.

"It's too dark," Jeanette said. "Ouch."

"I'll get a fire going." Hugh knew where the fireplace was in this room. This was the place Larkus took Hugh each time they left a town, or after they got another artifact. In a way, this was Hugh's home too.

The fire blazed bright, illuminating the small bedroom. Jeanette stood near the side table holding her foot. She looked beautiful in the golden glow. Even with frazzled hair and her torn and blackened silk nightdress. He watched and admired her every move as she turned and looked around the room.

Desire pulsed through his veins. She had saved him. He stood close behind her, moving the hair away from her neck and kissing her in that spot. She arched her neck as an invitation. He would not disappoint, and continued to kiss down the nape of her neck.

A sigh escaped her lips as Hugh pulled her close. He felt the curves of her hips against him. He slipped the strap of the nightdress off her shoulder and grazed her soft skin with his fingertips. They were finally free, their future in front of them. Hugh wanted to embrace the moment. He turned her to face him and kissed her soft lips, nibbling on her bottom one. Jeanette released a moan.

"Um..." Jeanette's breathy voice broke the air between them.

"What is it?" Hugh whispered.

"This feels weird, we're in Larkus's bedroom."

"Actually... we're in mine." Hugh smirked. "This was where we would retreat between..."

"Between?"

Hugh sighed. "Between hunting down artifacts."

"Oh," she said.

Hugh turned away. He didn't like that part of his past. He hated that he had tricked other sorcerers and caused their demise. It was no use though, Hugh could never have disobeyed Larkus's orders.

He felt Jeanette's hands on his back. "I'm sorry."

He turned to face her once more. "For what? It's not your fault."

"Maybe not," she paused, "but I am the one who turned Mapleshire into a small town. If it was still a kingdom, Larkus wouldn't have kidnapped you."

"Perhaps, but I'm the one to blame for you having to turn it into a small town."

"What do you mean?" Jeanette's face turned worried as her brows came together.

What would she think if he told her the truth about what happened that night? No. He couldn't do that— not right now. That story would have to wait. He looked into her eyes and down at her dress. It was dirty and damp. She needed to get warm.

"Here," he said as he grabbed the large quilt off the bed and wrapped it around her. "This will keep you warm. I need to go check on Phyre." He kissed her once more and left the cabin.

Jeanette awoke, curled in the blanket at the foot of the bed. She had fallen asleep waiting for Hugh to come back.

"Hugh?" she called. She stood and kept the warm blanket around her shoulders. The fire had died down and the room felt cold. A yawn escaped her lips, when was the last time she had a decent night's sleep?

"Oh good, you're awake." Hugh poked his head in. "Are you hungry?"

She nodded. She was hungry, and tired, and confused. She still didn't have time to think about what happened the night before. She'd obviously made a mistake by interrupting their moment and killing the mood. But she couldn't help the weird feeling she had.

Hugh motioned for her to follow him. He was dressed in new clothing that wasn't ripped or stained with blood. She kept the blanket wrapped around her as they walked out of the cabin, where she saw Phyre in his full glory. Hugh had told her he was originally red, but the way his scales glowed against the sun and reflected in the snow was more stunning than she had imagined. There was a small campfire. Hugh was cooking fish in it.

"Where did you get the fish?" Jeanette looked around, she didn't see a stream or anything when Larkus first brought her to the cabin, but she could've missed it in the dark.

"Phyre brought them. He can summon them with his dragon magic."

"Wow," she said. "He is quite talented."

Phyre puffed up in pride at the compliment from Jeanette.

"Come by the fire," he said as he pulled a cooked trout out of the flames and handed her the stick. The smell of it made her mouth water. She took a bite, her body relaxing as she savored the hot, flaky fish.

"This is the best fish I've ever had," she admitted. It was true, too. Clint never was a very good fisherman, and she had never learned. Needless to say, they never had much fish in their household.

After devouring two entire filets, her belly felt full and her body was warmed. The pile of artifacts, still sitting in the snow, caught her attention.

"What are we going to do with those?"

"Keep 'em."

"But, don't they belong to other sorcerers?"

Hugh looked up from the fire. "They used to. But in order to control the artifact, Larkus killed the previous owners." That made sense, but something still bothered her about just taking them for herself.

"He had my mother's necklace," she paused, "it should've been mine when she died. There could be others like me out there."

"That's true, but I'm not sure how we'd find them."

She wasn't sure either, but it seemed like that would be the right thing to do. She stood, picked up the pile of pouches, and looked around at the surrounding woods. The white trees with black markings were different from the woods near Mapleshire.

"Where exactly are we?" she asked as she dropped the pouches next to Phyre.

Hugh was quiet for a moment. His face turned concerned as he furrowed his eyebrows. "We're on the outskirts of Dovervie."

"Dovervie?"

"Yeah," Hugh nodded. "It's Larkus's home kingdom. He transported his cabin here after his daughter was murdered and he was banished. It was supposed to be their wedding day. The day Devlan became king."

"Devlan?"

"The one who murdered Angela."

"Oh," she said. She wasn't sure how to feel about being so close to a ruler who murdered his betrothed. "So, he's ruling alone? Or did he marry a different sorcerer?"

Hugh shook his head. "I believe he's ruling with a woman who was forced to marry him. He hated Larkus's daughter so much that he banned all magic in the kingdom."

Jeanette's shock made her eyes widen as much as they could. "That's terrible! Why would he do that?"

Hugh shook his head. "No one knows. Apparently he's not very fair either. He sits on a throne while his people starve."

A shiver escaped Jeanette. But not from the cold, from the fear and anger she felt. How dare someone so vile be able to rule while Hugh was stuck being the monarch of a kingdom that didn't exist anymore.

"Are you okay?" Hugh asked. "Should we go back inside?"

Jeanette shook her head. "So he... how does... why can..." Her anger fumed, it was hard to form her thoughts. She took a deep breath and tried again. "What happens if someone has magic?"

"Uh..." Hugh looked away and cleared his throat. "As soon as someone starts to show magic, or if a visitor uses magic..."

"Go on." She wanted to know. She needed to know.

"They get sentenced to death. Right then and there."

She gaped at Hugh. "But..." How could anyone be so vicious that they'd actually kill people over magic? She didn't understand. "If I started showing magic as a child..."

Hugh nodded. "Yeah. Anyone who has magic."

"I should go and turn that kingdom into a small town. Then he'd have nothing to rule." Although Jeanette meant for it to be a joke, part of her actually wanted to do it. "However, I don't remember how I did that to Mapleshire in the first place."

"I'm not sure that would be a good idea... even if you did remember."

"Yeah, probably not."

"It's getting late, we should head back," Hugh said. "We have a long trip ahead of us."

Jeanette stood and bundled in her blanket better. "I can't go anywhere like this though."

Hugh looked her up and down. "I know one place we could go." He winked, wrapped his arms around her, and kissed her. She loved the feeling of being wanted.

"I'm serious." She giggled.

He smiled and walked back into the cabin. She followed behind him and watched as he went back to the bedroom.

"Hugh, you said yourself that we need to head back. We don't have time for this."

A moment later, he came out holding a dress. It was beautiful and simple. Lavender in color, a row of embroidered flowers on the waistline, and long flowing sleeves.

"Where did you get that?"

"It was Larkus's daughter's."

"It's beautiful, but I'm not sure about that. What if Larkus had..." she paused, "I don't know, cursed it or something so no one would ever wear it."

Hugh shook his head. "He wouldn't do that, at least not to this one."

"Why not?"

"This was the last dress Angela had ever made," Hugh explained. "She never got to wear it."

"So, he kept it all these years?"

"Yes. He couldn't bring himself to throw it out." He laid the dress across the chair, next to where The Serpent Gauntlet still sat. "I think it would look beautiful on you."

Jeanette walked to the dress and held it up to herself; it looked like it would fit. "Can you hold onto this for me?" She handed the gauntlet to Hugh and changed into the dress. She appreciated being in warm, dry clothing, but not only that, she appreciated the time and effort that went into such a wonderful creation.

"She was really talented," she said as she twirled in the dress.

"You look lovely."

Hugh held his arm for Jeanette to take and escorted her to Phyre. As they approached, the dragon's head turned toward them, he crouched low and waited for them to climb on.

"Wait," Jeanette said. There was something she wanted to do first. She rummaged through the pouches of artifacts and felt the power coming from each one. She didn't notice the pulsing that came from them when they had searched through Larkus's storage room. The artifacts seemed to have transferred ownership to her when Larkus died. But she still felt as if she should find their rightful owners.

Finally, she found one that would help her accomplish what she wanted. She turned back toward the cabin and tried to cast a spell of what she felt in her heart for Angela.

A smile spread across her face as she watched the cabin become covered in dirt, and a beautiful lilac garden sprouted on the mound.

"That's a nice tribute," Hugh said and placed his arm around Jeanette.

She felt a burning in her chest and her throat tightened. It wasn't unusual for her to get emotional over things, and even though she never knew Angela, she felt a similarity to her. She wiped a tear from her eye and turned back to Hugh.

He smiled and squeezed her hand. "You ready?"

She nodded and they climbed on the back of Phyre.

"How do you hold on?" Jeanette asked as she continued to fidget against a horn on his back. Hugh sat in front of Jeanette and grabbed hold of the tendrils hanging from Phyre's head.

"Just hold onto me," he said as he wrapped Jeanette's arms around his waist.

When Phyre pushed off from the ground, her grip tightened as they soared high above the trees and into the clouds.

They flew for hours. Jeanette saw what Hugh had mentioned—she watched Phyre's scales turn from brilliant, scarlet red to deep black. It reminded her of the obsidian snake that remained coiled in Hugh's possession.

They landed in a clearing that Hugh informed her was the same place they stayed on his trip to search for her.

"We'll be safe here for the night," Hugh said as he helped Jeanette down from the dragon's back.

All three of them curled up together in the clearing. She was grateful for the warmth Phyre's glow gave them.

Hugh leaned against Phyre and held Jeanette. Snoring soon came from both of them and Jeanette smiled at her sleeping companions. As much as she wanted to sleep, she couldn't. There were too many things going on in her mind. All the new information she'd received over the past few days, all the new mysteries that she didn't have answers to.

Jeanette's eyelids soon grew heavy. She snuggled in deeper against Hugh's body and finally fell asleep.

The next morning, Jeanette awoke in Hugh's arms. She stretched and looked around the clearing. Phyre sat near the edge of the trees, his eyes fixed on the woods.

"What are you looking at? Is there something out there?" She shielded her eyes as she peered into the dark abyss. She didn't see anything, but Phyre seemed on edge. It reminded her of how he looked when Larkus used dark magic to hurt Hugh.

A low grumble reverberated through Phyre's chest. Jeanette knew it was time to leave.

"Hugh!" she called.

He jumped awake. "Wha— huh?" He looked around and came to her side. "What's going on?"

"Something's wrong, we need to leave right now. Look at him." She gestured toward Phyre.

"Um..."

"Trust me."

Hugh nodded.

They mounted Phyre again and he wasted no time pushing off from the ground. Once they were high enough, he circled the clearing once. Jeanette peered off the side of the beast and saw someone walk into the clearing; right where they had been standing. It looked like the same person that was at The Sanctum.

The one that made Larkus nervous.

Jeanette felt like cloud cover would help them. She closed her eyes and repeated that spell in her mind. She wasn't sure if it would work since she didn't have her amulet anymore, but it was worth a shot. When she felt Phyre relax under her, she opened her eyes, and they were flying above a sea of clouds.

She wasn't sure how she did it, but she was able to, once again, use magic without an artifact.

Something that was supposed to be impossible.

Chapter 22

The miraculous cloud cover provided enough protection to allow them to take off. Hopefully that woman hadn't seen them. Phyre flew hard and fast to get away from the clearing. He seemed more relaxed the farther he flew.

"I think we're safe now," Jeanette said.

"Safe from what?" Hugh asked. It was evident that he hadn't seen anyone. She wasn't sure if she should tell him, she wasn't even sure if there was anything to tell. He was finally free from Larkus, she didn't want to burden him with another mysterious person.

She took a deep breath. "There was a woman who entered the clearing who spooked Phyre. Larkus and I saw that same woman at The Sanctum, this magical circular area where he wanted to drain my power." She shuddered.

"I know of The Sanctum," Hugh admitted. "We used to go there sometimes when Larkus wanted to obtain an artifact."

"Oh." She felt bad for having brought up something she knew troubled him.

"What did this woman look like?" Hugh's brows furrowed.

"I didn't really see her very well," she said. "It was too dark at The Sanctum, and just now, we were too far away."

Hugh was quiet for a moment, but his shoulders were tense. "Well... I'm sure it's nothing to worry about."

They remained quiet the rest of the trip.

The day lapsed into dusk as they landed on the top of Mount Gravensburg. Phyre was shimmering black again, and panting hard.

"Welcome home, and thanks for the help," Hugh said as he patted Phyre.

"This is his home? He lives up here on Mount Gravensburg and no one in town has ever seen him?" That shocked her, but also made sense. Dragons were known to be wild and ferocious, and they used to be a lot more common. But no one had seen a real dragon in ages.

"Yeah, the red portal delivered me here. Right to him."

"The red portal? I guess Larkus hadn't thought about the portals when he took me away," she said. She thought it was strange that he'd leave them available for Hugh to use.

"Larkus? Those portals are part of the castle. They were your mother's magic. They remained through the transformation. Larkus had taken over the blue one and used the gold one for himself, but they were never his."

"They weren't? So, the house kept its own magic through everything. Leaving the portals, the magic painting, the magic bath baskets, and helping me when I needed things." She smiled at Hugh, but one of his eyebrows was raised. "What?"

"The house isn't magic. The portals and the baskets remained because they were magical... as is the painting. Anything that you thought the house helped you with was your own magic coming forward. You never lost the power inside of you. You just forgot you had it. I'm sure that happened a lot throughout the years that you just thought was a coincidence."

She thought about that for a moment. There were actually a lot of coincidences over the years that made sense to her now as being her own powers.

"I had no idea..." she admitted and turned away from Hugh and Phyre.

She had never been this high up the mountain before. She walked close to the edge and peered out over the scene before her. Mapleshire looked tiny in the distance.

"I wish I knew how to turn it back into a kingdom," she whispered. She wasn't really saying it to anyone, but it seemed that Hugh heard.

"It's okay." He appeared behind her and stroked her arms with his hands. "You'll be able to figure it out, just like you figured out how to break my curse."

She nodded. It was nice to be reassured, but this was different than his curse. There was a whole book full of spells she could try for that. However, she hadn't seen a single spell that talked about transforming an entire town. She didn't remember how she did it in the first place, and she wasn't sure if she'd be able to figure out how to undo it.

"I wonder why I can't remember," she said. It bothered her how much she was still unsure about. A small part of her had hoped that once Larkus was gone, her memories would come back and everything would make sense.

"It's your spell," Hugh told her. "It backfired on you when you cast it. You were so young, and that spell was too powerful."

"But I should be able to remember!" Her frustration built behind her eyes and escaped as hot tears on her cheeks. She hated that she couldn't recall this part of herself.

"All I can say is that when you transformed Mapleshire and split it into separate towns, you trapped everyone's memories as well. No one down there even knows it used to be a kingdom."

"Then, why can you remember?" She turned to face Hugh. "Mapleshire was your home too."

"Because Larkus had cursed me already," Hugh explained. "So, since I was his servant then, your spell had no effect on me."

Jeanette saw the pain in his eyes. A lifetime of homesickness that he could never get back. She was the one who tore the kingdom apart. She thought about that as she stared at the small town in the distance. She thought about Beth and Clint. They raised her as part of their family. But there were so many other families that were in the same kingdom, and because of her, those families were split apart. It was all her fault.

Her eyes scanned the valley. She saw the distance between the towns, the isolation she had forced on the kingdom. She barely saw Hempsure from the top of the mountain. The houses were tiny specks against the horizon. Stennton was closer to them on the southside of the mountain. The farmlands went on for miles. She gazed toward The Forest of Faiden Dell. The trees were so thick that, even from the height of the mountain, she couldn't see the town. No wonder there were so many stories about that mysterious part of the woods.

They were on Mount Gravensburg, but she didn't see The Gravensburg Pass nearby. No sign of a bustling market. No sign of life here at all. She turned away from the cliffside. Phyre lumbered over to the entrance of a cave.

Jeanette turned to Hugh. "Where's the mountain pass? You said I turned Mapleshire into five small towns, but I don't see the fifth one anywhere."

Hugh nodded. "It's under the mountain. They settled in the tunnels and caves."

The confusion that Jeanette felt must've shown on her face because Hugh just laughed.

"When the kingdom transformed, there was enough room for the other towns to continue with life as if nothing ever happened. Their memories shaped into thinking that's how it always was. But because the westernmost side of Mapleshire was against the mountain, they were pushed into the caves. They created an entire little village down there."

"How do you know this?" Jeanette was shocked at the amount of information that Hugh shared. It felt good to hear him be able to tell her things without getting punished. He must've enjoyed it too, since he kept talking.

"Larkus was furious at what you did. He dragged me to each town trying to find anyone who remembered the true kingdom. Maybe then your spell could've been broken through them somehow. Larkus never shared the workings of magic with me. I think he liked having a slave who couldn't fight back. I just did his bidding."

Jeanette interlocked her fingers with his and raised his hand to her lips. "I'm sorry. I wish I could fix this. I wish I could remember." She wanted to erase all of the pain he'd had to endure. If only she could remember the spell that shattered his kingdom. The very spell that had erased her memories, along with those of all the other townsfolk.

Memories.

"Huh..." Jeanette thought about what she could do.

"What?"

"I can't remember."

"You said that." Hugh studied her face.

Jeanette shook her head. "Larkus cast a spell that made me remember certain things, I wonder if I could cast it on myself."

Hugh's eyebrows furrowed. "Are you sure that's a good idea?"

"No," she admitted, "but I don't know what else to do. I heard the spell when he showed me a memory of us when we were children."

"I think you have to end that spell when you want to stop reliving the memory."

Jeanette didn't know about that, she had only heard Larkus cast the spell, and then she came back to the present when her vision ended. She wasn't sure if Larkus had done anything to bring her back out of it. But it was worth a try.

"What's the worst that could happen? It's not dark magic is it?" Jeanette chuckled. She wasn't sure if she actually wanted to know if something bad could happen.

"No, that one isn't dark magic," Hugh's voice was wary.

Jeanette wasn't sure how Hugh knew for sure, but she didn't question it. She dug through the bag of artifacts looking for one that would do the trick.

"Do you want to use this?" Hugh pulled the Serpent Gauntlet out of his pocket and handed it to her.

She held it, felt its power, but it didn't feel like the one she needed at this time. She shook her head and finally found one pulsing with the right power.

Although she had cast spells on her own, she didn't understand how it worked. She did, however, know how to use an artifact, thanks to her mother's magic books.

Hugh looked at her with concern in his eyes as he bit his bottom lip.

"I'll be okay," she kissed that lip and sat on the mountainside with her legs brought close to her chest. She placed the jeweled band around her head, a small ruby dangled, hitting her in the center of her forehead. She copied Larkus's words and felt her mind spin, around and around, until she thought she might be sick. Concentrating on the castle from her last vision helped her pinpoint the memory. Then everything became calm, and she stood at the base of Rosemont Castle.

No, not her.

Little, thirteen-year-old Jeanette was crying as she stared upon the vast castle. "I'm sorry," she whimpered. "I must do this to protect the people." Her tear-filled eyes saying goodbye to Hugh as Larkus pulled him away, gripping him by the neck.

Larkus was too far away to physically stop her. Now was her chance. She took a deep breath and held her arms high above her head. She chanted a spell over and over again, getting louder and louder with each repetition.

The earth trembled as she continued, she knew she couldn't stop until it was complete. Holding her ground, she watched as the castle morphed into a large mansion— still beautiful, but not as grand as before. She slowly turned in her spot and watched the resplendent kingdom change, spread apart, and become small, homey towns. Trees and roads sprouted between the new villages, keeping them apart. She watched the townsfolk's demeanor's change— once happy and vibrant people, now soulless. A sadness hung in the air about them.

Larkus was chanting something at the same time. His angry growl reverberated throughout the land, it sent fear trembling down her spine.

Her whole body began to shake as she continued chanting. The pain of the power was too great. Her arms faltered a moment and the spell sent her flying across the grounds, where her head collided with the base of the fountain.

"Jeanette!" Hugh's voice, but it seemed so very far away. How could that be real? She watched the monster disappear into thin air and take him away. His voice called to her again. She was crying and holding her head when Beth showed up.

Not the Beth she knew now, but young Beth.

She scooped Jeanette up and hugged the small child. "There you are! I've been looking all over for you. It's okay, I'm here. I'll take care of you. What are you doing here? At..." Beth's voice trailed off as she looked at their surroundings. "Rose Manor."

Little Jeanette thought it was a fitting name since there were so many rose bushes around.

"Jeanette!" Hugh's voice echoed in the distance, but felt close at the same time. Her world shook as if there was an earthquake.

No. Wait.

There was never an earthquake with Beth. Jeanette's eyes fluttered open and she saw Hugh hovering over her face. A cold sweat drenched her brows. Phyre's dragon breath calmed her nerves.

"What happened?"

"You went into a sort of trance. You were calm for a bit, but then you went pale and stiff. I thought you were having another seizure like you did when you were poisoned, but it also looked different. I tried to take that thing off your head, but it wouldn't budge. It was as if there was a barrier around you. Phyre breathed on you hard enough that you shook and fell over. That's when you woke up."

Jeanette blinked against the information that Hugh spouted, seemingly all in one breath. And she thought about the memory that came to her. If Phyre hadn't broken the spell, she would've been trapped in her memory, bound to repeat her entire life over again.

"Thank you for pulling me back," she whispered. Her breathing was shallow and her throat hurt.

"Did it work? Did you see the memory?"

Jeanette nodded, not wanting to speak.

"Can you try to undo it?"

"I think so, but not up here. I need to be closer," she rasped.

"I understand. We should rest before we head back, it's really late." Hugh's face was still worried about her. The creases on his forehead aged him. The evidence of a life he didn't deserve.

She nodded. She was feeling better, more anchored in her body the longer she spent back with Hugh. "But where are we going to rest? It's freezing up here."

"Hmm," Hugh looked around. "That's an excellent question."

Phyre grunted and pawed at the ground in front of his cave. They both turned and looked at the giant beast. He started walking through the entrance and paused to look back at them.

"I think he wants us to follow him," Hugh said.

"Well, the cave would be warmer than out here," she said and yawned. They followed Phyre into his home, and as he curled into a coil, they joined him and fell fast asleep.

Jeanette awoke to the morning rays peeking into the cave. Hugh was already up, staring out of the entrance of the cave. She rose and went to him, stroking his back.

"Good morning," she whispered.

Hugh smiled. "It is a good morning." His gaze seemed to be fixed on Rose Manor.

"So, how do we get down from here?" she asked.

Hugh finally turned away from the view and looked around. "I'm not sure."

Phyre let out a yawn that echoed throughout the cave. His footsteps scratched the air around them. He inhaled deeply, growing the dim glow in his chest into a bright light. As he exhaled, Jeanette witnessed him breathing fire into an orb that appeared to be floating near Hugh, illuminating the small cave around them. They saw a tunnel branch out of the circular room.

"Wow," she gasped. "But where does that lead?" Jeanette asked. "Does it lead to the mountain pass?" She wasn't sure what to think about following an unknown tunnel to a mysterious destination, but they didn't have much in the way of other options.

"Well, the mountain pass is mainly at the base of the mountain, but I wonder if the tunnel connects up here."

"Imagine if someone explored and came to this cave and found a dragon!" Jeanette couldn't help but laugh at the image of anyone in town stumbling upon a dragon.

"It would definitely be a story no one would believe." Hugh looked at the glowing orb. "This is amazing. Another bit of dragon magic and it never ceases to amaze!" Hugh agreed as he reached forth his hand and pushed the orb. It wobbled in the air, and continued to glow bright.

Phyre relaxed into a semi-circle.

Jeanette made her way to Phyre's head and gave him a hug and a kiss. "Thank you. You helped me realize the power I hold."

Phyre gave her a nod; she moved back to Hugh's side, holding his hand as they left the dragon's cave and entered the heart of the mountain.

As they walked through the dim tunnel, Hugh nudged the orb along in front of them to illuminate the path. They climbed down a rocky cliff into another great circular cave room. This one had multiple tunnels branching out.

"Which way do we go?" Jeanette was concerned that they were going to be stuck in the caves, bound to wander for days with no food or drink.

"I'm not sure," Hugh trailed off as he gave the orb another nudge.

They stood in the center of this room and watched the light. It wobbled again, but then floated toward the leftmost tunnel.

"I guess that way," Jeanette said and gripped Hugh's hand tighter.

They wound through more tunnels and curves and came to yet another circular room. This time however, it was not empty. Jeanette felt her eyes widen at the sight before her. There were thousands of orbs floating in the air. It made the ceiling of the cave look like starlight. Jeanette wondered how long it had been since the mountain pass villagers had seen real stars.

The two made their way to the center of the village, where the market resided. They observed all the wares for sale: fish, polished rocks, pieces of stalagmites. One stall sold shimmering shells labeled as dragon scales, but Jeanette knew from experience those were nothing like real dragon scales.

She watched the people buying and selling. She couldn't help but feel guilty for how gray their skin looked. If it wasn't for her, they'd never have been forced into the depths of the earth.

"Where did you get the fish?" One particularly silvery gentleman asked the owner.

"In the underground lake. What, do you think I'd head to the surface for these?"

It surprised Jeanette how disgusted the owner's reply sounded. It made her wonder what stories The Gravensburg Pass village had been told about the surface, and if they were anything like the stories she had heard about The Forest of Faiden Dell. She wondered how much was actually true.

Hugh gripped Jeanette's hand and brought her back to the present. She looked at his face, his jaw was clenched and his eyebrows were furrowed. As she looked around, she understood why. They were too tan. Even Jeanette's pale skin was much pinker than the gray skinned people who were staring at them. Then the whispering started.

"Hugh," Jeanette whispered.

"Just keep walking," he said as he quickened their pace.

They finally made their way outside the cave and Jeanette turned back. All she saw was the glow of their eyes. The villagers must've adapted to the darkness in the cave, having been in there for so long.

"Phew, finally!" Hugh seemed grateful to be out of the cave, his skin looked a little gray as well, but the color returned as soon as he was in the sun.

"Why did they think that the surface was so bad?" Jeanette hoped Hugh would have the answer.

"I don't know," he admitted. "But I felt really strange in there, didn't you?"

She thought about it. "No, not really. I noticed how gray they were, but *I* didn't feel weird."

"You didn't notice?"

"Notice what?" she questioned.

"Hmm." Hugh shook his head but didn't say anything else about it.

Jeanette looked around at her new surroundings. She had thought the mountain pass would drop them near Mapleshire, but she had no idea where they were. The trees were dense, and the forest floor had thick brush. It was hard to maneuver.

"I bet the mountain pass village made it nearly impossible to enter their cave," Hugh said as he stepped over a large, spiked plant.

Jeanette was quiet for a long time. They finally made it out of the brush, and a small cobblestone path lay in front of them. Jeanette felt better about being near civilization, but something was still bothering her.

"Hugh," she whispered his name. She wasn't sure if she actually wanted to know the answer.

"Yeah?"

Taking a deep breath, she voiced her concern out loud. "What's going to happen to them when I restore the kingdom? They've been underground so long, the sun is going to burn them to a crisp."

Hugh stopped and turned toward Jeanette. Taking both of her hands in his, he kissed her fingers and smiled. She felt a sense of comfort from the gesture.

"I think that your magic is powerful enough that it will restore the kingdom and protect the people. After all, that is why you changed it in the first place— to protect the people. You didn't want anyone else to get hurt."

Her heart swelled with gratitude for Hugh. He always seemed to know what to say.

"That's what I love about you," he said. "You care so much about everyone." He continued walking and pulled her to follow along.

They passed a tiny shack along the little path. And then another. Finally they got to a little market, with twinkling lights strung throughout the trees.

"Where are we?" Jeanette felt like she was in a fairy garden.

"The Forest of Faiden Dell," Hugh answered as he squeezed her hand. "Whatever you do, don't tell them your name."

"What? Why not?"

"You know how gray the mountain pass villagers got?"

"Yeah," she answered hesitantly, she wasn't sure if she wanted to hear what Hugh had to say.

"Well, I don't think you noticed their hands and feet."

"What about them?" Now Jeanette had a knot in her stomach.

"They adapted to their surroundings, their feet and hands became webbed. Like flippers. They became cave seals."

Jeanette's mind clouded with confusion as she placed a hand to her head. "Why didn't I notice? I don't understand."

"It's part of your spell. They look different to me because I'm not part of it. I'm an outsider."

She thought about all the stories of cave monsters from villagers who passed through Mapleshire. They were talking about the cave seals. The once-human villagers that she had forced to adapt into monsters.

The knot in her stomach twisted and threatened to never unwind. Her spell caused that. Somehow she knew they could never return to normal once she restored the kingdom. She had doomed them to live in the caves forever.

"And the villagers here adapted to their surroundings as well," Hugh continued. "They became—" Hugh stopped talking when a villager exited one of the tiny houses.

Jeanette barely contained her gasp.

"Hello, friends," the tiny fairy greeted them. Her wings sparkled in the sunlight. Her clothing was made of flower petals. Understanding what her spell had done made her see this cursed villager for what she was. Her proportions were off. This fairies head was nearly the same size as her own, but her body was too small, the size of a baby. Her wings were the largest thing about her, doubling the size of her entire body and head combined.

"What have I done?"

"Shhh," Hugh scolded.

"What do you mean, Dearie?" the fairy lady asked. "Oh, goodness me, where are my manners?" She paused to laugh. Her voice, her laugh, everything about her was inviting. "I don't even know your name, I can't keep calling you 'Dearie'. What's your name, Darlin'?"

"We're just passing through," Hugh answered. That received a glare from the fairy woman. For a split second, the glare showed her true image, dark and menacing. Jeanette knew this wasn't someone to trifle with, but also not anyone to trust.

"Oh, shucks. Why don't you stay awhile?"

"No," Hugh answered. "No, thank you." He pulled Jeanette into a run. She felt a danger there. She wondered if the missing travelers from the past had fallen into her trap.

Jeanette's spell had caused the villagers to physically change into something else, other creatures. She shuddered as she realized what she had done so long ago. The other three towns had been lucky. Stennton, with its abundant sunshine and rain, was a thriving farm town. Hempsure had enough shops and business to make a booming trade town. And, of course, Mapleshire benefited from its central location.

Travelers from other kingdoms told tales about the forest fairies and cave people, but no one ever believed them. Turns out the stories she'd heard as a child were true. But only because of her. She had caused this. There had to be something she could do. Maybe Hugh was right, if she could restore the kingdom and set it right, then maybe it would protect the people as well. She couldn't let those creatures possess the bodies of innocent villagers. If it wasn't for her, they never would've had to adapt like that.

"Finally," Hugh panted. "We made it."

Jeanette looked around once they broke through the thick trees. They were on the outskirts of Mapleshire. To the south, she saw Rose Manor in the distance, now that it was no longer shielded by Larkus's dark mist.

Her heart skipped a beat. They were home.

Chapter 23

Jeanette replayed the memory in her mind, refreshing herself on what the spell was in order to undo it. She paced the grounds in front of the mansion. She knew the words to say, but she couldn't bring herself to say them. Not without figuring out how to save those poor cursed townspeople.

"Are you ready?" Hugh asked.

Jeanette nodded. Then shook her head. Then crumpled to the ground in tears.

"What's wrong?" He knelt beside her. "Do you not remember the spell?"

"It's not that," she mumbled through her fingers. "I can't restore the kingdom without fixing those creatures."

Hugh's face fell.

She knew he was eager to see his castle again, to see his kingdom, his home. But she didn't feel right about it. "There has to be something that can help them too."

"I believe in you, Jeanette." Hugh's voice was calm, soothing. "I believe that if you restore the kingdom, with those wishes in your heart, then it will be."

Jeanette raised an eyebrow at Hugh. She was still learning how magic worked, but she wasn't convinced that wishing would make it so.

"What if I harm them more?" she asked. "What if I restore it, and then *they* harm someone?"

Hugh nodded. "I know it's scary, but I have faith in you and in your powers."

That was a really not helpful answer, but for some reason, it did calm her nerves. She took a deep breath and stood in the same spot she stood as a child.

She closed her eyes once more and pictured her child self... no artifact. She'd cast this spell all those years ago as a young girl without using an artifact. That would be something she would have to explore later, but at least she knew she wouldn't need one to break the spell.

But it did give her an idea... she rummaged through the artifacts again until the right one spoke to her.

"Here, put these on." She handed a pair of glasses to him.

"Um..." Hugh looked at the glasses and then back at Jeanette. His eyebrow raised again.

"I believe that these will work for you. It'll give you vast sight. I know how excited you are to see your kingdom restored."

Hugh smiled, put on the glasses, and started to look around.

Raising her arms above her head, she said the words she spoke twelve years ago. Her intent this time was to undo it though. The words from the magic book crossed her mind. *Spoken and broken at the same time.* She closed her eyes, reliving her memory but hoping to restore the kingdom. Hoping to save those poor villagers.

She felt the power grow, the same power she'd felt in her past that had caused the spell to backfire on her. It became stronger and stronger, until it was almost too much. She couldn't falter this time. A scream escaped her mouth as she felt the power peak.

Then peace.

A magical wave released from her center and expanded across the kingdom. The earth shook as Rose Manor transformed to its former glory. It grew higher and wider; the salmon-colored stone shedding the ivy that had concealed its façade for years. Before them stood Rosemont Castle, gleaming in the sunlight.

"Wow," Hugh breathed. "It's just as I remember it, though, somehow better." He looked so happy, so excited, so relieved to have his home back. To be able to finally become the man he was supposed to be. The king he was destined to be.

"I'm glad," she whispered as she swayed on her feet. She wanted to be as thrilled as he was, but her energy was completely drained by casting the spell. Dizziness overtook her mind and her vision blurred. She collapsed to the ground.

Hugh turned in a circle as he watched the distance between towns collapse, the trees of The Forest of Faiden Dell broke apart, and to Hugh's relief, he saw the fairies' wings disintegrate and their proportions return to normal.

He turned toward the cave entrance of The Gravensburg Pass. With the forest now gone, and the magic glasses he donned, he was able to see the entrance without any obstacles in the way. His heart thumped against his chest as he waited to see if the cave seals had returned to their normal selves.

It took a few moments before he saw one of them poke their head out of the cave opening. A young man with shaggy brown hair and gray skin exited. He looked down at his hands and feet and started frolicking in the grass, hooting and hollering. The longer he was in the sun, the more color returned to his skin. A small boy joined his celebration, then a little girl and her mother, and then in a rush, what seemed like all the other mountain pass villagers.

"Jeanette! You did it!" Hugh turned to give her a joyous embrace, but saw her crumpled figure on the ground.

"Jeanette!" He cried out in alarm and ran to her side. He was relieved to see that she was still breathing, but she didn't wake at his touch or his voice. He removed the glasses, lifted her, and took her inside to lay down on her bed.

As they crossed the threshold, Hugh was amazed. The castle was just as he remembered it from when he was a little boy. The walls were gold with silver filigree. The floor was covered in red velvet carpet and lavish golden rugs. He carried her past the sitting room picture and wished that she could have fixed that as well. But that wasn't her magic, and he wasn't sure if it was possible.

He stood outside the bedroom that used to be his parents'— the one that Jeanette had used when the castle was transformed. As a boy, he had hardly ever been allowed inside. But now, it would be their bedroom, together. He shouldn't feel hesitant about entering anymore.

Opening the door revealed the monarch's suite. He laid her on the opulent four poster bed. Jeanette relaxed into the plush covers. He straightened and stretched as he looked around the room. Jeanette's single wardrobe had transformed back into the two used by his parents. He opened the one on the left and saw his father's clothing, still hanging in color coordinating order. He took a deep breath, he could still smell his father's cologne.

"I'll do you proud, Father," he said as he closed the door.

"I'm sure you will," Jeanette whispered.

He turned and smiled at her. "I'm glad you're okay."

She rolled onto her side and returned his smile. "Did it work?"

Hugh knew she wasn't asking about the spell, they both watched the castle return. He knew she was asking about the creatures.

"Yes," he answered. "It worked. The fairies turned back to humans. I watched their wings melt and their proportions return to normal. The people of the mountain pass were frolicking in the fields with their tanned skin and unwebbed hands and feet."

Jeanette closed her eyes and smiled. "Thank goodness."

Hugh lay next to her, stroking her arm to soothe her. "How are you feeling?"

"I'm..." Jeanette wrinkled her forehead. "I'm feeling better. The energy the spell took is returning, and relaxing in this bed is helping." She smirked.

"That's good." He kissed her forehead. "But, I meant... how is your memory?"

"Oh." She thought about it. "I don't feel any different, hang on." She sat up in bed and closed her eyes. A smile spread across her face. "I remember," she whispered.

"What are you thinking about?" Hugh wanted to know which memory she thought of first.

"My mom." A tear streamed down her face. "She was teaching me magic. She was beautiful."

"You look like her," Hugh said. "I'm glad you have your memories back. It felt unfair that I could remember her and you couldn't."

"How strange you think it's unfair for me to not remember her, when I took your entire kingdom away."

"You had to." He shrugged. What had happened wasn't her fault. If anything, he felt like he was to blame.

"Some things are still a little fuzzy." She placed a hand to her head.

"Like what?" Hugh sat up as well.

"Where was her tower?" She shook her head. "For some reason, I can't place where it was."

Hugh laughed. "Do you remember when I told you that our parents were destined for each other, but made an arrangement so they could marry the ones they fell in love with?"

"Yes," she said.

"Come here." He stood and held his hand for her to take.

She followed suit and he led her to the mirror wall. She looked at him with a quizzical brow, which made him laugh again.

"Trust me," he said. Hugh felt along the edge of the large mirror that now had an ornate wooden frame. His fingers paused at a low spot.

"Right here," he said as he grabbed her hand to feel.

"A key hole?"

"Where did you hide that key I gave you?"

Jeanette's eyes widened. "I hid it under the bed... but what if it disappeared when everything changed?" She moved to the bed and knelt down.

"Do you see it?"

She was quiet for a moment. "Ah hah!" She held the bronze key above her head. "I was so nervous that it was gone. I had tucked it between the board and the frame, but since this is a much bigger bed, it was harder to find. Still there though!"

Hugh took the key from her and twisted it in the hidden latch. They heard a click, and the large mirror swung inward, revealing a grand circular room.

"This was her tower." He held his hand open for her to enter first.

"So, her tower was attached to the master bedroom because they would've been married if they hadn't fallen in love with other people." Jeanette chuckled.

"That's right."

"I bet your mother really loved that," she teased.

"She did. She and Gloria were best friends."

Jeanette looked at Hugh in awe. He was worried though. He'd thought breaking the spell would bring her memories back, but it seemed some were still missing.

"I should be able to remember that." Jeanette's face was pensive. "Did I not break the curse fully? Or is the memory loss permanent? What if no one can remember?"

Hugh shook his head. "I don't know. You remembered your mother. Maybe it just takes time to come back?"

She nodded and let out a heavy sigh.

They entered the tower, a large oak desk sat near the door, with books open and strewn about. A layer of dust on the surface.

"I can feel her here," Jeanette said as she walked around the circle. The rest of the room had four tall mirrors floating in a semicircle. "I don't remember these."

"Hmm..." He felt bad that she was still missing a part of her. He remembered them playing in here as children, sneaking in through the secret passage. She'd spent many days in this room with her mother, training in the ways of magic to become his sorceress.

"These look like mirrors, except I don't see my reflection."

Hugh stood behind her as they stared into the glassy, silver surfaces. "I remember your mother standing here, staring into them as if she was searching for something."

Jeanette turned toward him with a strange look on her face.

"What?"

"I remember her doing that at home, but maybe it was actually here, maybe my memory warped into something that made sense to me." She turned back toward the mirror in front of them and stood just as her mother did. It made him smile seeing that. Seeing her standing as regal as her mother, searching the mirrors just as she did all those years ago.

"Nothing's happening," Jeanette said with disappointment in her throat. "I don't know what she was searching for, she never told me."

"You'll figure it out someday." He squeezed her hand to encourage her.

A shimmering came from the glass and caught their attention. The surfaces shifted and morphed as words formed on each of the four mirrors.

They started with the one closest to the desk, it read:

Your past can hold useful knowledge. The next hovering surface read: *Decisions can be trapped in the middle.* They continued to the third one. *Your path may be different than your plan.* Lastly, they reached the final mirror. *The future is always changing.*

"What does that mean?" Jeanette reached her hand toward the glass but hesitated a moment. "I wonder how all of these work."

"Well, they *are* magic mirrors, why else would they be in your mother's tower?" Hugh said. "In your tower," he corrected.

She smiled at him. "I hope I can do her justice. I wish I could've learned more from her."

"You will." He leaned down and kissed her. "These mirrors could be a great gift... or a terrible one. We must be careful how we use them."

"I agree." She turned her back to the mirrors and stepped away from them. "I can feel the power that lies in each one. They're strong. It's scary."

Hugh nodded. "We've gone through scarier apart; we'll get through this together."

Jeanette left the tower and sat on her bed.

"Do you need to rest more, or do you want to go see the rest of town?"

She smiled. "Let's go."

As they walked downstairs, Jeanette paused at the sitting room portrait. "I'm glad this is still here," she said as she stopped to admire it.

He wished he could tell her why this particular item remained, but he didn't feel like it was the right time.

As they got to the center of town, she saw the entirety of Mapleshire, no more separate towns. Everyone in town was celebrating and hugging each other. Families reuniting and long-lost friends chatting. Chills went through her body as she thought about the last twelve years. It seemed the other villagers' memories had no problem coming back. She was glad for them, but still worried about herself. Everyone seeing Hugh bowed or curtsied out of the way so they could walk past.

"What is going on?" she asked.

"They remember who I am." Hugh nodded to each of them as they passed.

A sense of pride grew in her bosom as she watched Hugh fall right back into his royal training. He was born a prince, and he will rule as a king. The people already respected him.

"Jeanette!" Beth called to her, the heavily pregnant woman waddling over to them.

"Oh my goodness, look how big you've gotten." Jeanette hugged her mother-figure. "Hugh, this is Beth. She was the one who raised me after my parents died."

"Good to see you again." Beth held out her hand.

"Again?" Jeanette questioned.

"We ran into each other at Dr. Caldwell's office," Hugh explained. "I didn't think you'd remember who I was, it was such a quick passing."

"I never forget a face," Beth laughed as she curtsied to Hugh. It was ironic since Jeanette's spell had made it impossible for anyone to remember.

Once they got to the center of town, Hugh announced that he wanted to have a celebration dinner now that the kingdom was restored.

Every villager brought their favorite meal to the castle and gathered in the ballroom. It was simple, casual, and a perfect start to reuniting the kingdom. Everyone was laughing and eating— making up for the time they had lost.

Jeanette enjoyed seeing everyone reconnecting and playing. There were so many children running around the ballroom, it seemed as though the other towns had no problem conceiving. She wondered if the fertility issues were a repercussion from being in the center of the kingdom and so close to where the spell was cast, but it didn't matter now. Looking around the room, she felt comfort knowing the happy people here would help Maplshire become, once again, a thriving kingdom.

A little boy fell and skinned his knee. He ran to his mother crying for comfort. She noticed how her own knee didn't hurt at the little boy's injury. She had felt others' pain for as long as she could remember, but thinking about it now, that wasn't true. It only started happening after her spell backfired. It was a side effect. Among all the other side effects, feeling others' pain marked as a reminder that something was amiss. And now that the spell was fixed, it had resolved.

Hugh stood and thanked his subjects for coming. "It's been our pleasure to get to know each of you again and hear your stories. We have quite the tale that other kingdoms just don't have!" That filled the ballroom with laughter. "And it's all because of this beautiful woman right here beside me." He gestured to Jeanette. "I owe it all to her. She was always on my mind these past twelve years, giving me hope and strength while I was cursed to serve another. If it wasn't for her wonderful, magical abilities, we wouldn't be here today."

Jeanette smiled and stood next to Hugh so she could give him a kiss on the cheek.

"And," he paused and pulled out a beautiful ring, "if you'll be my queen, we can serve these wonderful people together, and become the rulers this kingdom deserves."

"Yes!" She barely heard herself answer over the cheering of the villagers.

Over the next few weeks Jeanette packed up her little cottage. The first time she went back to get things to move to the castle, she was surprised to see that even her home had changed. There was an entire library full of magic books that had been her mother's.

Today she was going to gather her last few items and leave her beloved home behind. She smiled at the thought that Beth and Clint would be living there. After all, it did have more room than their small house near the center of town. Their baby would be able to grow up in the same cottage that Jeanette did.

As she got to the patio, she was about to walk inside when she noticed a flower on the mat by the front door. It was beautiful, with crimson and creamy white petals. She had never seen a flower like this before. The sweet scent penetrated her senses.

She placed the flower on top of a pile of books she had been packing, and as she pulled a magic book off the shelf, a letter fell out.

My Dearest Jeanette, I know it must be hard without us now, but you are strong. You have a special gift, use it wisely.

I know you will grow up to be a confident and capable woman. You won't be spared hard trials, but I know you will get through them without any problem.

You are unique, from the first time you used your gift, I knew you would be a great sorceress. I might not have had enough time to train you as well as you deserved, but you can do things no one else can.

We love you.

"Thank you," she whispered as she finished reading. Seeing her mother's handwriting made her think of that feminine handwriting in the magic book she had studied. It was the same; her mother had written those notes. Her mother had continued to help her even after she died. She had no idea how this letter from beyond the grave appeared in her books, but she had no doubt that it was her mother's magic. Beautiful magic.

"Jeanette?" Hugh's voice came from the living room.

"I'm in here, just packing up the last few things," she called.

Hugh entered her little library and leaned against the door frame.

"I found a letter from my mom." She handed it to Hugh.

"It seems like she knew what was in store for you," he smiled as he read it.

"Thank you for the flower, by the way." She stretched, she had been sitting in the same spot for far too long.

"What flower?"

"This one." She lifted the blossom. "I've never seen one like it before, where did you get it?"

He looked at the flower, and the color faded from his cheeks.

"I have seen it before, but I didn't leave it for you."

"What do you mean?" she asked. "Then who did?"

"A witch."

Chapter 24

Jeanette was officially moved in just in time for the Spring Bloom. Being in the Castle now made it a lot easier to plan the festivities. Hugh had hired an amazing chef, Charles, who had lived in Hempsure. He was planning all the fixings, and Jeanette's favorite foods were a high priority.

Beth was grateful that she didn't have to spend hours in the kitchen like they used to with her baby being due any day. Jeanette didn't mind. This gave them the opportunity to relax and spend time reminiscing on forgotten memories. Beth would go on and tell stories for hours. Jeanette was grateful to hear them.

"I'm so glad I remember bits and pieces of her," Jeanette said as they finished up another of their many conversations about her mother.

"I just hope that I can be a good mother to this little one," Beth said as she rubbed her belly.

"You were a good one to me!"

"Are you lovely ladies ready?" Hugh entered the great hall where Jeanette and Beth were relaxing and kissed her on her head. "Charles says dinner is ready."

Jeanette helped Beth up, and they walked to the restored dining room. As they entered the room, she smelled all the mouthwatering food that was presented, and was glad to spot her favorites. She made sure to grab a couple hot buns to start with.

"Do you want me to load up a plate for you?" Clint asked Beth as he helped her sit in a chair.

Dinner was full of lively conversations as everyone ate. The most popular topic seemed to be the upcoming Spring Bloom.

"I love seeing the flower colors glow against the leftover white snow, the contrast is so beautiful!" Beth smiled and she took a deep breath.

"I like the warmer weather," Clint's response caused a chuckle to ripple through the room.

"I love seeing the snow melt into water droplets and float away," Jeanette shared.

Everyone shared their favorite part, except for Hugh. Jeanette noticed how quiet he had been during the conversation.

"What's wrong?" she leaned over and asked.

"I haven't experienced a Spring Bloom in such a long time," he admitted.

"Oh," Jeanette said surprised, "I thought you would've had it with Larkus, just like the Winter Slumber."

Hugh shook his head. "The Spring Bloom was when Angela died, he never let us celebrate it."

Heartache pinged in her chest. "Well, now you can enjoy it with me."

"Ooh," Beth gave a soft moan. "I'm so full, that was delicious. Thank you."

"It's my pleasure." Hugh gave her a small bow. It made Jeanette smile; she had told him about how Beth had raised her, and he treated her with great honor.

"It's almost time. Is everyone ready?" Clint asked as he got Beth's coat for her.

They nodded and walked to the garden. Hugh had arranged a sitting area for them to use instead of sitting on the ground like they had done in previous years. They didn't want Beth to be uncomfortable.

"Oh, thank you," Beth said. "I wasn't sure how I was going to get back up off the ground." She grabbed her tummy.

The sun came out from behind the clouds and shone brighter than any other day.

"It's starting," Jeanette squealed.

The bright light sparkled against the snow, which glimmered as a tulip popped out of the ground. The pink petals glowed against the white, just as Beth said they would. Then a purple daisy joined, and a yellow daffodil. They watched as more and more flowers bloomed instantly, fighting their way through the thick white blanket.

Everyone shed their coats as the temperature grew warmer, and the ice and snow melted into water droplets. They floated in the air and barely touched their skin and cheeks, giving them slight kisses as they floated into the sky and turned into fluffy white clouds.

The new clouds blew away in the wind and the sun dimmed back to normal.

"It's officially spring!" Jeanette exclaimed.

"That was beautiful. Better than I remember when I was a kid!" Hugh nodded and smiled at the group. "Beth, are you okay?"

With that, everyone turned to Beth. She had her eyes tightly closed and was breathing heavily, her hands on her stomach.

"Oh, dear." Clint knelt next to his wife.

"It's time," Beth sounded out of breath.

"It's time? It's time." Clint jumped to his feet and turned to Hugh and Jeanette. "It's time!"

"I'll send for Dr. Caldwell," Hugh said and ran into the castle.

"Come on Beth, let's get you comfortable." Jeanette helped her into one of the many plush bedrooms while they waited for Hugh to come through the blue portal with the doctor.

Jeanette was glad she had learned enough magic and was able to reactivate it. They had stored the other artifacts back in the golden closet and kept the blue portal open, without the caveat.

Clint waited for them in the hallway to lead them to the correct bedroom.

"You'll do great," Jeanette tried to calm her.

Beth tried to smile, but her face remained tense as she nodded through breaths. She tried relaxing on the bed but couldn't get comfortable, so she paced around the room, leaning on furniture between contractions.

Dr. Caldwell and Clint came running into the room, they were both out of breath.

"Looks like we've got an extra special celebration today," Dr. Caldwell smiled at Beth.

"I'll leave you to it." Jeanette smiled at the soon to be family of three and left to find Hugh.

Jeanette found him standing in the garden, near the fountain that spouted water accompanied by blue mist. He had his fingers interlocked behind his head.

"She'll be just fine," Jeanette said as she approached.

Hugh nodded.

"Is something wrong?" she asked.

"It's just," he paused, "I've been thinking about that flower."

"Which one?"

Hugh chuckled. "The one the witch left."

"Oh," Jeanette should've known that would bother him, but they had seen a lot of flowers today. "What about it?"

"How did she know that was your cottage? Why would she put it there? Why would she care?"

"Hmm..." That was something that had been bothering her as well. "Do you think it's still safe for Beth and Clint to move in?"

Hugh shrugged.

Jeanette bit her lip and twisted her skirt in her fingers.

"I'm sure they'll be just fine in that house." Hugh took her hands in his. "If the witch was tracking us— you— then I'm sure she'd know that you don't live there anymore."

"I'm not sure that makes me feel any better."

"Come here, I know something that will," Hugh said as he kissed her.

They sat at the fountain, watching the water and the mist. The spring mist tasted of wet stones, she loved how it changed with each season.

Hugh played with the mist; it seemed to obey his commands as it morphed into different shapes.

"Dolphin," Jeanette guessed the animal the mist had turned into.

Hugh nodded and contorted the mist again. "What about now?"

"Hmm..." Jeanette looked at it from different angles. "Crab?"

"Yes!" Hugh laughed.

"How did you learn to do this?" Jeanette asked. She had never seen anyone control the mist before, especially someone without magic.

"It's something that your mother actually taught me," he explained. "She called it a great 'party trick'."

Even though she could mostly remember her mother now, it was still nice to hear stories of her. It seemed like Hugh was able to spend more time with her than anyone else. Sometimes it made her sad, but Hugh was more than happy to share as many stories as Jeanette wanted to hear.

"What about this one?"

Jeanette looked at the mist. "It looks like Phyre."

"Well, it's just a dragon—"

"It's a girl!" Clint came running out, his brow visibly sweaty. "It's a girl." A smile spread across his face.

"Congratulations!" Jeanette hugged her father-figure.

"Do you have a name picked out yet?"

Clint nodded. "Flora."

"Aww, it's beautiful," Jeanette smiled.

"Very fitting," Hugh said.

Jeanette left the two men chatting and found Beth in bed with her new baby singing a song with the same tune that she heard from the music box. "How are you feeling?"

Beth turned to face Jeanette and smiled. "I'm wonderful. Come," she motioned for her to enter the room. "I'd like you to meet Flora."

Flora, wrapped in a blanket, lay sleeping on Beth's chest. Her delicate features framed by a wispy mop of red hair.

Jeanette smiled at the tiny infant. "What was that song you were humming to her?"

"It's the kingdom's lullaby," Beth said as she closed her eyes. "The late queen wrote it for Hugh when he was born. It's a beautiful melody."

"It is." Jeanette wanted to be grateful that Beth was able to tell her where that song was from and why it was familiar to her, but something bothered her. Why wasn't she able to remember it herself? Her frustration must've shown on her face, because Beth took her hand.

"What's wrong?" she asked.

Jeanette shook her head. She didn't want to talk about her problems when there was a new life to celebrate.

"Come on, you can tell me."

"I still can't remember everything," Jeanette said at last. "I thought that when I restored the kingdom, I would regain my memories just as the rest of the kingdom has."

"Oh, sweetie." Beth sighed. "It'll come back to you. It's just going to take time."

"But it hasn't taken time for everyone else."

"Well, of course not."

"What do you mean?" Jeanette asked.

"How can I explain it," Beth paused, "it's like you trapped all of our memories in a little box. They were all there, and when it was restored, the box opened and we had them back."

Jeanette stared blankly at Beth.

"But with your memory, it's not like that. Because your spell backfired on you, your memories got scattered. You'll have to search for them, but they'll come back."

In a strange way, what Beth said helped. Even though Jeanette wished she had her full past back, it was comforting to know that she would eventually find them.

H ugh came to the bedroom that night and saw Jeanette already laying down; she faced the window and was looking at the stars.

"You look beautiful tonight," he said as he climbed in bed beside her.

"Thank you." She rolled to her back and kissed him. "Today was such an amazing day, thank you for taking care of everything."

"It was my pleasure." He returned her kiss. Her lips felt soft against his.

"I hope Beth, Flora, and Clint are doing okay." She smiled and had a wistful look. "Flora is so precious."

"I'm sure they're quite comfortable. I told Charles to tend to anything they need while they're here." He stroked her forehead and into her hair; something he'd learned always helps to relax her.

"Thank you for that too," Jeanette said as she closed her eyes. "I know Clint was trying so hard to get the nursery ready for the baby, but..." she chuckled. "He's not the best when it comes to projects like that."

"Well, they can stay here as long as they'd like."

Jeanette rolled to face him, her eyes staring into his. She wrapped her arm around his waist and pulled him close.

They kissed again, longer this time. A slight moan escaped her lips as he moved his kisses to her neck. He saw the vein in her neck throb and kissed it, feeling her pulse quicken as his hands moved to her body.

Hugh felt the soft silk of her nightgown between his fingers. He slipped the straps off her shoulders and caressed every curve on her body, until she was breathing heavily. She pulled at his tunic, so he obeyed her wish and threw it to the ground.

Her hands grasped at his body, begging him to come closer. Her fingers grazed his spine and pulled him nearer to her. She moaned again as he pressed his firm muscles against her soft thighs.

The rise and fall of her bare chest against his drove him wild. She slid her hands through his hair as he kissed down her body. He grabbed her hand and pushed it against the bed as they built their passion in that moment. They gave themselves to each other fully and each felt a release of ecstasy.

"I had been wanting to do that again," he whispered in her ear and kissed her cheek.

Jeanette lay there, unable to move, smiling at him.

He lay next to her, grateful to finally be free, and for both of them to belong to one another.

The next morning Jeanette got out of bed and put on Hugh's tunic, taking a deep breath of the fabric. It smelled like him. The scent of the fire, wood, and something mysteriously familiar. Smelling it again, she tried to place it in her mind.

"Ocean waves." Jeanette smiled at finally figuring out what it was. All this time, it'd felt just out of reach.

"What's 'ocean waves'?" Hugh walked in the bedroom wearing his pajama pants, carrying a breakfast tray.

"You." She smiled. "You smell like fire, wood, and ocean waves. I finally figured it out."

Hugh laughed. "Have you been trying for a while?"

"Yes, actually." Jeanette furrowed her eyebrows, hoping she looked as annoyed as it caused her to feel every time she couldn't place it. "I couldn't figure it out. The ocean waves are familiar to me... but I don't remember ever going to the ocean. I mean besides when I was running from Larkus."

Hugh paused as he set the tray on the large table that occupied part of the room now. "Actually, you have."

"What?" Jeanette's eyes widened and she shook her head. "Another thing I don't remember?"

"It was when we were kids." Hugh explained. "Right before Larkus. Right before our parents died trying to stop him." He breathed out a long, heavy breath.

"There's more isn't there?" Jeanette prodded. "More you're not telling me."

He nodded. "I guess now's as good a time as any."

"Tell me." Jeanette didn't know what to expect.

"It was a family trip to the beach house, and since your mother was my father's sorceress, we all went together."

Jeanette nodded. That made sense to her. If her mother was needed while the king was away, she would have to be with him.

"Well, Larkus followed us," Hugh sighed. "Although we didn't know at the time who he was, or what he wanted."

"Why don't I remember any of this?" Jeanette tried to think of the time Hugh was describing. Normally, when she'd hear a story, she would also regain that memory, reliving it as it was being told. But not this time. That memory was still lost.

"Your mom wanted to protect your memory of this incident, so she sealed it away." His brow was knit together.

"Incident?" Jeanette asked, shocked. How could her mother take away a memory from her? That wasn't like her.

"Come here." He held his hand out for Jeanette. She took it, and he led her down the hall and stopped in front of the sitting room portrait.

"I don't understand, this is just a picture," she said. "A magical picture, but a picture all the same."

"It's not just a picture," Hugh told her. "This is the beach house we went to."

Jeanette felt confused. "So, this is an image of the beach house?"

"Not exactly..." Hugh paused.

"Well, what do you mean?" Jeanette asked. Her mind felt dizzy.

"Your mother saw the danger that Larkus posed. He tried to attack us at the beach; he made a huge wave smash right into us while we were swimming. We almost drowned. I remember getting tossed around in the waves. It felt like something was pulling me under." Hugh wiped his hand over his face.

Jeanette searched her mind for this memory, but the deeper she dug, the more her head spun.

"Your mother summoned us out of the waves, and we ran to the house. I remember looking back and seeing him slowly stalk toward us. She told us we needed to escape right then and made a portal in the house that let us get back here to the castle," he paused, "but something went wrong."

"What happened?" Jeanette asked.

"My sister got trapped." Hugh looked at the portrait with tears in his eyes.

"Your sister?" Jeanette couldn't contain her shock. "Why don't I remember her?"

"Same thing." Hugh shrugged. "Your mother trapped your memory of the incident and everyone's memories of her away, except for our family. She wanted us to always be able to remember her. She made the locket also forget her. I wished that she didn't. I haven't seen her face in twelve years."

"Why didn't you tell me before?" Jeanette scolded. She didn't want Hugh to keep things from her anymore.

"There wasn't ever a good time. I've tried, but didn't feel like it was right to bring it up. I even tried with the mist. Dolphin, crab—"

"Dragon?"

"Yes, even a dragon."

Jeanette saw the hurt in his face. "How did she get trapped?"

"She went back to get her stuffed *dragon* in the bedroom of the beach house. Your mother didn't know and closed the portal. She told us after that she enclosed the entire cabin in the photo so no one could follow us. I think she actually hoped to trap Larkus there."

"Oh." Jeanette was quiet.

"Then we noticed that my sister was nowhere to be seen. We couldn't find her anywhere."

Jeanette gasped and stared at the photo. "Is that why things change and move in there? Because she's still inside?"

"Yes." Hugh touched the photo. "We saw her stuffed dragon sitting on the table while we were looking for her. Then we realized what had happened."

"But," she paused, "I've never seen anyone there before. Although, I think I have seen that stuffed dragon."

"It's part of your mother's spell." Hugh nodded. "She can leave notes, and messages, but she's hidden to the outside world. She's been all alone for so many years. Your mother tried to reverse it, but we know now that breaking a sealed spell is hard. She said she would figure it out, and I know she studied different magic books to try to get her out... but then she died. I haven't seen her in twelve years, I don't even know if she's just stuck in the portrait, or stuck in time."

"You mean," she paused thinking about Hugh's words. "It's possible she never aged? She could still be that little child that's been all alone? All these years?" Her heart ached at that thought. She hoped it wasn't true. She couldn't bear to think she was trapped as a small child, but the alternative wasn't much better— having to grow up alone. She felt a pang of loneliness thinking of her own past.

Hugh nodded. "It's possible. I honestly don't know."

"Oh, Hugh." Jeanette squeezed his arm. "I'm so sorry. What's her name?"

"Helena. Her name's Helena." Hugh looked at the photo again and turned away. She watched him walk down the hall and up the stairs toward their bedroom.

Jeanette looked at the picture again. "I'll fix this. Somehow, I'll fix this."

* * * End of Book One * * *

Acknowledgements

I want to thank my alpha readers, Holly Morgan, and Rebecca Walton for helping me with each chapter and the process to get this book pretty much ready.

I want to thank my beta readers, Christy Boughan, Lisa Martineau, Chelsey Jones, Jayson Angell, and Sarah Matamoros for going through this book, giving me their input, and finding problems in the manuscript so that I was able to fix them.

I want to thank my editor, Courtney Hanan for all of her hard work in getting this book as perfect as we could.

And most of all, I want to thank my husband, Chance Dixon for all the support and wrangling our children so I could have time to write. If it wasn't for the spousal support, this book wouldn't be here today.

About the Author

Kimberleigh Dixon lives in San Tan Valley, Arizona with her husband and children. She has always loved reading fantasy, mystery, and romance novels, and in turn, loves to write the same.

When not reading or writing; she loves to bake, cook, throw themed parties, sew, and play an absurd amount of board games.

Connect:
Website: seamaidenpublishing-kimberleighdixon.company.site
Instagram: @authorkimberleighdixon
Facebook: Author Kimberleigh Dixon

Milton Keynes UK
Ingram Content Group UK Ltd.
UKHW040642070424
440548UK00005B/11/J